Blood Library

Calum France

First published in 2023 by Blossom Spring Publishing
Blood Legacy © 2023 Calum France
ISBN 978-1-7393514-9-6
E: admin@blossomspringpublishing.com
W: www.blossomspringpublishing.com

For Nicola

Chapter One

Deep in the recesses of the Hoia Forest, two campers named Lloyd Sealy and Arianne Derron found a small clearing to rest for the moment.

Both placed their packs on the damp grass and took a seat on a brown log which was no doubt infested with bugs.

'I'll put together a fire in a minute,' Lloyd said. 'I just need to sit for a moment.'

'I don't like this,' Arianne replied, standing, and looking around the clearing. All around them, they were blocked off by thick trees, illuminated by a bright white full moon. 'We shouldn't have gone off the trail. We should head back to Napoca.'

Lloyd shook his head and wiped his wet black fringe out of his eyes. 'We can't. We're too far from the city and it's too dark to find our way. We should make a fire and ride out the night.'

Arianne nodded. 'Fair enough, but can we get the fire going soon? The sooner we get some light and warmth the better.'

Lloyd agreed and grabbed his pack, pulling out a lighter

and testing it. Despite the small flame, he felt the warmth radiating through his skin.

'I'll just need to collect some wood and hope it's not too wet to light a fire.'

Arianne smiled. 'Thanks. I have a magazine in my bag that we can burn. It's dry and should burn.'

'Brilliant.'

Lloyd took a small torch from the pack and set off looking for some dry wood. It didn't take long. The wood amongst the thick trees had been kept mostly dry from the canopy of branches above them.

He looked up at the trees and appreciated the view. Even in the darkness of the night, it looked beautiful with the glow of the moon shining through.

Lloyd was a young man, aged twenty-four and had been with Arianne for two years going on October next month. They had met at Cardiff University while they both studied Communications but they both longed to travel the world, so after they graduated, they had decided to head off and explore.

It was that decision that brought them to Romania, especially Cluj-Napoca and now the Hoia Forest.

They had no idea it was that decision that would bring the end to their relationship.

Lloyd picked up a handful of sticks and logs and traipsed them back through the thick vegetation towards the clearing where he had come from. He could feel his socks becoming wetter with each step.

He froze where he was walking when he heard something moving in the bushes to his left. He glanced over, but wasn't sure what he was even looking for? *Probably just a rabbit, Lloyd thought.*

The Welshman continued on his path back to Arianne, confident the noise he had heard was just an animal.

Arianne was waiting for him – she hadn't moved from the log where she sat. In the distance, she looked tiny and cold.

The fire would fix that.

'Lloyd,' she said. 'I have to be honest with you. I don't feel safe here. It's too dark and I keep hearing noises.'

'Yeah, I keep hearing noises too. It's just animals, Arianne. Once the fire is on the go it will scare them all away and we can get some sleep. In the morning we can head back.'

'I don't know.'

'We're off the main trail, babe. A lot deeper in the forest than we should be. We'd just get lost trying to get back at night. It's better if we stay here and get some heat in us with a fire and go back in the morning.'

Arianne nodded and pulled her hood up over her head, covering her black hair.

'Besides, I thought this is what you wanted? Some adventure, you know. Are you worried about the stories?'

She nodded again. 'You know we came here because of the legends. It's a hot spot for the paranormal, apparently.'

'That's what they are,' Lloyd said, smiling as he put together a bunch of sticks on the driest patch of ground he could find. 'Just legends.'

Arianne nodded but Lloyd wasn't sure she was convinced. He could tell from the way she played with her fingers.

Lloyd ignored her for a few moments while he got the sticks in position. He used his lighter and tried to set the pile ablaze. He failed. The sticks didn't catch like he'd hoped they would.

'Can you pass me the magazine you mentioned?'

Arianne picked up her pack and ruffled through the contents, eventually bringing out *Hello* magazine. She had read it through on the plane twice over, and she always enjoyed reading about the lives of B-list celebrities.

'Thanks,' Lloyd said, reaching over to her and taking the magazine. He ripped it into shreds and laid the pieces down – some at the bottom of the pile, some in the middle and others at the top. He was no boy scout, but he was sure the fire would light now.

Thankfully, he was right. It was slow and small, but the flame had caught, and the pile was on fire. Despite its diminutive nature, the flame lit up the clearing and Lloyd enjoyed the heat entering his body.

'That better?' Lloyd said.

Arianne nodded and put her hand to her stomach. 'You got any food in your pack? I had the last of mine an hour ago and I left the rest at the hotel.'

An hour ago, they had taken a seat next to a large tree and had scoffed two Mars bars and shared a packet of Walkers Ready Salted before washing it all down with a can of Coca-Cola.

'Let's see,' Lloyd said, reaching into his pack and rummaging around, looking for anything at all. To his delight, he pulled out a Grenade protein bar. 'Salted peanut, happy with that?'

'Shall we half it?'

Lloyd nodded and broke the bar into two pieces. He handed Arianne the largest piece and tucked into his own one, enjoying the taste of the salt and the melting chocolate.

'Do you have the time? My phone doesn't have a signal,' Arianne said, shoving her iPhone back in her pocket.

Lloyd shook his head. 'No signal.'

'What was that?'

Lloyd looked at her – she was staring at a dark space

4

behind where she was sitting. From where he was standing, he couldn't see anything moving and he hadn't heard anything either. 'You're imagining things, Arianne.'

'I'm not,' she spat back. Shrouded in the fiery light, she looked petrified. 'I heard something there.'

'You want me to go check it out?'

Arianne continued to stare at the spot where the trees broke off into a small pathway. Lloyd joined her and touched her arm gently, which did not stop her from almost jumping out of her skin like a bloody kangaroo.

'Will I stay here?'

'You stay here,' Lloyd agreed. 'I'll go check it out. It's probably just an animal or something. If it is a rabbit, I'll try to grab it and we can have a nice midnight snack.'

'That's not funny,' Arianne said, she had been vegetarian for a while and didn't seem to appreciate Lloyd's attempt to lighten the mood. 'Can you just go and check and I'll keep the fire burning?'

Lloyd nodded and grabbed the torch he had left by the fire. 'I won't be long.'

Lloyd set off into the thick trees once again – this time in the opposite direction to where he had gone to find the sticks. Lloyd didn't scare easy – he didn't believe the stories they had read online about Hoia Forest. *A load of crap*, he thought.

Some of the stories were creepy while most of the stories were downright stupid. He read one where someone said a huge stick animal walked the forest at night looking for victims to transform into sap for the animal to grow larger. Stupid.

He walked for a few minutes – in a straight line so he knew how to get back. He was about to turn back when he was sure he heard something like a whistle. What kind of animal would whistle? It was low and struck a chord in his stomach. For the first time that night, Lloyd second guessed himself.

There it was again – the whistle.

Lloyd stopped in place, frozen to the spot. He knelt, trying to keep his shape low and turned off his torch to prevent whoever was seeing him. But then he thought about it for a minute – what if it was a camper in trouble? Or maybe someone had been sent to find them? The hotel knew where they were in fairness. Maybe they had realised they weren't back yet and sent a search party?

Lloyd listened – waiting again for the whistle to occur and after a minute of listening to his own breathing, the whistle came, this time sharper and louder. The idea that he was imagining it crossed his mind. They hadn't eaten much during the day and the fumes from the fire may have had an impact.

Lloyd turned, looking to walk back in the direction he came from but in his distraction, he had forgotten what way it was. All he had to do was turn a hundred and eighty degrees... but what if he had turned while trying to locate the whistle.

Damn it, he thought. This is not the way he was hoping the night would go. He had hoped they would explore the forest, then head back and have a nice meal at the hotel then head to the bedroom and do what happy couples do.

He started walking straight ahead, less than sure he was going the correct way. He walked for what seemed like an eternity – using his torch to light the way, but despite that he stumbled a few times, landing in the grass and mud, staining his bright blue jeans.

Finally, he came to a clearing. He sighed in relief at returning to Arianne but that turned out to not be the case. The clearing was a different one. No fire. No Arianne sitting on a log waiting for him.

Straight ahead – directly ahead, was a large wooden cabin, lit up by a small beacon of light hanging from the doorway. This wasn't on the map. No one had mentioned a cabin in the middle of the woods.

Lloyd couldn't move. He tried his utmost to take a step towards the shack, but he simply couldn't do it. His legs were as heavy as iron, trapping him in a prison of his own dread. He tried again to move and almost managed to shift forward until he saw the cabin door creaking open.

Lloyd stared, squinting hard to see and pointing his torch at the dark abyss in the doorway.

He struggled to see anything but then he was flying. Thrown from behind by his neck – landing on the soft ground. He rolled over onto his back and looked up, shining the torch at his attacker.

The last thing Lloyd Sealy from Wales saw in life was not the love of his life – it was a dark twisted creature with orbs of suns for eyes and the sharp teeth of a Sabre Tooth tiger.

That night – Lloyd Sealy died.

Chapter Two

The wind picked up outside, sending creaks up and down the wood inside the cabin, almost as if the building was shivering with the drop in temperature.

In the centre of the room, under candlelight, sat Mikael Lungu and Adrianna Popa.

Mikael was a man of average height with deep blue eyes, matching the eye colour of Adrianna almost flawlessly. Both were over five hundred years old and had only been awake for a couple of weeks.

All around them were artefacts and remnants of the previous occupiers' stay. The man who kept them underground for so long, bound by magic so neither Mikael or Adrianna could move nor shout nor scream.

'Do you remember what it was like?' Mikael said, leaning back on the comfortable green couch the previous owner had obviously used a lot, judging by the indent on the cushion. 'Waking up, after all that time.'

Adrianna pushed her long red locks back, behind her ear. 'I can still feel my bones creaking every so often,

Mikael. It is not a great feeling and one I hope to never feel again.'

'The witch is dead,' he replied. 'From what the witch said, he was the last one alive, so we are in no danger here.'

'Do you remember anything before the battle?'

'No. Do you?'

'I remember screaming and I remember blood,' Adrianna whispered. 'I remember Vlad being ripped apart by the witches' spell and the animals they had recruited and controlled under their magic.'

'Vlad deserved it, Adrianna. Do you remember what they called him?'

Adrianna nodded. 'Vlad the Destroyer. I remember.'

Mikael and Adrianna were both members of the first ever vampire coven to be created. Formed in the fifteenth century, they followed their leader around Europe like lapdogs, doing whatever he said they had to. It had taken a large group of witches formed of covens from all around Europe to stop them.

'The destroyer, exactly. The killing of him was justified. We both know that.'

'Do not let Dragoslav hear you saying this, Mikael, he is the oldest and strongest among us.'

Mikael nodded. 'The first Moroi ever if the stories he tells are true.'

In Romanian folklore, vampires were known to be called Moroi. The group crossed the entirety of Europe, picking up languages and knowledge, eventually settling in England.

'What is that?' Adrianna said, standing up and peering out of the small slit-like window. She squinted her eyes in the darkness, hoping to see whatever it was she heard. 'Looks like Nicolas and Velkan are outside.'

Mikael had never been a friend to the two brothers, and they had never been friends to him. He knew he was stronger than both, so he never saw them as a threat on their own, but when both were together, they were a danger. One that Dragoslav appreciated and used to put to good use – he would use them as a small hunting party on their trek across Europe, bringing in groups of humans to slaughter and feast on.

Mikael saw blood only as a means to an end – he didn't like feeding on humans, rather he would hunt animals in the woods.

Sometimes though, the lust for warm human blood was too much.

Mikael followed Adrianna out into the clearing next to the cabin.

'Look what we found,' Velkan said, with a disgusting shiny white smile, lit up in the darkness by the lights from the cabin. He was slightly taller than his brother, but he was more erratic and had more kills to his name.

In his grasp stood a young woman shouting in an accent Mikael didn't recognise. She was yelling and screaming for someone whom Mikael assumed was her partner. 'Lloyd! Lloyd!' she kept shouting, repeatedly.

Nicolas grabbed her by the neck and turned her to face him. He leaned in towards her and slowly licked her neck from the bottom to her chin. The girl shuddered and cried even harder than before.

'Lloyd's dead, girl,' Nicolas whispered, loud enough for Mikael to hear.

Mikael turned away, shaking his head, clenching his fist. The two brothers knew how he felt about – not only killing humans – but toying with their food.

'My friends,' came a booming voice from the doorway to the cabin. A man with long dark hair walked into the moonlight and smiled a grin almost as wide as the clearing itself. 'Nicolas, Velkan – you brought a meal. I knew I could count on you. A few more meals and we'll be strong enough to leave this forest and bed ourselves into society.'

'The girl is all yours,' Velkan said. 'We've had our fill.' Velkan looked at the girl and laughed. She was still crying and trying to pull away from the vampires, but their grip was strong as iron.

'Come, girl,' Dragoslav said, holding out a white hand with long dark fingernails.

Mikael watched the girl take a step closer – scared but following orders, likely hoping if she acted submissively, it might help the situation.

Dragoslav spent the next minute admiring the girl, circling her like a group of hyenas in the wild. He watched her closely, but her eyes were trained to the ground. She didn't dare look up.

Suddenly he reached forward, quick as lightning and used his long nails in a swiping motion to rip her red jacket into pieces. Beneath, her t-shirt was slightly ripped but still hanging on.

Mikael could smell the fear off her and he could see the goosebumps even from the distance he was from her. In that moment, he felt an almost overreaching desire to grab her and feed on her.

Unfortunately, for the girl, Mikael managed to suppress his need to kill and drink from her – he would have made it quick and relatively painlessly. Dragoslav, on the other hand, made it slow and most painful. It was like he enjoyed it – a little too much.

Mikael watched the young girl experience the torture Dragoslav had learned from working with Vlad during the fifteenth century. She was stripped naked and fell to the floor as the leader of the Moroi Coven slowly scratched her to pieces with his long sharp nails.

Finally, Mikael had enough of watching. He stepped forward, standing between Dragoslav and his victim. The girl kept her eyes on the floor, sobbing away like a small child just out the womb.

'Stop this, Dragoslav. If you are going to kill her then finish her off. Don't prolong her suffering.' Mikael heard the comments from Velkan and Nicolas suggesting Dragoslav teach him a lesson. He ignored them and tried to remain brave in the face of the creature that created him.

Unlike Dragoslav, neither Mikael nor the rest of the coven were able to create new vampires. For this reason, Dragoslav had created a tight group of people to do his bidding, including turning Vlad into one of the most feared legends in Romania before he fell in the war of the witches and vampires.

Dragoslav didn't take note of Mikael. 'Get out of my way, Mikael. You know you are no match to battle with me.'

This was true and Mikael knew this – and at that moment, he'd rather not die. What he did next went against everything that he stood for and went against what his brain was telling him. He stepped aside and let Dragoslav approach the girl.

Mercifully, Dragoslav did end the girl's suffering.

He wrapped his hands around her neck and lifted her off the ground so that her body looked as if it was hanging in the full moon. Mikael watched him rear his head back and watched his eyes turn bright red.

Dragoslav opened his mouth, showing off two large canine teeth, sharp as nails and he stuck them into the chest of the girl, just above the heart.

To her credit, the girl tried to fight it, pushing against

him but she wasn't strong enough and after thirty seconds of sucking and drinking – Dragoslav added the girl with the strange accent to his long list of kills.

It was that moment that Mikael knew he had to leave this place and start a new life. One far from Dragoslav and the rest of the Moroi Coven.

Adrianna took a step closer to him. Both of them watched as Dragoslav tightened his grip on the girl's neck, snapping it in two and beheading her. He held up the head by the hair and raised it in the moonlight.

Velkan and Nicolas whooped and hollered in excitement.

Mikael turned his back on his adopted family and walked back to the cabin for the last time.

Chapter Three

'Another drink?' The Wet Whistle had been around since Chris could remember. A small, quiet pub with a couple of tables and a long bar area with a pool table at the back. The walls were adorned in Oakley memorabilia, for the tourists. Above the bar, next to a shotgun that Chris hoped had been unloaded decades ago, was a large canvas print of a black wolf with a thistle painted beside it.

'I'm not sure,' Ashley replied. 'We have the lecture early tomorrow.'

'Come on,' he said, trying not to sound desperate but failing. 'We've only been out for a couple of hours and it's not even that late.'

Ashley smiled. Chris would be lying if he said he didn't have a soft spot for her. They had gotten close over the past couple of months since they met at their first lecture together. They were classmates. Friends. Besides, she had made it clear already she wasn't looking for any relationship.

Despite that, they had grown close and often could be

seen hanging out together, studying mostly.

'Come on,' he said, egging her on with his best puppy dog eyes.

'Fine,' she said, rolling her eyes, then she pointed a slim finger at him. 'But you're buying.'

'Fine by me. Usual?'

'Usual.'

Chris traipsed his way across the sticky floor and up to the bar. He glanced back at Ashley who was checking her phone. Ashley was the same age as he was – twenty-two. She had long black hair which fell towards her elbows with striking blue eyes that drew a lot of attention from people around her.

The barman, an older gentleman with a handlebar moustache approached him while cleaning a pint glass.

'What you for?' he said, in a thick Scottish accent. Chris couldn't quite place it; it certainly wasn't from Oakley. Inverness maybe? Higher possibly?

'Pint of cider and a vodka and orange please, mate.'

The barman did his duty, pouring the pint and filling the glass with vodka and orange. He laid the glasses down and told Chris the price. Under a fiver, not bad for the centre of Oakley.

The town was a small one, with a population of just under five thousand people, but it had a good number of tourists coming and going due to its central positioning and the famous Oakley Castle to the north of the town. If you headed south, you would come across a large loch five miles wide, however deep.

'Here you go,' Chris said. 'Keep the change.'

'Cheers, bud.'

Chris did his best waiter impression, trying to make it over to the table without letting the glasses hit the floor. The bar was busy. He had to change direction a couple of times to avoid dropping them, saying 'Sorry,' every time he had nearly walked into something or someone.

He made it to the table, plopping the drinks down and taking a seat.

'About time,' Ashley said. 'You looked a bit like, what's that saying?'

'Here we go.'

She snapped her fingers. 'Bambi on ice! That's it. Thought you were going to drop them at one point, especially when that big fella wouldn't move for you.'

'Aye. Well. I made it, didn't I?'

'You did,' she said and took a sip of her vodka.

Chris did the same with his pint, and he closed his eyes and allowed the suds to wash down his throat.

'You know, you've never told me about your family,' Ashley said, and Chris imagined his heart sinking through his body and rolling onto the floor. 'What are they like?'

'I don't have any,' Chris said. 'I mean, I do. But none that I speak too.'

'Oh,' Ashley said. 'Sorry, I shouldn't have asked.'

'Don't worry,' Chris said. 'Besides, it's not your fault. My mum and dad died a couple of years ago, just after High School finished.'

'Oh no,' Ashley said, putting her soft hand on top of his. 'Sorry to hear that.'

'Yeah,' Chris said, taking his hand away and taking another drink. 'The rest of the family live far away so we don't talk much. I took a few years off after I found out.'

'Explains why you're a bit older than normal the rest of the class,' Ashley said, doing her best to lighten the mood.

Both Chris and Ashley were a couple of years older than the students they shared their degrees with. Most of them attended University straight from High School whereas Ashley had gone on a gap year, travelling around the world, visiting wonders of the world and Chris had spent his time earning money to both pay for a place to live for University.

'Older? You're the same age as me! Twenty-two.'

'True,' she said. 'Doesn't change the fact we're both the elders of the class. It's probably why we connected so easily.'

'Very true,' Chris said, and despite the subject matter he found himself smiling. He noticed Ashley pushing the inside of her cheek with her tongue, an action she would only do when she was thinking about something important. 'You want to know how they died, don't you?'

'If you want to talk about it, then I'd be happy to listen. You know me, I'm a great listener!'

'I'll keep it short,' he said, surprising himself that he was talking about it. He hadn't told anyone how they had died. Mainly because no one had asked. He remembered the funeral – it was a strange occasion. It almost felt like something was being kept back from him, since no one spoke to him. He remembered standing by the grave after the ceremony, feeling the raindrops fall on his skin, successfully masking the tears dropping down his cheeks. He wasn't close with his parents – they were away a lot – but the death hit close to home, as you'd expect. 'It was one night in June; I had got my exam results that day and I got a phone call from my Uncle Danny in Australia. But he wasn't in Australia, he was calling from the airport.'

Ashley took a drink of her vodka, which allowed Chris to take a drink of his. He swallowed down the liquid and the golf ball size lump in the well of his throat.

'He told me they had been killed in a car crash.'

'Where were they?'

'Not sure,' he answered, and that was the truth, his parents were very secretive about where they would head off too. He'd known they were very busy people, and because of that he spent a lot of time by himself, wishing he could be part of their adventures. 'Norway, I think. Although, it could have been anywhere. They were very adventurous.' – *Secretive*, he thought.

'Guess that's where you get it from,' Ashley said and flashed some of her pearly whites.

Was he adventurous? What about his life had been exciting? Nothing, really, if he was honest. He'd done the correct thing – get good grades in school, head to University. The years between High School and University saw Chris get a call-handling job at a company called Full Stop Insurance, selling all sorts from car to building insurance. He had hated it but at the end of the day, it paid the bills and let him rent a small one-bedroom flat near the centre of Oakley.

After his parents died, he'd called the life insurance company that his uncle mentioned, and asked the rep on the phone what the process was for claiming.

'I'm sorry to tell you this, Mr Winters.' The representative's voice seemed to shake on the phone. 'Your parents cancelled their policy last year. There are no funds to claim.'

It had been another punch in the gut. He'd lost his family and now he'd have to support himself, much sooner than any teenager should have had too.

At least now, being twenty-two, he had carved out a solid job in sales and had enough saved to get a decent one-bedroom flat and enrol at the University of Oakley.

His parents had wanted Oxford or Cambridge. What a joke that was, Chris told himself after filling out his registration forms.

'I wish I was more adventurous,' Chris heard himself say after almost downing his pint. 'Life's very boring right now.'

'Thanks very much,' Ashley said with a hint of sarcasm, the edge of her mouth threatening a smile. 'I know what you mean though. When I was a kid, I'd imagine I was a pilot or an astronaut or a dinosaur wrangler.'

'Hold on,' Chris said, nearly spewing his drink from his mouth. 'Dinosaur what?'

Ashley held her hands up. 'Aye. I know. Stupid, right?'

'I mean, it'd be a hell of a career.'

There was a moment of silence, where for a second they had been the only two people in the bar. No longer could they hear the group of lads shouting at the pool table, or the older couple by the door arguing over who was to take the bins out in the morning. Chris knew Ashley was one of his only friends – since all his friends seemed to disappear when his parents died, too hard for them apparently. He appreciated her more than words could say.

Ashley had finished her drink and glanced at her watch. Neither of them had their phones out, too engrossed in the conversation. 'I better get going, I want to get a good night's sleep for tomorrow. Meet outside the lecture hall?'

'Sure,' he said. 'Bright and early, as always.'

'As always,' she repeated, grabbing her leather coat and slipping it on over her black shirt. 'I'll get a taxi. What are you doing?'

'Probably have one more, and then head back. You want me to walk you to the taxi rank?'

She shook her head. 'It's only a minute down the road. Text when you're back home.'

Chris nodded, and watched her leave the pub, squeezing past a couple of guys at the front door, and past the arguing couple who now seemed to be ignoring each other. He looked at his phone to check the time, it was now eleven PM and he figured he better get some sleep, but one more pint wouldn't hurt.

'Another pint?' the same barman said on Chris's approach.

'Got it in one, mate.'

The barman nodded to the table. 'Walk out on you, did she?'

Chris laughed. 'Early start in the morning.'

Instead of taking the pint back to his table, he sat at the bar on a small stool.

For the next thirty minutes, Chris nursed his pint, savouring the taste and dragging it out. He would be lying if he'd say he was looking forward to heading back to the flat. The rent wasn't too bad, but there was a reason for that. It was small, dark, almost falling apart. More importantly, it was lonely. He didn't speak to the upstairs resident, probably because he hadn't seen them. He could hear them, but he had never seen them.

'You alright, mate?' the barman said, tossing his dirty, white cloth over his shoulder.

'Eh? Aye. Never better,' Chris said, finishing off his pint.

The barman placed another pint down by the finished glass.

'Sorry? I never ordered—'

'On the house,' the man said, smiling. 'Think of it as my good deed of the day.'

'Thanks, mate. Appreciate it. What's your name?'

'Colin Scott,' he said and grimaced. 'I know – who names someone Colin these days?'

Chris smirked. 'Chris Winters,' he said, extending his hand and shaking the man's hand. 'Cheers for the drink.'

Colin nodded and almost bowed, which Chris found amusing. A punter at the other end of the bar had shouted for some service, prompting Colin to roll his eyes and then he was gone, talking to the man, and taking his order.

Chris, despite being in the hub of a relatively busy bar, felt alone still.

* * *

"Home! Text when ur back! X"

Chris opened his phone and typed back a quick message saying he would do just that.

He finished the pint, stepped off the stool and left the bar, not before giving Colin a wave.

Instead of heading home, he decided to take a walk to clear his head. Speaking of his parents had taken its toll.

He missed them dearly, despite all the secrets and lies.

Water had begun to fall from the heavens, and he was now soaked through, but still he walked. He walked down a narrow street, not far from Oakley Castle, with many independent shops on each side of him. The road was too small for two cars to fit, but he hadn't seen anyone use the one-way in a while.

Oakley was his adopted home. One that he used to get away from his past, but tonight he realised he would never be able to escape the love – or lack thereof – that his parents had for him. He had longed to go on trips with them, but each time he asked he was told to stay at home like a good boy.

Screw being a good boy, he had thought. He wanted adventure and excitement, not what his life was like now – mundane and a slog to get through.

Looking into the sky, he imagined them up there, and imagined them appearing like something out of *The Lion King*, telling him what to do and how to do it. But the image never appeared, and he found himself thinking how stupid he must look.

Or how drunk.

Suddenly, he was whisked off his feet at a pace no human could have experienced before. He'd been dragged into the alleyway and pushed up against the stone wall. The alley was dark, and, despite being a little drunk, Chris realised this was no joke, and he was in real trouble.

He tried to break the grip of his attacker, but the person holding him by the neck had the sharpest and strongest grip he had ever experienced. The darkness of the alley made it difficult to make out the attacker's features, and Chris tried to speak, but had a hand clasped around his neck and he was sure his neck would snap at any moment.

The pain was one of the worst feelings he had ever felt. It felt as though his very life was being squeezed from his body and the worst part about it was, he could barely see the person doing it. It was agony and he tried to scream for help, but no words came through the vice-like grip around his throat.

Thunder echoed overhead, illuminating the alley, and showing for a split second, the man holding him in place. The man had pure red eyes, like orbs of sun, only dark, evil shade of crimson.

'Wait,' Chris managed to stutter out, despite the hand around the neck.

The man seemed to lift Chris in mid-air, effortlessly.

'Do not scream,' the man said, in an accent Chris hadn't ever heard before. It was very proper and didn't fit the profile of an attacker in Scotland.

'I don't have much, but here, take it.' It was a struggle, but Chris managed to choke out his attempt at begging.

He had reached into his pocket, and yanked his wallet out but accidentally dropped it into the puddle underneath his feet. 'I don't want any trouble.'

'Quiet,' the man snapped, and Chris could see his formerly red eyes change to a normal shade of brown. The man grabbed him and held him in place again, but the clutch wasn't even close to being the breath-destroying grip from before. The man placed his other hand on his head and seemed to be fighting with some inner quarrel.

'Please,' Chris said, attempting to pacify his attacker. 'Just let me ago, I won't say anything.'

The man turned to Chris, and almost looked sad. 'I am sorry,' he said. 'I did not want to do this. But I had to. I need to.'

Chris's eyes widened as his heart sank and suddenly the raindrops on his skin felt like little needles stabbing him. He was going to die.

The man reared his head back, and emitted a guttural, almost other-worldly scream, then opened his mouth, fangs slowly appearing on either side of his mouth and his eyes turning the familiar shade of red.

'Vampire,' Chris whispered.

The man had heard him, and immediately stopped, closing his mouth, and cocking his head to one side, like a confused animal. 'What do you know of us?'

Chapter Four

'Why have you not killed me yet?' It had been the question he had rolled around his head for the past five minutes. The man had taken him roughly by the arm into one of the independent shops on Belford Street. Katie's Emporium sold a lot of gifts that he was sure the tourists would have loved. Items like bobble heads in the shape of the Oakley or of the only famous alumni from the city, Aaron Davis, who went on to become a decent football player for one of the Old Firm teams. Katie also sold bottles of water with special designs to celebrate the town, which Chris used to his advantage by downing a couple of them.

The man had seemed perplexed at the fact Chris knew what a vampire was. The supernatural was real. Or at least, Chris, in his drunken state believed him to be vampire. Chris had been sitting at the counter where the till was, and he had a brief thought of using the register to fight his way out. But the creature was far too powerful for him, and Chris questioned whether he could even pick it up in the first place. He wasn't as scared as he should be and part of him found it rather exciting. Maybe the world wasn't so mundane after all?

The man, dressed in a black evening suit, complemented by brown tie and black trousers, stood with his hands on the wall – he had been like this for the past minute, glancing at Chris every few seconds.

'You don't want to kill me, do you?' Chris said. If it were true – a real vampire – then he could easily have done it without saying a word, but he had paused and dragged out the moment of death. *If he was going to kill me, I'd be dead already, Chris thought.*

'No,' the man said finally, before punching the plasterboard, making Chris jump. His fist went straight through the wall, but the vampire didn't even flinch. His fist was covered in scratches, but he paid no mind. His skin was the colour of a Siberian tiger's fur.

How wild was it? A real-life vampire. Chris knew he should be hightailing it with the state the vampire was in, but he was intrigued by the whole situation, and he was confident he was in no danger. At the minute, at least.

'I do not want to kill you,' the man said. He turned to face Chris and held his hands up in a display of non-threatening behaviour. 'In fact, it's the last thing I want.'

'Why did you attack me then?'

The man shook his head and looked at the floor. He seemed almost ashamed of his actions, bringing his hand up and shaking his head from side to side. He said, 'I understand. But for a human such as yourself, you must understand that to a vampire you are prey. I was... I am hungry. Starving.'

'What's your name?' Chris found himself asking. 'Where are you from? I don't recognise the accent?' He figured if he made small talk, tried to connect, then he could live to survive another day.

'Mikael,' the man said. 'It does not matter where I'm from. What matters is I am hungry, and I need blood. But I don't want to kill you. I could drink from you. But I do not trust myself to stop. I've fended off the cravings for a long time with animal blood but my body cannot sustain that any longer.

'You don't need to kill me,' Chris said. 'Just let me go, I won't tell anyone.' The creature could have killed him easily, but he had shown impressive restraint. He would keep it to himself, no one needed to know he had an encounter with a vampire.

Besides, who would believe him?

'Go,' Mikael said. 'I do not want to hurt you, and I am sorry if I scared you.'

The understatement of the century award was decided there and then, Chris thought. He walked towards the door, and reached out with his hand, about to turn the golden knob when he heard the vampire keel over and start coughing. *He should keep going*, he thought.

But something deep inside told him to turn and help him. Mikael had been gracious enough to let him go despite looking as if he was on death's door.

Chris took the three paces to reach the vampire, and placed a hand on his back. His body was cold, colder than anything he had ever felt before – even colder than the shoulder he was given by his parents.

'Are you going to be okay?'

'What does it matter to you? Why does a human like you look to help a vampire?'

Chris grabbed his arm, and wrapped it round his shoulder, before taking Mikael over to the counter and leaning him down beside it. 'Because,' he said, standing up and puffing out his chest. 'You let me live. And to be honest, mate, I'm a little drunk and I'm not even sure if this is real or not.'

'It's real,' the vampire said.

'What do you need?'

'To live? Human blood. I have not had blood in a very long time, which explains my aggression towards you earlier. If I do not get blood in time, I die.'

Chris looked at his wrist, then back at the vampire. *What the hell was he doing,* he thought. He could easily leave and live the rest of his life in safety, but hadn't he just been complaining about how boring his life was? How the lack of adventure in his life had ruined him? If only his parents could see him now? Shooting the breeze with a dying vampire.

'Get away from that vampire,' his mother would say. Just like she would say whenever he wanted to try something new. Skateboarding, basketball, or football.

'Here,' Chris heard himself say, his mouth was running quicker than his brain could keep up, and there was a small delay before he thrust his arm out and offered his wrist to the vampire, who now was writhing in pain and clenching his teeth together. He'd been showing amazing resolve to avoid tearing Chris apart.

The vampire pushed the wrist away. 'No,' he said. 'If I do it, I won't know if I will stop. And I'm finished with killing and finished with treating people like cattle.'

'What do you want to do?'

'Just leave me here,' Mikael said. 'This death is nothing compared to the treatment I will receive from the coven if I am found. Better a slow painful death than decades and centuries of torture.'

Chris had no idea what Mikael was talking about. He realised his heart was pumping at a rate of knots, but even in his panic state, a light bulb pinged in his mind like a microwave going off and an idea flashed across his brain.

'I can save you,' he said. 'You need blood, right? Oakley Infirmary isn't far from here. If you come with me, I can distract the staff which will let you sneak and grab some blood bags.'

'You keep blood in bags? Whatever for?'

'Blood transfusions mostly,' Chris said. 'If you run into anyone, just use your spooky powers to tell them to piss off.'

'Piss off?'

'Christ, you really aren't from around here, are you? How old are you?'

'Centuries,' Mikael said, and struggled to stand up. 'I was born in the fifteen hundreds.'

Mikael stumbled and tried to use the wall to prop himself up and failed. Chris managed to grab the vampire before he hit the deck and was suddenly acutely aware of how close he was to the vampire's mouth.

'We humans are a fragile bunch. You either do this with me now, or you die?'

Mikael seemed to be thinking his over in his head, or perhaps he was thinking about cutting his losses and killing him and getting it over with. Less hassle. Instead, he said, 'Okay. But again, I must ask, why are you helping me?'

'Because,' Chris said, opening the door, allowing the sound of the rainfall to fill their ears. 'You let me live, and in all honesty, this is the most exciting my life has been in a hell of a long time. And I'm still not one hundred percent sure if I'm drunkenly imagining this or not.'

Chapter Five

Ten minutes had passed since Chris led the way out of the emporium and up the narrow street, onward to the infirmary. The clock had struck one AM, and Chris hoped there would be hardly anyone between them and the hospital. It would be a short one mile trek from the centre, heading north east towards the hospital.

The night air was chilly, but the sky was clear, clouds had disappeared. The rundown streetlights created a maze-like pattern, illuminating their path. Across the street, a group of people – six, maybe seven – stumbled past. Chris felt the tension in the air, as Mikael stared at them, the vampire possibly thinking about his next meal. The blood bags would do the trick. A simple case of distracting any reception staff whilst Mikael tracked down the blood. He'd just hope he didn't sink his fangs in to any hospital staff on his way there.

It was absurd, really. Here he was, walking down the street, still half drunk, with a supernatural being, one which he should fear and, by God, he was scared before, but he had calmed now. He felt on edge still, wondering if the vampire would cut his losses and chew him up, saving the hassle, but on the journey to the hospital, he never did.

Oakley Infirmary was dark, besides the writing above the main door. To the right was the outpatients' department – they wouldn't keep the blood in there. The infirmary used to be a lot bigger than it was, but with budget cuts and the lack of funding in the first place, the hospital downsized, and now it was only used for Accident and Emergency, Outpatient Departments and Sexual Health. Chris was glad he had never had to use any of them, especially the Sexual Health area, better known as the sexually transmitted diseases clinic.

Chris made a judgement call and reasoned the best place in the hospital to locate blood bags would be in the Accident and Emergency section. Surely that would be the place?

The two of them knelt behind a low wall, directly ahead of the main door.

'What is the plan?' Mikael said, before clutching his chest. 'We need to do this quick.'

'Thanks for the motivation,' Chris said. 'We'll go in, I'll make a scene to get rid of the reception staff and if you head down to the Accident and Emergency section, there should be some blood bags, just look for a big freezer.'

'Freezer?' Mikael said and turned his head as quick as a wink.

Chris quickly explained what a freezer was, then said, 'You ready?'

Mikael nodded.

The two of them turned to the side of the main door, so no one could see their approach. The hospital seemed to increase in size the closer they got, and as they skulked around, Chris had the fear someone would see them and wonder what the hell they were doing. What was he doing? This was insane. He'd wanted adventure, but sneaking a vampire into a hospital was next level. The dynamic duo – one on his last legs and the other seeking excitement – pressed themselves up onto the stone wall beside the main doors. Was that the *Mission Impossible* theme song he could hear?

Chris looked around briefly, and into the hospital. It was quiet. 'Let's go,' he said, pushing the double doors open and immediately clutching his chest. He yelled out in pain, screaming like a banshee, and fell to his knees. His eyes were closed, and he couldn't hear anyone running to help him, all he could hear was Mikael walking up behind him.

As if to drive the point home, he screamed, 'HELP!' But no help came. Or at least, he couldn't hear anybody. By now, he'd fallen face down on the cold white floor. A brief thought of how dirty the floor would be flashed through his mind, then the more important thought of why no one was coming to save him.

'Chris,' Mikael said, with a hint of impatience. 'It might be better if someone saw you doing this?'

'Eh?' Chris said, pushing himself up into a sitting position. 'Oh, right. Aye. Good point.'

The reception area was deserted. Clearly no one was operating the security cameras because, despite being pointed in his direction, no sod had come to his rescue.

He stood up and brushed his jeans. 'Right, well. You head off to look for the blood bags and I'll wait here.'

At that moment, a young receptionist seemed to have appeared from nowhere at the wooden desk, although she had not noticed the two men yet.

'Chris,' Mikael said.

'Aye?'

Mikael nodded towards the lady with the curly blonde hair, who looked like she was on her last breath before sleep would take hold. Chris exclaimed a number of expletives, then immediately fell to the ground again, clutching where he thought his heart was. He'd have been a couple of inches off.

'Oh,' the receptionist finally noticed. 'Are you okay?' She rushed round from her desk towards Chris.

About time, Chris thought.

The receptionist had a long white smock on, and a pair of black dolly shoes, and her hair was tied up in a taut ponytail. She appeared to be around Chris's age, but he couldn't tell for sure. As the receptionist knelt beside him, he looked at Mikael and met his eyes, he could see the vampire's eyes turning slightly crimson.

Chris had realised how idiotic he had been, he'd taken a vampire, a blood-sucking creature – a hunter, to a place where people would be, people in proximity who likely smelled of blood.

Things seemed to turn quiet. All he could hear was the mundane drone of the air conditioning. He stared at Mikael, urging him silently to control himself, and go find the bags.

The receptionist tried to help Chris to his feet, but he barely noticed. He was too engrossed in watching the vampire's internal struggle. He could see it on his face, and he saw his fists were clenched tight.

Finally, Mikael rushed from the scene, quicker than any human could, down the corridor, disappearing and Chris could only hope he'd not run into anyone else.

'Your pal's got some speed on him,' the blond woman said in a thick Scottish accent. 'Shame he's just left you here.'

Finally, the receptionist had gotten him to a standing

position, and leaned him against the reception table.

She looked him up and down. 'Now,' she said, raising an eyebrow. 'What's the problem with you?'

Chapter Six

Two hours ago, he had been sitting drinking an ice-cold pint of cider, chatting away with a close friend of his, and now? Sitting on his couch, watching a vampire gulping down a bag of dark, congealed blood like his life depended on it.

Chris studied the creature in front of him. He looked like a human, moved like a human. You wouldn't know he was a vampire passing him in the street. *Only when he was about to rip your throat out, you'd notice*, Chris thought.

Mikael finished the last drop of the blood, not allowing any of it to go to waste. He sat across from Chris, then looked around the room. The flat was nothing special. As you walked in the front door, a narrow hallway greeted you and halfway down on the left was a small closet and further down the corridor opened into a square living room with an open-plan kitchen at the far end. On the immediate left was his bedroom and the door next to that was the bathroom. It had been painted fully white to make the place look modern.

Chris followed his eyes, and wondered what Mikael was used to in terms of accommodation. Where did vampires live? What did they do? Was Dracula real? He had a lot of questions, but he found himself saying, 'It's not much, but it's a roof at least.'

Mikael looked at Chris for a moment longer than Chris was comfortable with, but the vampire's face slowly turned upwards in a smile.

'Thank you for your hospitality,' Mikael said, in an accent that Chris still had trouble placing. 'And, for your help with the blood. These bags will ensure no deaths tonight and no deaths in the future.'

'You're welcome,' Chris said.

'I must leave,' Mikael said, standing up, but Chris stood up too and the two men stared at each other like old gunslingers in the West.

'Stay a little,' Chris said. 'Can I ask you some questions? You must understand, this isn't normal. Will you sit?'

'I cannot,' Mikael said. 'It is never good for a vampire to be around a human. We were created to hunt and to kill.'

'I understand that, but you haven't killed me yet, and I have so many questions I want to ask. Please. Remember, mate, I saved your life tonight and I won't tell anyone about this.'

'You did save my life,' Mikael said, sitting back down. 'I owe you a debt. What would you like to ask?'

Chris started to speak, but then stopped. He had so many questions that it was difficult to narrow them down. He looked at the man across from him. Would he be insulted at some questions?

'I guess,' Chris said, shifting uncomfortably in his seat. 'I know it's true, the fact that you're a vampire. But I'd be lying if I said I wasn't a bit shocked. You have to understand that this isn't normal.'

Mikael nodded.

'Where did you come from? Why are you here? And I suppose, the biggest question is why am I still alive?'

'Well,' Mikael said and then stood. He crossed the living room towards the window and peered out into the street below. 'My name is Mikael, as you know. I was created – born, as you would call it – in the fifteenth century and I was turned on the full moon of January 7th. I am - was - part of the Dragoslav Coven. Created by a man named Dragoslav after he had been created by a coven of witches in Romania.'

'Witches?' Chris said, blurting it out before pressing his lips together and stopping himself from saying anything else.

'Drago was and is the very first Moroi. As far as I am aware, in the world you have, there are five vampires. I am one of them.'

'Where are the rest of them?'

Mikael looked towards the floor, then turned to Chris, before saying, 'I do not know. I do not want to know. We were put to sleep many centuries ago after a battle with the witches, and we were awoken months ago.'

'You mentioned you were turned? Was it this Dragoslav who turned you?'

'Yes.'

'Can you turn people?'

Mikael looked at Chris. Chris looked at him and found a little bit of sweat trickling down his forehead. He wiped it away with his sleeve, then took a deep breath.

'No,' Mikael said. 'Only the leader of the Coven has the power to do that. On the night of a full moon, the coven leader can turn a human by making them drink vampire blood.'

'So, you can't turn me?'

'No. You do not want this life, Chris. Living in the shadows, living in fear for your life. Living with the cravings, the incessant desire to kill.'

'When you put it like that, I suppose not. I have to say, mate, this is all very fascinating. Is that accent Romanian?'

'Yes, and no. We travelled all around Europe in our time before we were put to sleep.'

'What made you come here?'

'My partner – Rose – lived here. Dragoslav turned her for me, but she did not survive the battle in the Hoia Forest.'

Chris recognised the name from a documentary he had watched about supposedly haunted places around the world. Hoia Forest was a forest on the outskirts of a city in Romania. Perhaps they weren't far off the haunted aspect.

'Are the stories true that vampires cannot go out in sunlight?'

Mikael nodded. 'That is correct. Part of the spell the witches created ensured we could only roam around at night. Otherwise, we would die.'

Chris leaned back in his chair. There was a lot to process. Witches and vampires? *It was wild*, he thought.

'This must be very overwhelming for you,' Mikael said.

'Aye, you're not wrong,' Chris said. He raised his wrist to his head but noticed his watch showing the time as three AM. 'Damn it. Listen, I better get some sleep. You're welcome too... eh... I don't know, make yourself at home.'

Chris got up, and took the short strides required to reach the bedroom door. He opened the door and stepped inside, before reaching his head back out.

'Will you stay? I have a lot of questions.'

Mikael considered it for a moment, glancing Chris up

and down before looking at the pile of blood bags – there must have been around fifteen there. He nodded.

Chapter Seven

His eyes slowly adjusted to the box room before him. The walls were mottled brown and there were damp patches on the ceiling. Chris slept peacefully, and, for the first time in a long while, woke up with a pep in his step. His small window allowed just enough light to pop through. Chris wiped the sleep from his eyes and grabbed his phone. Using his dirty fingernails – he'd not had time to shower last night – he turned the phone on, and he suddenly jumped from the bed. He was late. Very late.

The lecture had been due to start at eleven, and it had already gone ten minutes past. Reaching into his bedside drawer, he yanked out a white t-shirt and a pair of blue jeans. He slid one leg into the jeans whilst trying to get the t-shirt over his head, resulting in a very poor fall, landing and bruising his knee.

Once he was dressed, he grabbed his phone, smoothed down his hair with a lick of his hand and opened the bedroom door.

The living room was deserted – he had expected to see

Mikael there, but the vampire was gone. Not just gone, but it was as if no trace of him ever existed. The blood bags were gone, the cushions on the chair were immaculately presented and the chill in the air had disappeared. What had he expected, exactly? Perhaps he had expected to see Mikael stretched out on the floor, like a body in a coffin?

Did the events of the previous night even happen? Did he really meet a supernatural being, raid a hospital for blood bags and learn about the origins of some vampire coven?

Or was it all an alcohol-induced dream?

Had he dreamed up the whole thing? Just to make his life seem that bit more exciting.

He had no time to think about it now. The door was unlocked, meaning either someone had left, or he had just forgotten to close it in his drink induced stupor.

Oakley had two Universities for a small town. Oakley University and City of Oakley University.

The former was the prestigious one, the one where all the students who went to High School in the city wanted to go too. But Chris had ruined his chances to get in when he'd been late for the interview and turned up stinking of booze. *Just a few shots*, he had decided the night before, and what a mistake that was.

He'd reach City of Oakley quickly. The roads were deserted, and the weather was clear. It was silent, hardly any traffic. It made sense, most people would be in work or already at school by now. He approached the building; it was just one campus. Unlike Oakley Uni, which had different buildings for each discipline, Chris's Uni didn't have such luxury. All the lectures were held from one building, with most lessons being done on Zoom or Teams.

Chris never truly trusted Zoom or Teams – he'd always

have his camera and his microphone switched off, and even place a white sticker over his web cam.

He would say one thing for the Uni though, when he told them he didn't have a laptop, they had provided one. An Acer something or other, it wasn't great, but it was serviceable.

The building was silver with black roofs, and the windows were square like an old Victorian building. The Uni was established in 1999. Created to give the lesser students of Oakley somewhere to go. Most high performing students travelled outwards to Edinburgh, Glasgow, Stirling or even Aberdeen. The level below went to Oakley University and the level below them went to Chris's University.

He walked into the building, past the receptionist table and into the right wing of the building. This was where his lectures were held. He'd been studying English with the view of writing his own screenplay or novel. That would get him up on the alumni board, giving him the privilege of sharing the stage with a football stud.

Approaching the doors to the lecture hall, he smoothed his hair once again and tried to act nonchalant. The one thing he'd hated about High School was if you were late for a class, the whole student body would stare at you like you'd killed someone.

He knew Ashley would have saved him a seat, so at least he'd not have to sit by himself. Although how she might have felt about being stood up was anyone's guess.

He opened the white doors, as if he was a God coming to see his disciples.

The lecture hall wasn't big as by standard University sizes, it wasn't the type of University that could afford huge rooms to teach in, but from where Chris stood, it seemed massive. Because just like in High School, everybody in the room turned in his direction. Some smirked, some couldn't have cared less, and others shook their heads.

Down the steps, the lecturer, Mr Connors, stood with his pasty hands on his hips. He was an older man, losing his hair and he had recently started wearing glasses. He didn't look angry, just disappointed.

'Nice of you to join us, Mr Winters,' he said, and ushered him into the room.

Chris muttered some form of apology and scanned the room for Ashley. She was to his right, dressed in a green jumper. Her long hair fell straight as a ruler from her head, and she shook her head at him as he approached.

'Sorry,' Chris whispered, allowing Mr Connors to get back to his class. 'Slept in.'

Chris got in close beside Ashley, and she immediately put her fingers to her nose, closing her nostrils with the ferocity of a clothes peg.

'Chris,' she said, sounding like she had a stuffed nose. 'No offence, but you stink of alcohol. Have you not showered?'

'I—'

'Chris!' Mr Connors shouted from the bottom of the hall, this time his face was a picture of aggression. His right eyelid twitched, and his mouth was pointed down. 'You have arrived late to your lesson. Please sit down and don't interrupt the rest of the lecture.'

Chris held his hand up in apology. He made sure to keep his armpit pressed down to ensure no other bad smells made their appearance known. He didn't have the time to shower this morning. *Besides, with the water pressure in that shower I'd have struggled to get clean even with the wash*, he thought.

He made a mental note: buy a new showerhead.

The lesson carried on for the next forty-five minutes,

and Chris spent the time taking hand-written notes in his journal.

The rest of the class, most of them at least, had tablets or small laptops, but not him. He'd taken longhand notes, and Ashley did the same, although he imagined hers were out of preference rather than circumstance. The lesson consisted of speaking about Thomas Hardy. Then, switching pace, they spoke about bringing a piece of writing to the next lecture, albeit on Zoom.

Chris was an avid reader, when he wasn't out drinking or watching a movie, he could be found with a book in his hand. He fell into the habit of reading after his parents started disappearing for days and weeks at a time. They would always give him a new book to read: Tom Clancy, Dan Brown and, when he was older, Stephen King. It was their way of pacifying him and allowed them to avoid the awkward conversation of where they had been.

Mr Connors signed the lesson off and allowed the students to leave. Ashley stood and packed her bag. She hadn't spoken to Chris since he arrived, but he'd hoped that was due to the fact they were in a lecture, not because she was annoyed he'd been late. He imagined her, standing outside waiting, watching as all the younger students went in.

'Mr Winters,' Connors said. 'A moment of your time?'

Chris had just put his notebook into his bag, then zipped it up. He laid it on the seat and turned to Ashley and said, 'Wait outside for me?'

Ashley nodded. 'Don't be late this time.'

She wasn't pissed. The words were said with an air of sarcasm, as she showed the million-dollar smile Chris had become such a fan of over the past months. He'd known nothing would ever happen between them, she made it perfectly clear she wasn't interested in a relationship. Chris decided he'd rather be friends than not be in her life at all, so he accepted it. Did he still hold feelings for her? Yes, but not in the way he'd expected. He now saw her as a close friend rather than someone he could try to date.

He had no dating experience. One kiss at a High School dance with Matilda Robson didn't count, not that he remembered it well. The booze some of the kids sneaked in saw to that. Most of the students had left now, and Chris took the steps two at a time, being careful not to fall onto his face.

'Mr Connors,' Chris said, smiling.

'Hold on,' Connors said, looking at the final student, who was a moment away from leaving. Now that he was gone, the teacher continued: 'We need to have a word.'

He showed Chris to the leather seat at his desk and told him to sit. Connors took the seat opposite him. The desk was covered in white papers, some unmarked, some marked. Chris had no idea how the man kept himself organised with the haphazard way his desk was laid out.

But then, was he any different? If you looked at his flat, you'd think the exact same thing.

'Chris, I have to say, as your teacher, I'm a bit worried about you.'

'Oh,' Chris said. He had no idea how to respond, instead he rolled his thumb in his hand and chewed the inside of his cheek.

'Your grades at the start of the year were good, but with every assignment they have regressed. You're late for class, you always look as though you're stressed, and, might I be so bold, you don't look like you have had a good night's sleep in days.'

'I'm sorry, Mr Connors.'

'Don't be sorry,' he said. 'Can I help with anything?'

You could keep your nose out of my business, Chris

thought, but then said, 'Not really. I'm just struggling a little with the coursework, but I'll get there.'

A part of him told him to be angry. What gave the tutor the right to question how he was doing? Chris found it both amusing and sad that Connors had showed more of an interest in his studies than his parents ever did, and perhaps that was the problem. A small part of him blamed them for how he'd turned out. He was annoyed he was not living the lifestyle his parents had – travelling everywhere, meeting new people, the life of mystery he had used to call it.

Now, he was a former office worker, struggling to live in a disgusting one-bedroom flat, studying a degree from a University that barely broke the top sixty of Universities in the United Kingdom.

'Your mother and father would be very disappointed to see the level of work you're putting in.'

Chris hadn't expected the scathing words from the teacher. Chris felt something rise from his feet, up his legs, through his stomach and out of his mouth.

'Screw you,' he said, standing up, smashing his thighs on the edge of the table. He ignored the pain in his legs and pointed at the tutor. 'Don't tell me what my parents would think of me. I know you knew them, and, let me tell you this, they weren't the fantastic parents you and everyone else thought they were.'

'Chris—'

Chris closed his fist and slammed it on the table, sending papers flying. Connors tried to catch some of them, but most of them ended up on the floor.

'My parents were never there for me. They would have sooner put me into care than looked after me! Do you think it was easy? Being left by yourself for weeks with no clue why? Why they left their little boy for days and days by himself, just with a visitor every so often to make sure I had food?'

Chris's chest was moving up and down now, and his face had turned a dark shade of red.

'Christ,' he said, shaking his head and almost laughing. 'I'm not sure that's even legal, leaving a minor by themselves. But it doesn't matter because they're gone and I'm still here. You have no right to tell me how my dead parents would think about me.'

Chris stormed up the steps of the lecture hall, grabbing his backpack on the way past his seat. He shook his head. How dare he question him on what his parents would want? No one had the right to do that.

He turned to the teacher, expecting to see anger, but the man had his head in his hand, perhaps he had realised he was out of line? No matter though, Chris was far too pissed off to make Connors feel better. His heart was pumping blood around his body too quick, he felt as though he would have a heart attack at any moment.

He imagined the anger stemming from the fact that, the night before, he'd had a taste of what his life could have been like. Even if he had dreamed it all up, it was excitement, it was meaning, and it was doing something with his life that helped somebody.

The truth was, since his parents died, Chris had felt empty. Living a life with no purpose, other than to go to school and get a decent grade. But then what? It's not like his job prospects would be great with a degree from City of Oakley, especially in English. And after that outburst, he may not even get the degree in the first place.

He pushed open the main doors of the lecture hall and stepped into the corridor.

Chapter Eight

Outside of the University, Chris had not made eye contact with Ashley for a few minutes – he'd not been able to. She would have heard his outburst in the lecture hall. He didn't regret it, but he was frustrated at allowing his emotions to get the better of him. He'd been running low on sleep, confused about the events of the previous night, unsure if they had even happened, and he was hung over. He took a deep breath in, and then let all the air out through his mouth, enough so his lungs were completely empty.

'Are you okay?' Ashley said.

Chris didn't speak for a moment. He looked away, then back. 'I'm fine,' he said.

Ashley nodded and let the silence hang in the air a moment, before asking, 'What time did you get home last night?'

He wanted to tell her everything. He made a promise to Mikael that he'd keep him a secret, that he wouldn't tell a soul. But was Mikael even real? What harm would telling Ashley do, it's not like Mikael was around anymore. If he was real, he would have disappeared, and Chris believed he'd never see him again.

'I met a vampire,' he said and almost winced. It truly was absurd.

Ashley stared at him, unmoving and unblinking. 'You're not still drunk, are you?'

Chris found himself smiling at that. He knew she wouldn't believe him – who would? Nobody would believe it, and he wasn't sure he believed it either.

Chris softened. 'I should really apologise, eh?'

'To Connors?' she said, and stood up, checking her phone then looking back at Chris. 'From what I heard he was out of line, but it might save your degree if you suck it up and say sorry.'

'I suppose.'

'Listen,' she said, getting a little closer. 'You know we're mates, right? You can talk to me about what you're going through. I might not have answers for you, but I can at least listen.'

'I know,' he said. 'Thanks, Ash.'

'Now, we were talking last night about how boring our lives were, so I was thinking we do something to spice it up a bit.'

His issue wasn't just that his life was boring, it was the lack of love and the lack of caring his parents showed him. He blamed them for how he turned out – and deep down he blamed them for dying.

'What did you have in mind?'

'Well,' she said. 'Let me organise it, it'll be a surprise. Just keep next weekend free.'

He looked into the distance, half excited by what the plan would be, but the other half wondered what Mikael was doing.

＊ ＊ ＊

His flat was nothing to write home about. He'd lived there for a year, and still he'd never seen the upstairs neighbours. Sometimes he thought he could hear somebody up there but other times it was dead silent.

The rent was decent, around two hundred a month which he could afford with the savings he had from the job he took to get himself by until starting University.

His parents didn't have life insurance, or rather – they did, but they had cancelled it. Likely to get money to travel the world. He had no clue what his parents did for work.

He opened the front door and felt the door groan, he was almost sure it was about to snap off its hinges.

Chris turned towards the bathroom. He grabbed a pink towel off the radiator and turned on the shower and let the water heat up before stepping in.

He washed the alcohol smell off, and the felt the frustrations of the day cascading off. He'd been wrong to yell at his tutor, but he still felt Connors didn't have the right to say what he did. He'd write an apology after the shower, he thought. His next lecture wasn't for a week, and it was on Zoom, so an email would be best for everyone. *Save the awkward face to face conversation,* he thought.

He thought back to the night before and how much of a thrill he'd had.

He pressed the off button and the water trickled to a halt. He stepped out, pushing the white shower curtain back and proceeded to dry himself with the towel. It was an old one, but it still did the trick. He was dry in minutes, and then shoved a t-shirt and shorts on. As he was getting dressed, his stomach rumbled.

He opened the fridge in the small kitchen, and he was met with nothing but a couple bottles of beer and some cold meat, ham, and turkey. He could order food, but he needed to save money. Especially if Ashley's surprise ended up costing him. He was looking forward to what she had cooked up, but depending on what it was it might mean dipping into savings reserved for his rent. The weekly payment from SAAS was not enough to cover the rent, which meant he was slowly losing money each month. He grabbed the cold meat and a bottle of beer. He sat down on the couch and switched the TV on. It took a few seconds for it to warm up, and when it did there was some daytime movie on. A western it looked like.

He picked up his laptop and, as he waited the five minutes for it to boot up, he wired into the cold meat before using the edge of the wooden table to crack open the beer.

He took a deep gulp before exhaling loudly.

The laptop booted up. Chris opened Outlook and opened a new message.

Mr Connors,

I would like to apologise for my outburst in your class today, and for being late in the first place. As you said, my parents died and, like you also said, they would be very disappointed in how my life has turned out.

But I shouldn't be taking that out on you. Again, I'm sorry, and hope I can continue in your class. I understand our next lecture is on Zoom in a week's time. If I do not hear from you, I will assume I am still enrolled in the course.

Thank you,
Chris Winters.

He read the email over multiple times before deciding to bite the bullet. He wasn't confident that it sounded genuine, but it was difficult when he didn't believe what he was saying. He needed to say sorry, but he felt he was owed an apology as well.

He closed the laptop.

He zoned out and watched the film for a few minutes. A movie he had never seen before called *Deadwood* entertained him for a while before he lay down and stared at the ceiling. It needed a good wash.

Did last night happen? He asked himself. He was still unsure. The alcohol didn't help. It had felt real at the time, but there was no trace of the vampire when he woke up.

Shame. It was the first bit of excitement and first time he truly felt alive since his parents died. He was almost vampire chow, but despite that, he loved the experience of meeting something else. Meeting something that wasn't human.

Maybe he could use it as a story idea?

He threw the bottle to the side; it was now empty so didn't spill any of the liquid. He perked up like a meerkat and grabbed the laptop again. After five minutes, he booted up Microsoft Word and started writing his story. At least, now, he could document it on paper and maybe turn it into something to publish.

He started typing and spent the remainder of the evening on that. He became so engrossed that the clock had struck midnight before he even noticed. He had written about five thousand words and was looking pleased.

He was no Stephen King or Dean Koontz but, reading back over it, he was pleased with what he had wrote.

Chapter Nine

The Audi sped down the motorway with Ashley at the steering wheel. It wasn't her car; she couldn't afford a car just yet. She'd explained how her dad allowed her to borrow it.

'Can we roll the window down a little?' Chris said.

'Go for it,' Ashley replied.

'Thanks,' Chris said, clicking the window icon on his armrest and watching the window slowly drop to the bottom. They had been on the road for about half an hour now, and still Ashley hadn't let slip what the plan was. Every time he'd ask, Ashley would smirk and say nothing.

For the first time in days, Chris felt excited and felt like he was enjoying life. Since his outburst at the University, he'd spent his days writing his idea for a short story, which had quickly turned into a novel with how much he was trying to write. He'd not thought about the vampire besides writing the book. He couldn't tell anyone – no one would believe him – but he could write about the experience. Get it down in writing and it might seem more real to him. With every passing day he started to believe he'd imagined the whole thing.

'I haven't seen you in ages,' Ashley said.

'Aye. It's been a while.'

'Did you hear back from Connors?' Ashley said, pressing the indicator down and pulling into the left-hand lane, past the sign for Glasgow.

'Yeah,' he said. 'He said he was sorry, so hopefully tomorrow's lecture won't be too awkward.'

'Just keep your camera and your microphone switched off. He probably won't even notice you're there.'

'Good plan. Aye, that's what I'll do. So, where are we off too?'

Ashley smiled. 'I told you already, you won't know until we get there. But believe me, it'll be a good laugh.'

'Fair enough.'

Ashley drove in silence for a few minutes as Chris scrolled through his phone. He'd been looking through Instagram then settled on Facebook to kill time.

'Can I ask you something?' Ashley said.

'Go for it,' Chris replied, sliding his phone back into his jeans pocket. He'd opted for comfortable blue jeans and a non-attention-seeking white shirt.

'Would you be up for coming to my parents' house at the weekend? For dinner, I mean.'

Chris found himself without words for a moment. This was the last thing he'd expected to hear. 'Did they ask?'

'Well,' she said, focusing hard on the road and watching a Renault overtake her. 'They know that we're good pals, and they wanted me to ask if you were interested. My mum makes a mean steak pie.'

'If steak pies are on the menu, then how can I say no? I'll come. Is it Saturday?'

'Sunday,' she said and struggled to hide a smile.

'Thanks, they'll be glad.'

'Good,' Chris said, staring out of the window at the fast-moving trees flying past them.

The idea of meeting Ashley's parents didn't faze him because it wasn't done in a 'let's meet your boyfriend' way. Chris knew, without getting confirmation from Ashley, she would have told them about the death of his parents, and no doubt they felt sorry for him. Hence the invite.

He appreciated the invite though.

'We're about fifteen minutes away,' Ashley said.

* * *

'You're absolutely mental,' Chris said. They had arrived, and were close to the River Clyde, and standing in front of them across from the car park was a large crane. 'Are you for real?'

'Yep,' Ashley said, full of pep and raring to go. 'You wanted excitement and adventure. Well, here you go.'

'A bungee jump?'

He looked towards the top of the crane; it must have been at least a hundred feet high. In front of them was a small hut-like building, where some staff members were milling around. They spotted the two of them coming, and one of them, a smaller man with black hair, went out to greet them.

'Ashley?' the man said and Ashley nodded. 'Great. I'm Angus and I'll be your instructor today. Hope you both are ready for it, it's good fun.'

'I'm sure,' Chris said, regretting the sarcasm in his voice.

'Worried?' Angus asked. 'Everyone is when it's their first time.'

Ashley walked forward, with Angus, towards the entrance of the hut, and then said, 'First time for everything. So how do we do it?'

'We'll take you to the top of the crane,' he said, grabbing some ropes and what looked climbing equipment from behind the small wooden reception desk. 'Then we'll strap you in and you'll jump. Simple, right?'

'Is it over the river?' Chris asked, as he was handed some of the equipment.

'Aye, that's right. We'll then hoist you back up with the winch and I guarantee you'll want to go again.'

Chris doubted that very much, but Ashley had been right, he had wanted some excitement in his life, to do something out of the ordinary.

Angus led the two of them to the lift. It seemed to be like one of those platforms window cleaners used, but it was automatic and when they stepped on, Angus pressed a button, and they were slowly lifted to the heavens. The air seemed to get thinner and, for a moment, Chris felt light-headed, he steadied himself on the railing of the platform, looking out into the distance, avoiding looking down.

Across from his view, he could see one of the three big football stadiums in Glasgow, but he wasn't sure which one. He'd liked football, but he'd never ended up supporting one of the two Old Firm teams like everyone else had.

The platform reached the top, and Angus opened the platform gate and said, 'Ladies first.'

Ashley took a tentative step onto the orange crane and used the railing as a guide. At the end of the crane was a modified stage, big enough to fit a group of people on it. On the stage was the winch, and another couple of staff members waiting.

'Not sure how they could be waiting there,' Chris said. 'The air's so thin.'

'You get used to it,' Angus said.

They spent the next few minutes putting all their gear

on. Angus and the other two staff members made sure they were all tightly packed in.

'Right,' Angus said, clapping his hands together. 'Who's first?'

Ashley looked at Chris. Ashley looked back at Angus and said, 'Can we do it together? Like a tandem one?'

Angus shook his head. 'Sorry, we don't have the equipment for a tandem jump, but hopefully in the future.'

'Right,' Ashley said. 'Aye. Well, I'll go first then. Ladies first and all that.'

Chris looked at Ashley and smiled. He would have been fine with going first, but it was always good to see how it was done. Ashley was much braver than he was.

Ashley shimmied over to the edge of the stage where the barrier gave way to a small corridor she could edge out on. She looked down and smiled. Ashley looked at Angus, who gave her the nod.

Suddenly, she disappeared. Chris peered over the edge, as did Angus and his staff. Ashley was plummeting to the river below. Despite it being water below, Chris knew that if she hit the water at that speed that she would – at best – end up with a broken neck with the speed and angle of the fall. But she didn't hit the water. The bungee cord reached its longest point, and did its job nicely, effectively stopping her in mid-air and rebounding back. Ashley screamed, but it was a yell of joy. She bounced up and down a couple of times before Angus hit the button on the winch, and the rope began to roll back up.

'Wow,' Chris said.

'It's something isn't it?' Angus asked.

'Not half.'

After about a minute of being wheeled back up – she did have over a hundred feet to travel – she was pulled back onto the platform and detached from the rope. 'That was amazing,' she shouted and gave Chris a big, tight hug.

He hadn't expected it and he took a moment before he returned the favour.

'Right,' Chris said, slapping his hands together. 'My turn, eh?'

Chris walked over to Angus and allowed the man to strap the bungee cord and the safety rope onto him. His body was tight, partly because of how much all of the equipment weighed, but also because he was a bit nervous. His brow had begun to sweat, and he hoped no one had noticed. *Anybody would be nervous*, he told himself.

Despite watching Ashley do it with no problem, his brain went into self-preservation mode and gave him many reasons why he shouldn't do it. *The rope could snap. You could hit the water. The winch might not work, and you'd be stuck. Then what?* He took two timid steps onto the edge of the stage, shuffling like a zombie. He peered over again. The last time he peered over he had been focused on Ashley and the enjoyment she was having. But this time, all he could see was the water below, and his imminent death.

Stop it, he told himself, and if no one was around he would have given himself a good slap. He had handled a freaking vampire and handled the loss of his parents – not well, granted, but he had handled it. This was nothing. He imagined himself diving off the board at the local swimming pool, he used to practice diving off his couch when he was a kid when he was bored. Just do the same, just close your eyes and think of that.

He counted down from five in his head, and on number one he leaned forward and let gravity do the rest.

All his weight disappeared, and he felt lighter than air. His body launched itself towards the ground, streamlined like a shark moving through water.

He kept his eyes closed tightly.

He would reach the end of the rope soon, so he steeled himself for the bounce back. But it never came. He continued to fall, he felt like he was falling for what seemed like hours. His brain showed him images of his parents and their dead bodies at the funeral, showed him the image of Mikael attacking him, complete with his crimson eyes. Finally, it showed the image of a smiling Ashley.

He opened his eyes and saw the water crashing towards him.

He expected to hit the river, to be thrown into the dirty, disgusting Clyde. He didn't want to imagine what was hidden beneath the liquid, who knows what the residents of Glasgow dumped in it.

But he didn't hit the water.

The rope did its job - stopping him a few feet from the surface, and springing back, sending him rising into the air like a phoenix from the ashes. Chris yelled out a scream of relief, but also of happiness. His heart was rapid, and his breath was short, but he was loving the experience.

After reaching the top of the rope, his body fell back towards the water, this time at a slower speed but gravity was pulling him towards it again. It stopped, and he felt the blood start rushing to his head. He'd felt light-headed before, but this time the blood caused his brain to pulse like it was under attack. He felt like he had a headache, right in his left temple, but he put it down to the adrenaline pumping through his body.

The winch did its thing now, yanking him upwards, towards the platform.

He reached the top and was helped by Angus. He took off the cord and the safety rope, then Chris leaned against the barrier and breathed a loud sigh.

'Exciting, right?' Angus said, rolling up the ropes.

'Aye,' Chris said, looking over the edge again. 'Can say that again.'

Angus finished rolling up the rope, and led the way to the platform that would take them back down to solid ground.

Ashley tucked in beside Chris. 'Well, enjoy it?'

Chris wrapped his arm around her waist and pulled her in close, giving her a quick hug and saying, 'Thank you.'

Angus opened the gate to the platform, and the two of them climbed in. He pushed the button at the side, and the contraption lowered. Chris looked over the side again, this time not afraid.

At the little hut, they handed in their helmets and said their goodbyes. 'Here you go,' Ashley said, handing Angus a ten-pound note.

'You paid already when you booked it?'

Ashley shook her head. 'Little tip.'

Angus took the cash and placed it on the counter. 'Thank you. And hey, tell your friends!'

Ashley nodded and led Chris to the car park.

'I'll need to square you up for my half,' Chris said.

'The hell you will,' Ashley said. 'It was my idea, so I'm paying.'

'I can't let you pay for me, besides it was great fun, so I should pay for my own.'

'No chance.'

Chris sighed as they reached the car. He'd known Ashley to be generous, and she was aware of his trouble with money, but he still felt like he should pay for his half.

'Come on,' Chris said, climbing into the Audi and clicking his seat belt in. 'How much?'

'Chris, stop. It was my idea, so I pay for it. Besides, I didn't book it just for you. I had a blast.'

'Aye, I know, but—'

Ashley held up a hand. 'Are you busy tonight?'

Chris made a show of thinking of his answer, looking up. 'Upon checking the diary, I'm not. How come?'

'How about you buy me a drink? And we'll call it even.'

'Fine, but it will need to be a lot of drinks to cover that experience.

'Aye,' she said, turning the engine on and putting the gear into first. 'Well, who said it would just be one?'

She lifted the clutch, and they joined the motorway, leading back to Oakley.

Chris found himself thinking of the jump again, how all those pictures flashed through his mind, and despite the great experience, one image stuck in his head. Mikael. Would he ever see him again? Was it even real?

Maybe he'd find out tonight, maybe he'd go to the spot where he was attacked.

Or maybe he'd just focus on having a good time with his friend and forget about any supernatural nonsense.

Chapter Ten

'Remember, I'm buying.'

'Yes, sir.'

Chris opened the door to the same bar they went to the previous week. He led Ashley to a table, and the two of them sat down. It was only seven PM, meaning the bar wasn't full but it was starting to get busy.

'You want food?' Chris asked, picking the menu up from the table.

Ashley did the same and scanned the leaflet. 'Are you hungry?'

Chris felt his stomach rumble. 'After today? Aye, just a wee bit.'

'What you going to go for?'

Chris wasn't sure. He looked over the menu, the burgers caught his eye. He'd never eaten in The Wet Whistle before, just drinking, but he was ravenous and needed something in his stomach. The food wouldn't be up to much, but right now he could eat a scabby horse.

'Think I'll go with the burger,' he said. 'You?'

'I'll go with the chicken wings,' she said.

Part of what Chris liked about Ashley so much was how much she didn't conform to what was expected of her. People would have expected her to get pasta or lasagna; but she was very much like Chris, she liked her meat and she liked comfort food.

'I'll go order,' he said, grabbing both menus and heading to the counter. He shimmied by an older couple taking their drinks to their table and propped himself up by the bar. He nodded at a younger man with blond hair at the end of the bar, sipping what looked like gin or vodka.

'Alright, mate?'

His deep thoughts were interrupted by the thick Scottish accent. Colin stood before him, smiling with his hand towel flicked over his shoulder. He still had the same hair style, and this time wore a blue shirt with black jeans.

'Fancy meeting you here,' Chris said.

'Aye well,' Colin said, taking the hand towel and drying off a pint glass. 'Got to make the pennies.'

Chris nodded. It was nice to see a familiar face.

'Usual?'

Only regulars would get the fabled 'usual' from a bartender.

'Aye,' he said. 'Can we order food too?'

'Sure. What will it be?'

Chris placed the order, telling him the table number – 13 – and then waited for the drinks. Colin placed a pint of cider and a vodka and orange on the bar. Chris grabbed his wallet and paid for both the alcohol and the food, coming to a modest total of just under twenty pounds: the least he could do after what Ashley had set up. He had looked up the place they had gone to and it wasn't cheap. He'd made a mental note that she wouldn't be paying for anything tonight.

'It'll be around ten minutes,' Colin said, then went over to serve another customer. A loud shout came from the back of the bar where the pool table was, a group of men, three of them, were playing pool and one of them, a man with a tattoo on his neck, seemed to be winning, calling one of the others a dick for being so bad at the game. 'Watch them, they're bad news apparently. The guy with the tattoo is called Greg. Nasty piece of work, by all accounts.'

Chris looked at Colin then back at the pool table; he then glanced at the man with the blond hair who nodded back at him.

He took his drinks back to his table.

'Be around ten minutes,' he said.

Another bartender, a woman in her twenties, brought their food over after the ten minutes had passed.

They tucked in, neither of them had eaten all day, so it didn't take long before the food was gone.

The burger and wings went down a treat. Ashley used up a lot of the napkins given since the wings were greasy, but a great kind of greasy, the kind you love and want more of.

'Did you enjoy today?' Ashley asked, wiping her fingers on a clean napkin, and putting it to the side.

Chris took a long drink of his cider, then said, 'It was brilliant. Genuinely had no idea that's what you had in mind. Not going to lie though, my heart was going like a train, but it was amazing.'

'Good,' Ashley said. 'You did say you wanted some excitement.'

'I did,' Chris said and thought about the fact it wasn't quite what he had in mind. Maybe he would go to the same place tonight after sending Ashley home – Mikael was still skulking around.

'You're looking forward to the lecture tomorrow?'

'You're joking, right? It's going to be so awkward.'

'I thought you had buried the hatchet with the teacher.'

Chris took another drink. 'We did. Well, at least I think we did. It was via email, so I've not actually spoken to him.'

'It'll be fine,' Ashley said, brushing her long hair out of her face and then pushing the plate forward. 'Besides, it's on Zoom so just keep your camera off. He won't even know you're there.'

'Good plan. So, is it this weekend you want me round to your parents?'

'Aye.' Ashley smiled, then looked at the table. 'If that's fine with you. You don't need to if you don't want to.'

Part of him wanted to, but another part knew the reason they had asked is because they likely felt sorry for him. Alone and with no parents. He didn't know for sure if Ashley had told them, but it was the only reason he could think for their sudden interest in him.

'Happy to,' Chris said. 'Should I bring anything?'

'Like what?'

'I don't know,' he said, stretching his arms out. 'Don't people bring gifts to dinner parties?'

Ashley laughed. 'Dinner party? This isn't *Come Dine with Me*. It's just a dinner, you don't need to bring anything. Just maybe wear a shirt or something.'

'Fair enough, mate. Can I ask you a question?'

'Go for it.'

'Well,' Chris said, and part of his brain told him he didn't need to ask, but another part knew he had to. 'Did you tell your parents about the fact my mum and dad died?'

Ashley looked down and Chris knew immediately that

she had.

'It's fine if you did,' he said, smiling. 'I don't mind. I just figured it'd be good to know before the weekend.'

'They asked how you were, and I let it slip. Sorry,' she said. 'We weren't gossiping or anything.'

'I know,' Chris said. 'Besides, probably better they know to avoid any awkward conversations. It's not like it's a secret, I suppose. I mean, I felt a bit better after telling you last time we were here.'

Ashley looked up. 'Really?'

He nodded. 'It was good to have someone find out about it, and not disappear.'

'What do you mean?'

He sighed and started to twirl a toothpick in his fingers. 'Well, whenever someone finds out, they tend to treat you like a lost puppy. Like one wrong word might crack me. It's probably why all my old pals don't speak to me anymore. That or they have their own thing going on.'

'Is that why your relatives aren't around?'

'I don't have many to be fair. But the ones that I do have, my uncle and aunt, don't have anything to do with me. They live abroad anyway so they aren't fussed about me. To be honest, even my parents weren't too fussed about me. They were more interested in travelling.'

'Do you think that's why they cashed in their life insurance? To travel more?'

'Maybe.' He had to admit it wasn't quite what he thought they had cancelled the policy for, but it'd make sense. 'I never thought about it like that. I never knew what they did for money, but they never seemed to be short of it. Always travelling, never at home. Did I tell you, whenever they would come home, they'd always give me a new book? Like they were trying to pay me off.'

'Must have been difficult,' Ashley said, pausing for a

moment. 'Not seeing them that much and being left by yourself.'

'I had my friends, so it wasn't too bad. But there was always the part of me that wished they cared a bit more. Buying me off with a book wasn't quite what I wanted my relationship with my parents to be.'

'You said it was a car crash?'

Ashley had a knack for this. She would make you feel comfortable enough to talk about anything. 'That's what I was told and that's what's on the death certificate.'

There was an odd silence, like the pub had gone silent. The noise soon picked up, it was like he had lost his hearing for a second, but he realised it was because he was so engrossed in the conversation.

'We weren't close or anything so when they died it wasn't that bad on me, but them dying left me struggling with money and I couldn't stay in the house because the bank took it back. So, I'm just doing what I need to do to get by.'

'That's why you think your life's boring, isn't it? The fact that you wanted to live an exciting, extraordinary life but you're stuck in a rut.'

'I suppose.'

'I know you said that all your friends kind of disappeared after your parents died, and whenever you tell people they treat you differently. I think we have become good friends, don't you?'

Chris nodded.

She smiled.

'Well,' she said and paused. 'I'm still here. And I won't treat you any different. You'll still be a lovable idiot to me.'

Chris smiled at that. 'Thanks,' he said. 'I think.'

They both took another sip of their alcohol. The bar had now picked up, it was quite busy. The waitress that gave them their food came over and picked up the plates without saying much. She struggled past the crowd at the bar and disappeared into the kitchen. Colin was struggling with the number of people at the bar.

One of them was the skinhead with the tattoo. He was waving around a wad of cash and shouting at Colin for some service.

'Another drink?' Chris asked.

Standing up, he shimmied around the crowds who were now standing in the table area and reached the bar.

Colin – who at this point, was looking stressed – smiled at him and held up a finger, indicating he'd be a minute.

Chris leaned on top of the bar, avoiding the alcohol spillage from previous patrons and waited his turn. The blond man from before had left now, leaving an empty chair at the end and an empty glass.

Chris looked over to Ashley, who was nose deep in her phone, and smiled.

It had been a good day. The best day in a while.

'Usual, mate?' Colin said, approaching Chris.

Chris nodded. 'Busy tonight?'

'Not half,' Colin said, pulling a clean pint glass from the rack above the bar. 'You'd think it was pay day with how many people are in tonight. It's not normally as busy as this.'

'Have you worked here long?'

'About a month,' he said, filling the glass with the alcohol. 'Good tips and means my mornings are free.'

Colin placed the glass on the bar and poured the vodka. 'Here you go, buddy.'

'Cheers,' Chris said, using his bank card this time to pay for the drinks. 'Have a good night.'

Colin nodded.

Chris turned to walk back to Ashley, but as he turned,

he smashed into something. He tried his best to keep the alcohol upright, but the angle caused his grip to move forward, and both the cider and vodka tipped forward. Right onto the man standing in front of him, soaking his rough t-shirt, likely through to the skin.

'Damn,' Chris said, smiling to try to defuse the situation. 'Sorry, didn't mean—'

He looked up from his alcohol-soaked hands and saw the man staring back at him. It was Greg with the tattoo and the skinhead. The one he'd been warned about.

He felt someone appear beside him and realised it was Ashley. Sensing he needed some back up, she dived straight in. 'Let us buy you a drink,' Ashley said.

The man didn't even look at Ashley. He stared at Chris.

'Outside,' the man uttered coldly.

'What?' Chris said, and almost laughed at how absurd he sounded.

'You heard,' Greg said. 'Outside.'

'Mate, you joking? We'll buy you—'

Chris didn't have time to even register what had happened. He felt a solid impact on the left-hand side of his jaw. He staggered back, using the bar as a prop to keep himself upright, and realised he'd just been punched square in the mouth.

Tattoo Man was backed up by two of his cronies, and Chris knew it would be stupid to start a fight in a bar where he might end up beaten up or worse. They seemed like the type to carry something dangerous. Besides their fists.

'Hey!' Colin said from the behind the bar.

Tattoo Man turned to the barman.

'Enough of that,' he yelled, sounding like a teacher scolding a child. 'It was an accident. I'm going to have to ask you to leave.'

Chris rubbed the side of his jaw and watched the thought process behind the meat head's eyes. He was clearly weighing up his options, whether to leap across the bar and strangle Colin, or continue with Chris and use his goons to throttle him. Or both. Very possibly it was both.

'Out,' Colin said again, lifting his phone. 'Or I'm calling the police and judging by what I've heard about you lot that's the last thing you'd want.'

Greg exchanged a glance with one of his cronies, and then nodded. He brushed past Chris, knocking him backwards with his shoulder, and one of the other men stared a bit too long at Ashley for Chris's liking.

The bar – which had quietened down to watch and listen to what was going on – picked up again. Bar fights were a common occurrence, and entertaining for a minute, but soon everything was back to normal.

Chris watched the three men leave the bar, slamming the door closed so the person sitting nearest jumped. He looked at Ashley and said, 'We'll need new drinks.'

'I'll get that for you, mate,' Colin said and started pouring another pint.

Luckily for Chris, the alcohol splashed forward rather than backwards, so he was relatively dry, but Colin threw him a hand towel anyway to dry his hands off.

'You alright?' Ashley asked, touching the side of his face.

'Never better,' he said, putting on a huge smile, the truth was it stung like a mother. 'Just as well they left, otherwise I'd have taught them a lesson.'

Ashley rolled her eyes. 'Aye, so you would have, Rambo. Come on, back to the table.'

Chris nodded. Then grabbed the newly poured drinks from Colin.

'Got them?' Colin said with a smirk.

'We'll see,' Chris said. 'Thanks for helping there, appreciate it.'

Colin nodded.

Chris joined Ashley at the table, and they drank for the next couple of hours.

Chapter Eleven

The night was winding down and the bar had started to vacate most of the customers. Chris and Ashley stayed on, this time until closing, along with a couple of other regulars and a couple who seemed to be on a first date, judging by how touchy they were. They weren't as hidden in the corner as they thought, since Chris and Ashley almost had a direct line of sight at their sordid antics.

Colin had come over once it had simmered down and talked to them for a while about his plans for the next year. A holiday in Italy was on the cards, then maybe move to Greece for a year.

Chris wished he was that spontaneous. Nothing was tying him down to Scotland, or to his degree or, in fact, to his life.

He had to admit, his life had changed a bit since his experience with a vampire. Since then, he had had an argument with the man that controls his future, gone bungee jumping, and ended up in a bar fight.

Perhaps bar fight wasn't the correct term though, he

thought.

Wrapping up, Chris grabbed his coat and helped Ashley with hers.

'Ever the gentleman,' she said, slipping her arm through the arm hole and allowing Chris to help her with the other.

'As always,' he said.

He turned to wave goodbye to Colin, but upon turning, something – someone – caught his eye. He happened to look out the window, through the hole and into the darkness where he was sure he caught the image of red eyes staring back at him. He closed his eyes tightly, and when he opened them, they were gone. *Just my imagination,* he thought. What if Mikael was out there still?

Maybe he didn't like the blood-bag diet after all? Maybe he was hunting him. Angry because he didn't finish him off when he had the chance.

What was the story Mikael had told? Something about a witch? That certainly was not natural, and he wasn't sure he believed he had the encounter after listening to himself tell it in his own head. He wanted to rush out into the night and go searching for Mikael. He needed to know if what he experienced that night was real.

'You still in there?' Ashley said, nudging him in the side.

'Huh?'

'Finally,' she said, throwing her arms in mock disgust. 'I've been saying your name for the last minute. Where were you?'

'Right here, obviously.'

'You looked out of it. I thought maybe that guy's punch had given you a concussion.'

'He didn't hit that hard.' The pain still throbbing

through his lower jaw said otherwise. 'You ready?'

Ashley raised an eyebrow. 'Are you?'

Chris nodded, and the two of them waved goodbye to the bartender. Chris held the door open for Ashley, who graciously thanked him with a mock bow. They weren't drunk by any means, but tipsy would be the word to describe them.

'Shall we call an Uber?' Ashley said, just as the rain started to fall.

'Nah,' Chris said, pointing down the road. 'There's a taxi rank round the corner.'

The street was dead. Quiet. The silence cut through him.

As they walked, Chris peered down every alleyway, hoping for a glimpse of anything moving. Maybe Mikael was stalking him? Would that be so bad? Maybe then he could get more information out of him. Information about another life – one where immortality ruled, and you could do anything you'd want.

'It's freezing,' Ashley said, as they turned a corner.

'I'll help warm you up,' came a low, cold voice from the shadows.

Just ahead of them. One of the guys from the bar. The one who had stared at her for a bit longer than normal. Beside them was a black **BMW**, and whoever was inside the car swung the door open.

Chris and Ashley watched as Greg used the top of the car to pull himself out. 'Well,' he said. 'Figured you would leave eventually.'

Chris looked at the three of them, weighing up his options. He'd already felt the force of Tattoo Man's punch, and he imagined the other two would be just as hard, if not more so. Chris had never been in a proper fight. Let alone fighting three guys at once.

Instinctively, Ashley took a step back, trying to pull Chris back by the arm, but he stood still. *There would be no point in running,* Chris thought.

'Listen, guys,' he said, holding his arms out in surrender. 'I don't want any bother. What happened in the bar was—'

'Was a mistake,' the man who had been staring at Ashley said. He was a bigger man, with a large waistline and stomach to go with it. He looked as though he had one too many fried food meals.

'My pal here is right,' Tattoo Man said. 'It was a mistake. And it's one mistake you're going to regret.'

Chris almost replied with a sarcastic taunt about how the line sounded like it was from a straight-to-DVD movie, but before he could say it, Ashley tugged his arm again.

'Don't worry,' Fat Man said. 'Once we're finished with him, we'll have a good go on you.'

The words hadn't left Fat Man's mouth before Chris swung a right fist. It clocked the tear drop on the side of the nose. Chris immediately felt a tinge of pain shoot through his hand and up his wrist.

The third man grabbed him from behind, stretching his arms out so that his stomach was exposed.

Tattoo Man was laughing, but his laughter didn't last long, because, suddenly, Ashley swung her bag at the back of the third man's head, allowing Chris to break his grip.

He had no idea what he was doing, but he was able to swing his arm again at Tattoo Man whilst the third man was distracted.

He missed by a country mile, as Greg sidestepped him and grabbed him by the back, throwing him backwards onto his stomach. Before he knew what was happening, Fat Man was back in action, and had him pinned down. He dug his knee into the small of Chris's back, bringing out a scream of pain.

'You stupid piece of crap!' Greg said. 'This could've all gone quietly.'

Chris felt his body melting into the ground, his clothes soaking through to the skin. His hand hurt, and his back ached. His face was almost lying in a puddle of water, and he could smell the alcohol from the group.

Fat Man was strong. Chris tried to move, but he could barely speak from the pressure being exerted on him. He managed to move his head, forgetting about the pain from his skin scraping along the concrete, he looked around, and noticed Ashley was gone. *She must have run in the commotion, he thought.* Better that way. He'd rather she get away than watch what was about to happen.

'Hold him up,' Tattoo Man said.

Fat Man and his friend picked Chris up and pulled him into the nearby alley. With no one around to see, Tattoo Man went to town. He clenched his right fist and smashed it into Chris's stomach.

Chris lost all feeling in his legs, almost falling to the ground, but the two men held him firm. His stomach screamed, not used to this time of punishment.

What happened next was a blur.

Suddenly, he was no longer held by the two men, in fact one of them was lying on the floor in a heap. Fat Man looked around, then at Tattoo Man, they had no idea what had happened, and neither did Chris.

One second the third man was standing beside him, then another he was on the floor. Alive, but he had a lot of blood coming from the top of his head. He looked as if he had been smashed headfirst into a concrete wall.

Fat Man checked on his mate.

Tattoo Man grabbed Chris by the neck, bringing him to his feet and slamming him into the wall.

The back of Chris's head snapped back, and he felt a trickle of blood running down the back of his neck. His vision started to blur. Faces became specks in his eye line and he waited for the final blow to come.

'HEY!' came a voice from the end of the alley.

Chris didn't recognise the voice, but it was enough for Tattoo Man to let go of him.

He saw his opportunity. He pulled back his fist and smashed it straight into the side of Tattoo Man's nose. He heard a crack and found himself hoping he'd broken his nose.

Suddenly, a cacophony of shouts came, a mixture of Ashley's voice and the voice of strangers.

Chris felt his eyes go heavy and his body go limp, he fell towards the ground, and the last thought he had was wondering what happened to the third man.

With the rain battering down now, he felt his eyes close, and he felt his body hit the deck, sinking into the ground like he had fallen into quicksand.

Chapter Twelve

His vision came back slowly. For a moment, he thought he had died and gone to Heaven with how much light shone into his eyes. He struggled for a good minute with the brightness before he finally adjusted. He was in a bright room, still clothed in his blood-stained outfit and he could feel a bandage on his cheek. He realised he was in a hospital room.

To his right, Ashley noticed he'd woken up. 'How are you feeling?' she asked.

Chris adjusted awkwardly on the bed and winced with each passing pain point. 'I've been better,' he said, and it was true, he was in pain he'd never felt before. He'd kill for some painkillers. 'What happened?'

'You passed out and the police took you straight here. They're still outside waiting for you to wake up.'

Chris looked past her and could see two police officers standing at the window, not staring at him but talking with each other.

'I ran back to the pub and called the police from there.

Luckily there was a patrol nearby, so they sent them.'

'What happened,' he winced and coughed a couple of times, 'to the three guys?'

'Got away,' she said and looked down. 'Police tried to get them, but they were more concerned about you and getting you to hospital. The attackers carried their pal away; I didn't know you had it in you to knock someone out like that.'

Chris wondered what she was talking about for a second, then remembered the third man. Remembered him lying on the concrete with blood on his head. He didn't remember doing that. All he remembered was clocking the Tattoo Man with a right fist, then the lights going out and hearing sirens in the distance.

'Excuse me,' a voice sounded from the doorway. 'Are you feeling up to a chat, Mr Winters?'

Chris glanced at Ashley, then back at the policeman staring back at him. The policeman had the usual black-and-white uniform on but had taken his hat off to reveal a shaved head.

'Ready when you are.'

The policeman glanced at Ashley, who seemed to take the hint as she said, 'I'll give you a minute.'

The room was left to the two of them and the policeman took out a small notebook.

'Am I being arrested?' Chris asked and felt stupid for asking it.

'No, not at the minute, sir.'

'What's your name?'

'PC Jake Grange. Do you mind if I ask you a few questions?'

Chris nodded.

'Do you remember anything of the men who attacked you?'

Chris remembered their grotesque faces clearly. He remembered the sour smell from their mouths as they held him against the wall. He remembered the feeling of their fists pummelling into him.

'Description wise, you mean?'

Grange nodded.

'One of them had a star tattoo on his neck, and the other was quite a large man. Besides that, nothing distinguishing, except both being skinheads and both being absolute pricks.'

Grange nodded again.

'What about the third man?'

'I can't remember much about him,' he replied.

'He seemed in a bad way. Obviously, nothing is going to happen here, from our point of view it seems like your standard bar fight that got out of hand. Aside from the blood trail from the guy that has a busted noggin. But I need to give you a warning, if it happens again then it might be a criminal charge.'

Chris nodded. 'Understood, officer.'

'My colleague will be in soon to take your contact details, but I doubt we'll find the other people involved.'

'Sure,' Chris said, then spotted Ashley talking to the colleague outside.

PC Grange put the notebook and pen back into his pocket and looked as if he were about to leave, but then turned back to Chris. 'One more thing,' he said. 'Off the record, from the description you've told me. Those people aren't people you want to get involved with.'

Chris studied the officer's face, it seemed conflicted, like he didn't want to tell him. 'What do you mean?'

'I can't give you names, but if it's the same guy, then the man with the star tattoo is part of a well-known family to the police.'

'Oh,' Chris said, looking at his hands where he had scratches and scrapes from the concrete. 'Put it this way, officer, I won't be searching them out.'

'Good,' he said, rubbing the back of his head. 'For your sake, it's best not. My colleague will come in soon, and then you can check with the nurse if you can go. Thanks, Mr Winters.'

Chris nodded.

'One more thing,' he said, halfway out of the door before shoving his face back into the room. 'Did you bite one of them?'

It was as if the world slowed down. Chris felt his body go heavy and his blood quicken.

'No, why?'

'My colleague is sure he saw a bite mark on the guy who was knocked out.'

Chris shook his head. PC Grange left the room, and his colleague swapped in. Chris didn't catch his name because he was left in too much of a daze from, first, the beating and, second, the revelation that perhaps he'd been saved by Mikael. Judging from the way Grange spoke about them, Greg was not the type of man you wanted to be around. And judging by the fact he'd been put in hospital, the policeman was right.

He gave all his details to the other cop, who wished him a goodnight and explained he'd call the nurse for him.

Ashley entered the room after the cop had left and sat on the bed next to Chris. 'What a night, eh?'

'Do you think I can go home?'

'Guess we'll see what the nurse says. If she gives the go ahead, I'll order us a taxi.'

'What time is it?'

'Just gone two. I was thinking that I can go back to yours with you, get you cleaned up, I mean?'

'If you're sure? It'd be nice to have the company. You know, after the beating I just took.'

'A pretty big beating, I'd say.'

The door swung open, and both of their attentions swung to the nurse entering the room. She had blonde hair and blue eyes, with a hint of dark bags under them. Nonetheless, she smiled and seemed happy to be there.

'How are you feeling, Chris?'

'I've felt better.' He tried to smile. 'Can I go home?'

She glanced at Ashley then back at him. 'The doctor on call has signed you out, you're free to go. Just take it easy for a few days. Before you go, head to reception and you'll be given a prescription for some high-strength painkillers. I reckon you'll need them.'

'Thanks, nurse,' Ashley said, picking her bag off the floor and then standing up.

Chris said his goodbyes, then walked - stumbled - towards the door. He grabbed the knob, twisted, and took a couple of steps out.

Behind him, he overheard the nurse say, 'Keep an eye on him, will you? An attack like that can have longer lasting effects than just the physical ones we see.'

Ashley replied, 'I will.'

Chris didn't let on that he had heard. He imagined she was right though, a lot of people who are in fights or assaulted struggle with living after it. Living in fear of their own shadow or turning a street corner. Not him, though, that wouldn't happen to him. His life was boring enough as it was, let alone worrying about leaving the house. Was it that easy though? To simply decide to not let it affect him?

Chris and Ashley followed the signs towards the reception desk. The halls were white and cold, and he wondered why hospitals didn't paint their walls in warmer, brighter colours. It would sure liven the place up. The last time he was in this hospital was when he was pulling a blood-bag heist, working in tandem with a vampire. The news that one of his attackers had a bite mark, the one who had been holding him one second, then on the ground the next, had confirmed his belief that he had, indeed, had an encounter with the supernatural.

If that truly was Mikael, then why had he stopped with one of them? Why had he not taken out the other two? Had he regretted helping him? Chris didn't have the answers, and despite the pain flowing through his body, he smiled, because he knew now that he wasn't crazy and there was something else out there.

'Why are you so smiley?' Ashley said, walking close beside him.

'Just glad to get home,' he said, but as they turned the corner to the reception desk, his smile disappeared, and his face went red. The same receptionist who he had tried to con last time he was at the hospital was there. She hadn't noticed him yet, and he'd rather not have the awkward conversation about his audition for *Casualty*. 'Listen, could you get the prescription for me? I feel like I need some air.'

'Sure. You go order the taxi and I'll get the pills.'

Chris watched her go, sneaked past the desk, and opened the main doors. He stepped out and felt the cold air smack him in the face. It felt nice, so much so that it made him realise how hot the hospital room was. He pulled out his phone, surprised that it still worked after being thrown around in his pocket during the attack, and he swiped it open and opened the Uber app.

Ashley wasn't far behind. She brought the prescription and handed it to him. 'Freezing,' she said. 'Did you order the taxi?'

'Uber,' he said. 'Shouldn't be long. How are you anyway?'

'Better than you,' she said.

'Fair point.'

A couple of minutes passed, the two of them sat in silence on a low wall near the main path, staring at the road where the Uber would come from. Their bodies almost touched. He wanted to tell her about the bite marks, tell her that it confirmed what he had thought about the vampire, but she'd never believe him. What was the point in telling her? She'd either think he was concussed or insane.

He decided he needed to find Mikael, to investigate all of this, but first all he wanted to do was to go home, get cleaned up and get some sleep. He could do the rest in the morning – or in a few days after the painkillers did their job.

While waiting, Chris opened the bag and studied the contents. Co-codamol was named on the packet. It was a strong drug and the nurse had warned him of the effects. The pill itself was a mixture of codeine and paracetamol. An addictive substance but one that, if managed properly, wouldn't have any ill effects.

A few more minutes passed before a small Ford Fiesta turned the corner and pulled into the narrow lane, usually reserved for emergency vehicles. 'Winters?' the driver, a young woman with an English accent, asked.

Chris opened the door for Ashley. It took him a moment to get seated in the car, and Ashley had to help him with the seatbelt which embarrassed him slightly.

'Rough night?' the driver asked.

'What gave it away?' Chris asked.

'A couple of things,' the driver said, putting the car into gear and moving off, 'like the fact I've just picked you up outside a hospital, and the other thing being the fact you look like crap.'

'Thanks,' Chris said. There was no malice to the driver's statement, but Chris noticed Ashley didn't laugh, and didn't smile. She wanted to get back just as much as he did, and neither of them could be bothered with a chat with an overzealous Uber driver.

The driver drove in silence from then on, and after a twenty-minute journey, said goodbye to them and sped off into the distance.

Chapter Thirteen

The car approached Chris's home steadily and parked up. Chris had already paid the fee over the application and they both said their goodbyes to the driver. Chris struggled out of the seat and took a deep breath as he straightened up. The cold wind raised the hair on his arms, and he felt an overwhelming desire to lie down and go to sleep. It had been a very long day and the only thing he wanted to do was rest. Ashley joined him and looked up at the building. It was a small flat building with only two individual flats. Almost on autopilot, Chris walked into the entrance.

He paused at the bottom of the stairs, and said, 'Listen, you know I've not got a lot of money and how hard things have been, so don't go in expecting a lot.'

Ashley smiled. 'What? You think I'm loaded? I'm sure it'll be plenty nice. Come on, let's get you up there so I can clean you up. The blood started to dry in and you look awful. The driver had a point.'

Chris nodded and followed her up the steps to his landing and he inserted his silver key into the keyhole.

Twisting, he took a big sigh, preparing himself, then opened the door and allowed Ashley to go in first. The place didn't look untidy, it wasn't the place you'd want to spend much of your time. But it was cheap. And cheap was what Chris needed.

'Right,' she said, leading them to the living room. 'You want to give me the tour?'

'Living room,' Chris said, pointing in the general direction of the couch and chair, then pointed behind him. 'Bedroom, and beside that is the toilet and shower.'

He didn't need to point out the kitchen, it was an open-plan living room and kitchen so she could clearly see it.

'Told you it wasn't much,' he said.

Ashley waved his concerns away.

She was the first person – the only person – ever to be in the flat besides him. He noticed how wet her hair was, so much so that it stuck to her face, and he noticed how tight her dress was to her skin because of the rain.

'Here, I'll go get you a towel and a change of clothes.'

'Thanks.'

Chris opened the door to his bedroom, lifting some old clothes from the floor and throwing them in the clothes hamper at the end of his bed. He grabbed a towel from the radiator, and opened the chest of drawers, pulling out a t-shirt and shorts, quickly changing into them then pulling out another shirt and a pair of longer pyjama trousers for her.

'Didn't peg you for a pyjama man,' Ashley said, smiling as she grabbed the clothes after Chris's throw.

'A man of comfort,' he said, wincing as he sat down on the chair. He watched her dry her hair off with the towel. She sat down then, and pulled some make-up wipes out of the bag and used them quickly to remove the wet and wild make-up look she had, caused by the rain and the wind.

'Sit here,' she said, tapping the spot next to her. 'I'll get a cloth from the kitchen, and we'll give your face a clean. Your skin will be red for good before long.'

He moved positions, wincing at the pain as he moved from one seat to the other.

Ashley returned with a wet cloth and a dry hand towel. She sat in front of him and looked into his eyes. She smiled, then raised her hand up, taking his chin in her hand.

She lightly took the wrapped bandage off his cheek, sending shivers down his spine.

'Nurse did a good job tidying this up. Just needs a rinse. It might sting a bit.'

'I think I can handle – OW!' He immediately clutched his face where the scrapes were, which only served to cause him more agony.

Ashley raised an eyebrow. 'You were saying?'

He shook his head. 'Aye. Well, go a bit gentler next time!'

'Wimp.' She rolled her eyes, pressing the cloth into the wound, squeezing it slightly so some cold water leaked out onto the red scrapes. The wound had been caused by his face landing on the concrete then being scraped along it. He hadn't seen what his stomach and sides looked like yet, but from the way they felt it wouldn't be good.

A few minutes passed in silence. Ashley continued to tidy him up whilst he avoided staring into her deep blue eyes.

Once they were finished, she put the cloth to one side, and grabbed the prescription pills that the receptionist gave her. She unscrewed the white lid and popped two pills into her hand. She extended her hand to him and said, 'Take these. I'll just get you a glass of water.'

Chris did as he was told, throwing them into his mouth.

She returned with a tall glass of water and passed it to him. He used his tongue to push the pills to the back of his mouth, then took a large gulp of cold liquid. The water did its job and sent the pills down his throat and into his stomach where they would dissolve and make him forget about the pain. Hopefully quickly.

Ashley sat back down. 'How are you feeling now?'

'Not wonderful.' He leaned back and stared at the ceiling. He noticed a damp patch that he was sure wasn't there that morning. 'I suppose taking a beating would do that to you. Probably feel worse in the morning, likely with a hangover.'

'The pills might stop that from happening. Hell, I might take two.'

'You're not meant to take someone else's prescribed drugs; didn't you get taught that in school?'

'Alright,' she said, rolling her eyes. 'You should probably get some sleep.'

'Yeah, suppose you're right.'

There was a moment of silence that seemed to hang in the air like a bad smell.

'Can I stay here?' Ashley blurted out, and seemed to go a little red. 'I mean, it's really late and by the time I get a taxi—'

'You can stay,' Chris said. 'I assumed you were, actually. Far too late to be travelling back, and besides, we'll both need a good sleep to deal with that lecture tomorrow.'

'Damn it.' She shook her head. 'I totally forgot about that. I'll need to leave early in the morning to get ready for it. It's at ten, right?'

'Bright and early.'

'Damn,' she said, and glanced at the bedroom door then at the couch. 'I'll take the couch, you can sleep in your bed.'

'No, you take the bed—'

She held up a hand. 'You're the invalid. I'll take the couch, and you take your bed.'

Chris knew not to argue, he'd seen the look in her eyes that said, 'Don't you dare talk back.'

Chris laughed. He nodded then was about to stand up, but Ashley grabbed his hand.

'Thanks for standing up for me tonight,' she said, looking down. 'Those guys were dicks.'

She was referring to the third man, who Chris had to search his mind to remember what he'd said. It wasn't pretty.

For a moment, as the two of them sat there, only illuminated by the small lamp on the table, he had a sensational urge to move closer and kiss her. That would be wrong, he had decided. It would be taking advantage, and she had made it clear she wasn't interested in a relationship.

'I reckon you could've taken him,' he said, avoiding his urges.

Ashley smiled. 'I reckon so, too.'

They said their good nights, leaving each other with a hug which caused him some pain, but he withstood it to feel bodily warmth running through him.

Thirty minutes later, he had got underneath the covers, still feeling the cold draft coming from the window. For what seemed like an eternity, he lay there, staring at the ceiling and running through the events of the day.

It had been a long, hard day, and he was willing his body to sleep. Only a couple of hours and he'd need to wake up for the lecture, he couldn't afford to miss it, not after what happened at his last one. At least this one was on Teams.

He couldn't get it out of his head. He could have died tonight. He thought about the attack and wondered what would have happened if Ashley hadn't been there to call the police.

Or if the third man hadn't been attacked?

What was it the policeman said? Bite marks? It had to be Mikael, surely? Did it mean Mikael was watching him after all?

He tossed and turned, slowly due to the pain – the painkillers were just about to kick in, he could feel it, and thought about what he would need to do. He'd need to investigate vampires more. Myths were based around legends.

He felt his eyes starting to get heavy, and he wished for sleep, with the idea of searching for Mikael etching away on his brain. He had the experience of a lifetime bungee jumping, but it wasn't enough, he felt he needed to see what else was out there.

The last thing he thought of before sleep took him, was the idea of nearly kissing Ashley. He thought of her lying on the uncomfortable couch and wanted to go through and tell her to lie in the bed with him. But he couldn't bring himself to do it, because they were good friends and he wasn't sure if how it felt tonight was because of the mix of alcohol, prescription drugs and the comedown from adrenaline.

Mercifully, his brain switched off and sleep took him under.

Chapter Fourteen

The shrill sound of his alarm awoke him. He hadn't slept well, tossing and turning and only getting about an hour. For a moment, he was concerned his eyes were glued shut thanks to the fact it had taken enormous willpower to open them. He rolled over and checked his phone, noticing he had half an hour to get presentable for the lecture. He climbed out of the bed, grabbed a t-shirt and pair of jogging bottoms, then opened the door, expecting to see Ashley.

She wasn't in the living room. He checked the notifications on his phone and Chris read the message from her, telling him she had left early in a taxi to get ready for the lecture. The lecture was in twenty minutes, so he had time to make himself a slice of toast and pour a glass of water. The toast was dry – he had no butter. It felt like glass going down his throat with every swallow, but he ate it regardless, his stomach crying out for some sustenance after a night of hard drinking and even harder punches.

He hadn't dared look at his side and stomach yet, the pain when he moved was enough to tell him it wouldn't be a pretty sight. After finishing his toast and drinking the water, he sat on the couch and brought out his laptop. He laid it on the coffee table. As he put in his details and waited for the laptop to log him in, he had a coughing fit which racked his stomach. He felt like his insides were screaming at him. He leaned back in the chair and looked at the ceiling, noticing the damp patch again. He made a mental note to head upstairs and find out who his neighbours were and what they were doing up there to create that.

He knocked back a couple of painkillers – Co-codamol – and swallowed them down.

The nurse had warned him about the addictive nature of codeine. She had told him it was like morphine, and he found himself thinking of his High School Geography teacher. On a particularly slow day, he had told the class of his father, who was permanently disabled and had to have morphine drips daily.

The pain was too much to bear. The fact he knew it would be gone shortly gave him peace of mind and allowed his body to relax. He opened his emails and saw one from the tutor, Mr Connors. It was an email to the entire group, with a link to the Teams meeting room. He moved his cursor over the link and clicked it, after a few seconds he was thrust into a waiting room which told him the host would accept him shortly.

He had around ten minutes to wait, so he decided to stand up and give his face a wash and hair a brush. The pain had subsided now, for the most part, but still lingered. In the bathroom, he washed his face with cold water, letting it run off his skin and into the sink below. He looked at his face in the mirror and it was not a pretty sight. He looked like he'd been through a few rounds in a boxing match, like Muhammad Ali or Mike Tyson had been having a go at him.

He dried his face off with a towel and used a comb to brush his hair through. He'd have a shower after the lecture. Back in the living room, he had only a couple of minutes and used the time to get into a comfortable position. At least he had an excuse to keep his camera off if anyone asked. What a story that would be. 'Why isn't your camera on?'

'I got attacked by three men and put into hospital.'

Great story.

Connors wasn't the best at technology, so it would usually be a few minutes before he would begin speaking. Everyone else was on mute, but most had their cameras on. Chris noticed Ashley had hers on. She looked a lot better than Chris did, hair curly and make-up done.

Connors took himself off mute and ran through the checklist for what he would be covering in the lesson. Chris zoned out multiple times over the course of the meeting. His mind was elsewhere.

He wondered if Mikael was feeding on people, or if he was still stealing blood bags, or back to eating animals now. Blood was blood. Why would he attack one of the men? Was it because he was trying to protect him? But then why would he only take out one of them? Unless he had planned to take out all three of them? What did he say? He didn't want to kill people. He knew if he drank from a human, he'd end up killing them. *Maybe Mikael didn't want to risk it?* Chris thought.

The lecture ended right on time, and everyone said their goodbyes. Chris had not taken himself off mute the whole time, and nobody even noticed he had his camera off.

He washed himself in the tepid water from his shower head, but before that, he had taken his shirt off and looked at himself in the bathroom mirror. He had never seen such an awful sight. His ribs were black and blue, and he was sure his stomach looked swollen. His face wasn't much better.

In the shower, he let the water drip off him. Not a lot of pressure, but enough to clean himself. He brushed his teeth and took another glass of water. In the living room, he turned the laptop back on and scrolled over to the file where he was writing his book.

He was a few thousand words into it.

But he hadn't opened it to write more, to continue the story in a fictional sense, because this time he knew the story was real, and he wanted to continue it. He thought about it for a moment, then decided to delete the file, head to the recycle bin and permanently remove it from the computer. He didn't need to write a story, because it wasn't a fictional story, it was real, and he needed to continue it.

He shoved the laptop to the side and called Ashley.

'Hello,' she said on the first ring.

'You alright? Didn't hear you leave earlier.'

'I'm not bad, weird thinking about what happened last night though. I didn't want to wake you. Besides, needed to get my laptop and notebook. Noticed Mr Connors didn't say anything to you.'

'He didn't say much to anyone to be fair.'

'Sore?'

'Yeah, a wee bit,' he lied. The truth was he was in agony, the painkillers had started to wear off in the past ten minutes. He had thought about popping another couple, but again, he didn't want to get addicted. 'I'll be fine in a few days.'

'Hopefully,' Ashley said, and Chris could hear the smile in her voice. 'You don't call very often. What's up?'

'Just wanted to make sure you were fine after last night?'

'Yeah, I'm not bad. I'm not the one with bruised ribs and stomach.'

'You saw?'

'This morning,' she said quietly. 'I opened your door to say bye, but you looked peaceful so didn't want to wake you. The covers were down a bit, so I spotted your belly. Black and blue, eh?'

'Few days and it'll be back to normal.'

'White and pasty?'

'Exactly,' he said, laughing. 'Listen, I know you mentioned about having dinner at your place at the weekend—'

'You don't need to go,' she said immediately. 'Not if you're in too much pain.'

'I just wanted to check you still wanted me over?'

'Only if you're still up for it?'

'And miss your parents' cooking? Just send the address over and I'll be there. What time?'

'I'll let you know,' she said. There was silence. 'I'll need to go but speak soon!'

After their conversation, Chris spent the remainder of the afternoon trying to keep himself busy – tidying the place up a bit. Despite the pain, he managed to get the place looking good. It wasn't a place you'd bring a girl back too, but it was liveable. Every so often, his eyes would clock the damp patch and the more he looked at it, the angrier he got.

He thought about going up there, like he had decided earlier, but then he remembered what a state he looked. Imagine someone looking like him coming to the door and questioning what was going on? It'd look right dodgy, and a confrontation isn't what he wanted that afternoon. Not after the previous night.

That night, he ate a couple more slices of toast, and sat down in front of the television. He struggled to focus on the show he was watching, something about couples on a trip through Europe. Pain echoed through his stomach and side which made it difficult to focus. He clocked the prescription drug bag on the other chair and decided a couple more wouldn't hurt.

The drugs worked quickly. This time it only took ten minutes before he started to feel better, but the drowsiness came over him. Turning the TV off, he left the lamp on as he laid his head on the cushion. It was the first time since the last pill he felt comfortable.

As he drifted off, he thought about what the dinner would be like. He was nervous. This was an opportunity to make a good impression on Ashley's parents. They had asked because they felt bad about the fact his parents were no longer around. He was sure of it. But nonetheless, it was kind of them, and he felt he needed to repay that.

I should buy some flowers and some beer, he thought. He texted Ashley asking what they would prefer, but he never saw the response because his eyes closed, and he fell asleep.

He slept poorly, plagued by dreams – nightmares – of being stuck in a hospital, trying to find his way out and back to normality. Every hour, he'd wake up, most of the time because of the nightmares, but other times he'd wake due to the pain.

The night before the dinner, he went to bed at a reasonable hour. He barely got a couple of hours. He had avoided taking painkillers that day, through sheer determination alone – the pain urging him every second to pop a pill to take it away.

He lay in bed that night, tossing and turning.

He reached over to his bedside table, and, in the darkness, he popped a couple of pills filled with codeine, not caring if it was an addictive drug. He needed relief and the small yellow pills would give it to him.

The pain had gone, for the moment, yet he still couldn't sleep. Probably because of the nerves of the next day, partly because he was annoyed at himself for not following through on his decision to research the supernatural and try to find Mikael. The pain had been too much, and he was resigned to watching TV and killing time on his laptop.

The morning passed quickly, and he found it was time to get ready. He put on his best shirt and a nice pair of black jeans, complimented by a pair of white trainers. Ashley had said it wasn't a formal event, just a casual dinner, so he felt dressed for the occasion. He ordered an Uber through the app.

On his way out the door, he clocked the damp patch on the ceiling again, sure it was getting bigger.

It wasn't the rude driver from the hospital. This time it was a friendly guy named Paul who drove him to his destination. It was a pleasant enough journey, aided by the fact Paul had kept his mouth shut for most of it, and the fact he'd taken a pill before he left.

It had been his third of the day, after the two he had taken in the morning. He could already feel his body starting to crave them. He had no idea how addictive the codeine was, but he was worried about the effects when he planned to come off them.

In the car, he made a vow to stop taking them the next day. For today though, he needed them. Couldn't sit through a meal with his body racked with pain.

The driver pulled into Burton Street, where Ashley lived and pulled up to their house – number 12. Rain broke the clouds as he stepped out of the Uber and peered up at the house. Ashley was right – it wasn't a mansion, but it was a lot nicer than he had been used too. Detached, probably three, maybe four, bedrooms. Most likely a few bathrooms too.

The garden was nicely kept, the lawn tended to, and some nice delicate flowers were potted about it.

The wait seemed to go on for minutes, even though it was only a few seconds. A thought crossed his mind that nobody would be in, but just as he thought that the door would slowly open, Ashley smiled at him, dressed just as she said, casually: blue jeans and a white t-shirt.

'Come in,' she said, pulling the door a bit wider. 'My parents are in the kitchen. You're a bit late.'

'Am I?' He was sure he had left right on time. Then he noticed her smiling. 'Funny. Well, fancy giving me the tour?'

'Come meet my parents first, they're excited to meet you.'

'I bet.'

Ashley led him through the house. The front door had opened into a long narrow hallway, covered in nice wallpaper, and had a long chest of drawers on the left. They passed a door to the left which, upon successfully peeking, led to a small sitting room. On the right was another door, leading to what looked like an office room. Straight ahead, there was a staircase and down beside that was another narrow hallway, leading to a downstairs toilet and, from what Chris could gather, the kitchen.

He knew because he could hear her parents pottering about with trays and cutlery.

She opened the door to the kitchen and Chris stepped

in, in front of the two people.

'Hello,' Chris said politely.

'Hello, Chris,' Ashley's dad said, he was a tall balding man with grey hair at the back of his head.

Her mum, on the other hand, had long flowing dark hair, dyed most probably. She was more welcoming than her dad seemed, as she crossed the kitchen in a few long strides and brought him in for a big hug. 'Good to meet you, son.'

Chris caught Ashley's eye who looked mortified. 'Mum's a hugger.'

Chris nodded meekly, trying to forget about the fact she had her arms wrapped around his waist where much of the bruising still was. 'It's good to meet you, Mrs—'

'None of that please,' she said immediately, letting go. 'First name's Valerie and that's what you can call me. That there is George.' She nodded towards her husband, who nodded at Chris.

It was nods all around as Chris nodded back, then said, 'Do you need any help?'

'Oh no, not at all,' Valerie said. 'Ashley will give you the tour. It'll be about half an hour before everything's ready. You both can sit in the living room, and we'll give you a shout.'

'Come on,' Ashley said, grabbing Chris's arm and pulling him towards the kitchen door.

'Chris,' George said, opening the fridge, looking in it and then looking back at him. 'Are you a beer man?'

He was more cider, but he didn't want to make a fuss, so he said he was, and then he was handed a beer over the kitchen table. 'Cheers,' he said.

He hoped the alcohol wouldn't have any adverse effects on him, what with the codeine flowing through his system.

The house looked large from the outside, and inside it

seemed even bigger. The tour had lasted a good ten minutes, and, in that time, Ashley had shown him three large bedrooms and even an office room upstairs. That made two since he had already clocked the one downstairs.

Ashley's room was what he had expected – an adult room but with a hint of child-like wonder in it. He had noticed she kept a stuffed animal on her bed. Her room was painted grey, and her bedroom furniture was all white and her bed sheets were pink.

On the floor, there were a stack of textbooks and her laptop. She explained she liked to do her work sitting on the floor, because if she sat on the bed, then likely she would fall asleep.

'Why don't you do it in the room with the desk?' Chris had asked.

'That's where my dad does his work. He's the head of sport at the local newspaper.'

'A reporter?'

'Used to be,' Ashley explained, leading Chris down the staircase and into a decent-sized living room with an obnoxiously large television. It made his TV look tiny in comparison. 'Now he has a team to do his dirty work. They might be looking for more people soon, if you're interested?'

'Maybe,' Chris said, as he sat down on the cream leather couch. He wasn't interested in working for a newspaper, not for sport at least.

He and Ashley made small talk whilst he sipped his beer. He wasn't fond of beer. People say it is an acquired taste, but despite his best efforts, he never started to enjoy it. Not wanting to kick up a fuss, though, he took a sip every couple of minutes. Hoping to God it wouldn't affect the medication.

Half an hour passed before they heard the shout from Valerie, 'Food's on the table!'

The smell was divine. It was the first time in a while – ever, really – that he'd smelled a kitchen like it. He could smell a mixture of succulent meat and what seemed like roasted vegetables. The food was nicely presented in the middle of a circular table, sitting on a tablecloth with silver spoons at the side, ready to do their job and serve the delicious food.

Ashley and her dad were joking about something, and it was the first time he'd noticed her dad smiling. He felt a pang of sadness at that – the fact they had such a good relationship.

'Everyone take what you want, there's plenty to go around,' Valerie said.

'What is it?' Chris asked.

Valerie pointed at the tray covered in tin foil in the middle. 'Steak Pie here,' she said, then pointed at a couple of other trays. 'Roasted potatoes in there, Yorkshire puddings and sausage stuffing in those two. On the hob is a pot of peas if you want to grab them for me?'

'Aye, sure,' Chris said. He took the peas from the counter, still roasting hot, and placed the pot next to the trays. By this point, the rest of them were sat at the table. He took his seat next to Ashley.

'Do you say grace, Chris?' Valerie asked.

'Eh? No, not really. Never really been a thing for me. Do you?'

'She just wanted to check,' George said. 'We're not religious.'

'Right,' Ashley said. 'Well, help yourself.'

'Aye,' Chris said, and the four of them started taking their own helpings from the trays.

Chris piled his plate high with a bundle of roast

potatoes and a nice thick slice of golden-crusted pastry with brown bits of beef on top. He wasn't keen on peas, but he picked up a spoonful anyway and laid them on the plate. Finishing the masterpiece off were two homemade Yorkshire puddings.

'I'll just move the trays out the way,' Valerie said, and took them off the table, placing them off to the side on a kitchen countertop.

The four of them ate their meals, making small talk as they did so. They asked Chris what he did for a living, and he explained he was a student now, and he had savings from the job that he took the previous year to get him through.

George seemed to approve of his aptitude for saving money.

Chris asked them what they did – like Ashley said, George explained he worked for the local newspaper. And Valerie said she ran a day care for dogs in the town centre. Chris had no idea there even was a day care there, and the mention of the dogs took him back to when he would beg his own parents for a puppy.

'We can't, as we won't be here to look after it,' his dad had explained when he continued begging.

'I'll look after it,' Chris had said, but his dad laughed and ruffled his hair, telling him to forget about it.

Chris looked around the room and remembered he'd not seen any dog beds or toys there. He turned to Valerie. 'Do you have any dogs of your own?'

'We used to,' she said.

'We had a little poodle,' Ashley said.

'Yappy wee thing,' George said, smiling and taking a sip of his beer.

'Dad! She wasn't yappy at all,' she said, then turned to Chris. 'Don't listen to him. She was great. You'd have liked her.'

Chris was seemingly making a good first impression, so much so that George offered him another beer after he'd finally finished his first. He almost refused but out of politeness he said yes.

Throughout the meal, a little slice of his brain couldn't help but wish he'd had more of these experiences when he was a child, with his own parents. With his own family. He hadn't turned out badly by any means, but he always felt something was missing in his life. After all, his parents were his family in name only. He never felt like they were his parents.

And watching how Ashley interacted with her family only served to drive home the fact.

The fact that his mum and dad were bad parents.

Bad parents who left their son for days and weeks on end, only returning for a few days, bribing him with a new book or game and then running out on the next adventure. But wasn't that what he wanted now? To be adventurous, to experience what they did?

Yes, but I'd never put that in front of a child, he thought.

It had begun to get under his skin. He hated himself for admitting it, but the loving family here annoyed him. Why couldn't that have been his experience?

The mixture of alcohol and the medication wasn't helping, not to mention the fact he was starting to feel sore.

He gritted his teeth through it, and for the rest of the meal he was relatively quiet. He drank his beer and answered any questions they had before they moved to the living room. George turned on the TV and put on a football match – Scotland were playing Estonia in a friendly match, down one-nil with fifteen minutes played.

He wanted to leave. He had a decent experience, and

appreciated the invitation, but he was light-headed from the bad mixture of booze and codeine. He also had started to look at Ashley and her family with contempt rather than happiness.

He made a show of checking his phone, then slapping his hands on his lap and standing up, in pure British fashion. 'Right, I better be going.'

'So soon?' Ashley asked as she and George turned to him. Valerie was in the kitchen tidying up.

'I don't want to impose,' he said and immediately regretted it. What could he say? He didn't want to admit he was starting to feel pain. Didn't want to admit he was starting to hate the fact he was there, invited only because Ashley told her parents that his family were dead. 'We have that assignment due on Monday too, and I haven't started it yet, so better get home.'

'You want a lift back?' Ashley asked.

'Eh, no, it's fine, I've already ordered an Uber, should be here any minute so I'll go wait for it outside.'

He reached his hand to George who shook it firmly.

Ashley followed him as he walked towards the kitchen, shoved in his head and said, 'Thanks for the meal, Valerie. I'm heading off now.'

Valerie crossed the room and wrapped him in a hug. 'No problem. Figured you'd not had a family meal like that before. You'll come again?'

Chris had barely heard the last part, but enough to say, 'Yeah, bye.'

He felt bile churn in his stomach, and a bit of it came up his throat into his mouth and he felt a bit of beef float around too, but he managed to swallow it down, not looking to make a mess of their kitchen. He walked to the front door, waving goodbye to George in the living room and stepped out.

He was met with the cold air and a slight pattering of water from the clouds. Like he thought, the Uber was there, waiting on him.

'You alright?' a voice asked from behind him. Ashley had followed him to the door. She closed the door behind him.

'What did your mum mean when she said about that being the first family meal I had? Did you tell her what I said? About the fact they were never there?'

'Uh,' she said, stammering a little. 'I told them that your parents were no longer around and—'

'And you told them that they never really were,' he said, with a little bit more anger that he had expected.

'She didn't mean it like you think—'

He could feel his face turning a shade of crimson and his heartbeat booming in his chest. The raindrops fell on his skin like pinpricks. Despite his light head, he was able to stop himself from getting too angry. How dare she tell them that? It was bad enough she had told them that they were dead, let alone the fact that he was practically neglected as a child.

What was it George had said? He'd asked what his future plans were, and Chris didn't have an answer. He had mentioned something about family, but Chris didn't really hear it, but he realised what he did say.

'Shows you need a good family around you to have a future,' he had said. It was as if Chris's brain didn't realise what he said at the time on purpose, but now it was if his brain was on fire. He remembered that, and what Valerie had said, and he felt anger like he had never felt before, even more than when he had been assaulted.

He looked at Ashley. 'I better go. I had a really nice time.'

'I'm sorry,' she said. 'I didn't mean for—'

'I know,' he said immediately, cutting her off. 'Tell them thanks again for the meal. It was nice to have one for the first time.' He heard the bitterness in his voice and hated himself for it. It wasn't like him, but the alcohol, drugs and the pain were taking over now. He just wanted to get out of there and get home. To get some sleep.

He smiled at Ashley, and even to himself it felt fake. The Uber driver beeped their horn, which gave him the excuse to say goodbye and climb into the car.

He closed the door and watched Ashley stare at him as the driver drove off. Once they were round the bend, he looked forward and, as if the day couldn't get much worse, it was the same driver as the night he was at the hospital.

Chapter Fifteen

Chris spent most of the week resting. Lying on the couch and taking medication. He seemed to think the pain was getting less and less, but because of the painkillers he couldn't be sure. He was scared to stop taking them. Fear of not being able to sleep.

During the day, he'd focus on researching what he could about vampires.

At night, he'd pop a painkiller, then head out. The idea being he'd spend as much time as possible near where he had met Mikael. Rational thinking told him the vampire would have moved on. Somewhere new where no one knew he existed.

He spent his days on the Internet and on books taken from the Oakley library. It had been slim pickings, but he had managed to find some books on the occult. Most of them read like a fiction book.

The time spent alone allowed him to reflect on his dinner with Ashley. He had been in the wrong to walk out like he did, he knew that. It wasn't her parents' fault that his parents never cared about him.

She had phoned that night to say she was sorry again, and Chris, after a few days, had phoned her back to tell her everything was fine.

He still felt that she shouldn't have divulged so much about him, but he understood why she had done it. Better that her family know about the situation rather than put their foot in it and say something out of bounds. Would he see them again? Maybe. He and Ashley hadn't arranged anything else to do since that day, and he wanted to see her, to spend time with her, but all his focus and energy was on finding out more about Mikael, vampires and whatever else was out there.

He saw the search as a way to escape from his life. From living like this. The damp patch on the ceiling still angered him.

One night, he even went up the stairs to the neighbour. Fuelled with a vicious mix of medication, pain, and alcohol, he slammed on the door and didn't bother stepping back. He waited and waited, but no one came. Either no one was in, or they didn't want to speak to him. He imagined someone standing behind the door and staring out through the peephole, laughing at the drunken man chapping his door.

With one last knock, he turned and went back to his flat and texted his landlord. He didn't expect a response, because outside of the deposit and the monthly payments, his landlord never spoke to him.

Saturday night came around, but instead of heading out to do some more searching, he decided to stay in for a change. Order food and maybe look on the Internet for anything he could find. The night before, he had signed up to a forum based around the occult and had posted a thread, asking if anyone had any altercations with vampires.

He got the expected responses a few minutes later.

'Are you high?'

'Sparkling ones?'

He thought he'd get a good discussion going, but after looking into the website more, it seemed like a lot of the users were there to take the piss.

Any valid thread or question was down-voted and flamed.

After having dinner – Chinese – he opened the laptop. He opened the thread, expecting more negative comments and people talking rubbish.

Sure enough, more comments flaming him and some insulting his family. The joke was on them, he didn't have any.

But there was one comment that stuck out to him. A user by the name of Occult69 had commented, saying he had a friend who was on a camping trip, and came back swearing he had encountered a vampire.

Chris was hesitant to respond; he could be taking the piss too.

He saw a little green marker next to the user's name, indicating he was online. The benefit to this forum was it had a chat box, where you could invite users to speak. So he did. He waited for a couple of minutes before the chat popped up, stating Occult69 had joined the chat.

The chat box remained silent, unmoving.

Finally, Chris asked him what his friend had told him, asked him where it had happened and anything he could tell him.

Occult69 responded after a few moments. Telling him his friend was likely talking rubbish, but he had said he had encountered a vampire in the Hoia Forest in Romania.

The Hoia Forest rang a bell.

Occult69 couldn't provide much more information, just telling Chris to be careful. Apparently, his friend had gone a bit off the deep end because of this.

He closed the chat box and closed the website.

Hoia Forest.

Where had he heard that before?

Armed with this new information, he typed Hoia Forest into Google and also included the word vampire, which didn't come up with any meaningful results. Instead, he typed Hoia Forest Supernatural. Several results showed, and he spent the next few hours looking through them all.

It was interesting reading – articles ranged from serious news reports about people going missing to people's own accounts of what they thought was going on the forest. Allegedly, Hoia Forest was famous in Romania for being an interesting and supernatural place.

Some even compared it to Aokigahara in Japan. A forest known for people disappearing, named locally as the suicide forest. Hoia Forest seemed to be the distant cousin of said forest, with some people saying they were scared to enter for fear of what the forest hid within it.

Some websites mentioned the practice of the occult, arguing people had set up a cult in the forest, and would kill anyone who would enter. Others argued the forest was magical, entwined with the old magic of witchcraft where Romanian witches made their settlement.

The only mention of vampires was the age-old tale of Count Dracula.

Chris noticed the time; it had just clocked over nine. His head was hurt, and his stomach was painful. He closed the laptop.

He popped another pill and took a swig of water. A spark went off in his brain like a current going along a wire

– Mikael had mentioned Hoia Forest. That was what he was forgetting.

Despite there being no mention of vampires in the websites he read, he was sure that if he dug deep enough, either on the Internet or in real life, he'd find something.

He remembered the word occult and frantically pulled his laptop back. He opened Google and searched for Occult Studies in the UK. Hardly anything came up, it seemed to be more of an American thing with even some American Universities having degrees, or majors, on the subject.

He searched for witchcraft in the UK and added a degree at the end. The first result was a History of Magic and Witchcraft course held in London at one of the lesser-known colleges. *It's better than nothing,* he thought. He opened the page. It seemed well written and seemed to be taking itself seriously.

He clicked on the tutor's details and found the name of the person teaching the course, Bryan Robson.

His biography stated: 'Bryan Robson is a world-renowned expert in the history of magic in our world, and the previously forbidden witchcraft. Bryan travelled the world researching the supernatural to provide the basis of this course.'

The course had already started and wouldn't start again until September of that year. It was only February.

The course had a contact number on it, likely for the college, they would hardly put a direct line to the tutor on it. He dialled the number into his phone, and he listened to it ring out. Again, he realised the time, and the fact that no one would be at a college to answer a phone at this time of night.

His mind was racing, and he wanted to speak to Bryan, but he'd have to wait until Monday.

Not the best timing considering he had an exam to take on Monday. He was halfway through the semester, and this exam was key to getting a good grade, accounting for forty percent of the overall grade for his module.

He had done no revision and no studying. The only research he had been doing was for his own benefit, for his own studies.

Studying for the module was the furthest thing from his mind, but he figured he should at least try to try for the exam before contacting the tutor down south.

He stood up and took a quick shower. He popped another pill and climbed into bed. It wasn't too late, but he was tired from the late nights.

He dreamed he was running through a forest, chased by something he couldn't see. He reached the end of the forest, the trees becoming tighter and tighter until he couldn't move. He was cornered, and when he turned, he was face to face with what looked like Mikael, only this time his fangs were out and his eyes were red.

He woke up sweating.

He went about his Sunday in a haze. Still popping pills to combat the pain, he struggled to think of anything else except when his next pill would be. His prescription was running low – only a few tablets left, and he wasn't sure that he would be prescribed more. The nurse said they were only a short-term solution, expecting the pain to dissipate after time. Had the pain gone? Chris often thought he may have become reliant on the medication to the point he couldn't be sure whether he needed them, and he was too scared to find out.

It was a rainy day, perfect for staying inside. After he broke out of his brain fog with a cold shower, he started studying for the exam the next day.

His heart wasn't in it.

And it showed, because he would study for five minutes, then lose concentration and focus on other things, like watching television, reading a book, or looking at the Internet.

* * *

Later that evening, he ordered food, some place cheap and no valid health and safety certificate. The food arrived and he tucked in, taking a pill at the same time.

He finished his food. Then had another shower.

His plan was to head to the University, sit the exam, get back home and call the college in London. Hoping to speak to Bryan Robson. Likely he would get through to a receptionist, and if that did happen, he decided he'd make up a story about wanting to study the course to get information.

He had it all planned and he went to sleep that night, painless but with only two tablets left.

His alarm sounded, waking him from his slumber and he rolled out of bed. He had time to get dressed and get a bite to eat, but all he had was a-couple-of-days-out-of-date bread.

At the University, he followed the signs to the relevant room. He was one of the last to arrive.

Ashley was at the front of the room, already sat with her notebook and laptop, ready to answer the question. It was an online exam, but the University insisted they complete it in the building.

Chris took a seat at the back and turned his laptop on – he forgot to charge it the previous night, but thankfully it had some juice left in it. Enough to blast his way through the exam.

The exam time limit was one hour.

It didn't take him long to complete it. Despite the fact he hadn't studied much, he felt as though he had made a good attempt, and would at least get the required marks to pass. He was one of the first to finish, beating Ashley to the punch and standing up to make Connors aware. Connors only nodded at him.

Leaving the building, he wondered if he should wait for Ashley to finish, maybe discuss the dinner but he decided against it. She had said she was sorry, and he had accepted it, and that was to be the end of it.

Overhead, rain clouds formed, much as was the norm in Scotland. Instead of ordering a taxi, he jumped on the number 57 bus which took him to his flat. He was feeling good thanks to the painkiller he had taken in the morning. And because he was excited to make the phone call he had planned.

In his mind, he ran through what he would say to whoever answered his call. If it was Bryan, he'd go right into why he was calling, looking for information about Hoia Forest and the supernatural. If a receptionist or administration type answered, he'd pretend to be a student.

His phone buzzed and he had a message from the landlord. He hadn't heard back about the upstairs tenants. Opening it, he wondered what she would have to say. She didn't even acknowledge his message – just a simple; 'Rent due. Transfer by next week.'

Brilliant, he thought.

He poured himself a glass of water, took a sip then threw two bits of stale bread into the toaster. As the bread was warming up, he opened his laptop, turned the power on and typed in the London College web address. The page loaded quickly just as the toast popped, slightly burnt.

Toast was a staple of Chris's diet when he was younger, and not much had changed in that regard. He ate the dry toast, dropping flakes and crumbs onto his laptop, allowing them to fall between the keys.

He opened his mobile and typed in the number for Bryan Robson.

The number rang for a good twenty seconds before a female voice answered.

'Hello. You're through to London City College admissions, how can I help today?'

'Uh yes,' he said, stammering a little. 'My name's Chris Winters and I'm looking at your History of Magic course.'

'Right?' Clearly the receptionist was in a poor mood.

'Can I speak to Bryan Robson, please?'

'Are you registered or are you looking to register?'

'Looking to register.'

'In that case, you can fill out the form on the website and we will register you on the course. Can I help with anything else today, sir?'

He may have imagined it, but he was sure he heard exacerbation in the way she had said 'Sir'.

'I'm not sure if I'm ready to register,' he lied. 'I'd really—'

'That's a shame,' she said, cutting him off. 'If you look over the course guidelines it might help you.'

'Exc—'

'The next intake is in a couple of months, so you have plenty of time. Thanks for your time today.'

'Hold on,' he said, feeling a bit of anger in his voice. 'Can I speak to the lecturer, please?'

'Mr Robson isn't in the office. Why do you wish to speak to him?'

'For information,' he said.

'Sir, all of the information can be found on the website. No student can speak to the tutor before they sign up, I'm afraid.'

'Why not?'

'All of the information required to make an informed choice is on the web page.'

'I understand that the information is there, but I'd really like to discuss the course with—'

'Again, sir. Mr Robson is not available, and even if he was, I couldn't transfer you through. The History of Magic is one of our lesser-known courses, shall we say, and because of that Mr Robson is not often in the building.'

'Right,' he said, and almost resigned himself to failure. So much for his master plan of getting through the gatekeeper and to the prize at the end of the rainbow. 'Thanks, then.'

'Goodbye.'

The lady ended the call with no hesitation, leaving Chris sitting in his living room, upset and frustrated. When he worked in Customer Service, he knew to be polite and patient, and she was the complete opposite. He could have asked to speak to a manager, but he didn't want to turn into one of those people.

He looked on the web page, and checked to see if he could find anything else. A way to contact the lecturer without signing up. Maybe LinkedIn would have his details?

He opened LinkedIn and searched by his name, Bryan Robson, and a few results came up. He searched through City of London College, and he found some lecturers but not who he was looking for. Did the guy even exist?

He searched again for Bryan, this time adding quotation marks at the end of his search term, and this time it came up. Buried away on page four of the results, there he was. Bryan stared back at Chris, who clicked on his page and scanned the information. His profile picture showed an older man, probably in his thirties and with deep brown hair.

There it was – an email address. He wrote down the address on a bit of paper and closed the window.

He needed to think of what to say, he needed a moment. Alcohol was what he needed. He went over to the kitchen and looked in the fridge – nothing there. Frustrated, he took the pills from his pocket and put one into his hand. He stared at the little thing – and was amazed at the fact that this little tablet was the reason he was in no pain.

Chris thought back to the night he was attacked and shuddered before swallowing the pill dry.

He was starting to run out; only three more pills left, and he had to make them last. He double checked the prescription, and it didn't allow for refills – he'd need to speak to a doctor to get another prescription, but he didn't want to admit to anyone that he'd become reliant on them now.

Back at the laptop, he pushed those thoughts about the pills to one side and started typing up the email he would send.

Hi Bryan,

My name is Chris Winters, and I'm writing to you to hopefully arrange a chat to discuss something important. Upon researching the supernatural, you are the only person I have found who seems to know what they are talking about.

As someone who has experience with the supernatural, I would love to discuss the history of magic and witchcraft with you.

I'd be willing to tell you about my experience with the supernatural, in that I had a confrontation with a vampire, who said they were created by witchcraft.

Could we arrange a time to chat?

My contact details are below.

Chris signed off the email with his name and contact number, then clicked send, not expecting to hear back for a few days.

Suddenly, the shrill sound of his phone played in his ears, and he felt a rush of heat in the pit of his stomach. Unknown number.

'Hello?'

'Is this Chris?'

'Aye. Who's this?'

'It's Bryan Robson. You emailed me a few minutes ago.'

Chris paused for a second and couldn't quite believe his luck. 'I tried to call the number on the college page, but the receptionist wouldn't put me through. What made you call so quick?'

'You mentioned you had an encounter with a vampire.'

'You believe me?'

'I didn't,' he said, then there was a brief silence on the line. 'But then you mentioned witchcraft and either you've done extensive research, or you may have just confirmed a theory I have.'

'Oh, right,' Chris said, standing up and pacing around the living room. 'I was hoping to chat about what you knew about vampires and witches and all that sort of thing.'

'I can tell you what I know,' he said, then coughed. 'Sorry, chesty cough. A lot of vampire stories are folk tales, fairy tales, nightmares even. But there are accounts in the early centuries of people drinking blood from the veins of other people.'

'Right,' Chris said. 'I can attest to that.'

'What do you mean?'

Chris had made a promise to Mikael – to not tell

anyone about his encounter with him, but he hadn't seen the vampire in a few weeks, so what harm would it do?

'A few weeks ago, I was attacked by a vampire.'

Bryan didn't respond for a minute. The line was deathly silent, and Chris fully expected him to laugh.

He didn't laugh, but said, 'How can you be sure?'

'Because he told me so. When he attacked, he had red eyes and fangs that protruded from his mouth.'

'You spoke with him?'

'I saved his life,' Chris said. 'Then he disappeared, and I haven't seen or heard from him since. I know I'm not crazy and I know what I saw. I had a vampire in my living room for God's sake.'

'This is amazing,' Bryan responded, sounding almost giddy. 'For years I had my theories about vampires and witches but could never confirm it despite years of travelling.'

'What do you know about Hoia Forest?'

'A lot,' he replied instantly. 'You mentioned this vampire told you they were created by witches or witchcraft. One of the stories I heard whilst travelling was just that.'

'What? Witches exist and create vampires.'

'Existed,' he said and took a moment. 'In the early centuries, the world was a much different place and all around the world were what people would call witches. This is all hearsay, keep in mind. When I was in Romania, I heard stories of Hoia Forest and witchcraft.'

'Any mention of vampires?'

'Yes,' he said, and sounded almost angry that Chris had interrupted. 'A local fella I spoke to told me the story that his grandparents used to tell him. A story where if you went into Hoia Forest a Moroi would kill you. Obviously, there are stories like this all over the world, but he also said that these vampires were created by witches many, many years ago to protect them from humans who sought to kill all witches and forms of magic.'

'Did you believe him?'

'At the time, no. But after what you've said that this vampire told you he was created by witchcraft. Surely that shows some of the story to be true.'

'Well,' Chris said, rubbing his head. 'He never said he was created by witchcraft, but he said his coven leader had been.'

'Possibly,' he said, his voice shaking. 'This is all very interesting. Is there anything else you can tell me about the vampire? Anything at all?'

'All the stories I've heard about vampires paint them in a blood-thirsty, animal-like light. But he wasn't like that, not after he had drunk blood. In fact, he was fairly calm and polite.'

'They would be part human, so it's natural to assume many would enjoy human company, but it's also natural to assume others would take the power of being a vampire to heart and go in the opposite direction. This truly is amazing. Are you still in contact?'

'With the vampire? No, I've not been able to track him down.'

'You must!'

'I've been trying,' Chris said defensively. 'I'm not even sure if he would still be in the city.'

'There must be a reason why this has come to light now. I've read reports of people going missing in Romania and thought nothing of it, but now I'm not so sure. And why would this vampire have left his group? Where are you from again? I'm guessing Scotland by the accent.'

'That's right,' Chris said and looked out the window. 'You think there are more of them?'

'Certainly. If you manage to get in touch with this vampire, please let me know. I'd love the chance to interview him.'

'I will.'

'And Chris?'

'Yeah?'

'Be careful with this. All the stories say vampires are vicious creatures, who love nothing more than to kill and torture humans. This vampire sounds different, but tread cautiously.'

Chapter Sixteen

Since his conversation with Bryan Robson a few days prior, Chris had spent his nights on the hunt.

He would go to different places in Oakley, from the town centre through to the loch and even tried to sneak into the castle in the hopes Mikael would be hiding out in the dungeons. That would be where he expected to run into a vampire, but he never got a chance to get that close, thanks to the security guard walking round the grounds.

Each night he was left frustrated. He would trudge back to his flat, freezing cold and shattered. The only shimmer of positivity was each night he would come home and pass out into a dreamless sleep. Each morning he woke up feeling rested and relaxed.

The days were the hardest. With nothing to do, and running out of medication, he fell into himself and avoided speaking to people, especially Ashley when she would text to see how he was.

It was as if his brain was wired at night, hoping to find Mikael, then would spend the day recovering.

* * *

On March 4th, he woke up bright and early and took the second to last pill he had left. As he showered, he noticed all the bruising was now gone, and he had no scrapes left on his right cheek. After brushing his teeth, he opened the laptop, tempted to give Bryan a call to let him know he hadn't got any further forward.

As he was thinking, he noticed an email pop into his inbox from the University with his results from the previous exam. He scanned it for a moment before closing the laptop in disgust.

A poor fail.

The result screamed at him through the pixels in bright red font.

A poor fail.

'Damn it,' he said, standing with his hands on his hips and shaking his head. He knew he hadn't studied properly, but he was sure he'd at least get a decent pass. Certainly not a poor fail.

He could feel his face turning red and a deep feeling of regret running around his stomach. It was as if his stomach had butterflies, but if they were on fire.

Chris pushed the laptop off the table in frustration and rubbed his head. He walked over to the window and put his hands on the edge, leaning on it and looking down at his feet. He breathed heavily.

He turned. He looked at the laptop on the floor.

What was he doing?

Chasing a vampire when he couldn't even keep his life together normally? A University degree which could help him succeed in life was what he knew he should be going for, and that was what angered him, the fact his brain told him one thing, but he did another.

He sat down on the couch and rested his head. He was

entitled to a resit, at least. And it wasn't the end of the world, he'd just need to focus on the next one. A small part of him hated the fact he was at a poor University when he could be doing something much more.

What was his focus in life? Finding a purpose in life, excitement, and adventure? Or focusing on student life, getting a good degree, and doing the expected thing of settling down with a wife and kids?

Breaking his thought process, he heard the chapping of his door, rather loudly, he thought. He sighed, stood up, and walked towards the door. He looked through the peephole and saw Ashley standing on the other side.

He unlocked the door from the latch and pulled the door open.

'Alright?' he said, confused as to why she was there.

'Alright,' she said, and looked to be deciding whether she would take a step in. 'I was in the area and just wanted to check in. You've not been answering my texts.'

'Sorry, yeah,' he said, standing to the side and allowing her to take a step inside. 'It's been a rough couple of weeks. Come in.'

She walked into the living room and took a seat on the couch, spotting the laptop on the floor. 'What happened there?'

'Oh, that. Eh, might have got a wee bit angry at something. It's nothing, though.' He sat on the chair opposite her and turned the volume on the TV down.

She looked at him for a moment, almost studying him like a zookeeper would a wild animal. 'Seriously, are you alright?'

Chris gave his best winning smile. 'Aye, of course! Just been a strange few weeks what with what happened at the bar.'

'How are you feeling? Are you still in pain?'

'Not really,' he said, touching his stomach without noticing he had done it. 'I mean, I still get the odd twinge, but the medication helps.'

She paused for a second. 'You're still using then?' she asked with a hint of confusion. 'Have you got much left or are you off them now?'

'One tablet left,' he said, starting to feel a bit uncomfortable. 'I'm still taking them every so often.'

'How often?'

'Every few hours.'

Silence hung in the air like a bad smell.

'What happens after this last one?'

'I don't know,' he said. 'It'll be fine though. If it's sore, I can handle it.'

'It's not the pain I'm worried about...'

'What do you mean?'

'Well,' she said, stopping to lean forward. 'These pills can be addictive. From what I've seen, you're walking fine and speaking fine, and seem to be coping well. The nurse said you wouldn't need them for very long. I'm not worried about the pain because I know you won't have much, and even if you did a nice paracetamol would help, but codeine?'

'Yeah?'

'I'm just worried about the effects of addiction to it.'

Chris leaned back in his chair. If he was honest with himself, he was concerned about it too.

'All these late nights mixed with these pills can't be good for you.'

'Probably not,' Chris said and laughed, trying to lighten the conversation but it didn't work.

'Do me a favour? Take the last pill and try to forget about them. You don't need them and if you do feel like you are in a bit of pain, then get some over-the-counter stuff.'

'I'm scared,' he said, almost whispering. He felt stupid for saying it, for finally admitting it. More admitting it to himself than Ashley.

'I get it,' she said. 'I lost a friend to drugs and I know it's not the same, but I don't want to lose you too. If you need anyone to help you in the next few days when you're off it then please let me know.'

'I will,' he said. 'Do you want a glass of water or juice or anything?'

'I better not,' she said. 'I was just stopping by. Heading to the train station.'

'Oh really,' he said. 'Day out?'

'Suppose so. I'm meeting a literary agent to discuss a book that I sent them.'

'That's amazing,' Chris said, beaming. 'I didn't even know you were writing a book. You'll let me know how it goes?'

'Sure, I will. I better get going. Remember, if you need anything in the next few days, please let me know and I'll be here for you. Anything at all. We'll get another day like the bungee jump sorted again.'

'As long as we don't have a repeat of what happened that same night then I'm all for it.'

She stood up. 'Come here,' she said and stretched her arms out.

Chris stood and allowed himself to be hugged.

With a smile and a wave, Ashley disappeared out of the front door, down the stairs to the ground floor and out of the complex.

Chris closed his door and leaned against the wooden frame. Several things she said had hit home. He decided there and then he'd take the final pill later today after the allotted time on the prescription and it would be the last tablet he'd take. If he ended up in pain again, he'd get through it, or at a very last resort, he'd use some over-the-counter medication.

That moment came quicker than Chris had realised.

He poured himself a glass of water and put the pill in his mouth. The water did its job and washed the tablet down his throat and into his stomach where it would dissolve and the moment he swallowed, he felt at ease again.

That was until later that night, after he had time to think about what had happened with the exam and the news that Ashley may have a book deal in the works. As he went to sleep, he felt the effects of the tablet start to wear off, and he started to worry. The anxiety of not having any medication to hand prevented him from sleeping and he lay there, tossing and turning for over an hour before deciding it was futile.

His body was craving a pill now. He wouldn't say he was in pain; it was more discomfort, and it was something he knew would go away if he just had a damn tablet. There would be no place open right now where he could get over-the-counter meds. Maybe the twenty-four-hour Tesco, but that was the other end of the city and would be a pain to get to and back, especially at the time which had just struck two AM.

Instead of lying in bed, he got up and wandered through to the living area. He spent the next few minutes walking up and down, from kitchen to living room to the front door and back again. He did this at least twenty times, hoping it'd take his mind off it.

I really am addicted, he thought.

He found himself wishing he had one more pill left. Just one to see him through the night.

He'd call the GP in the morning, get another

prescription. They wouldn't ask too many questions, right? It'd be natural for someone who was assaulted to ask for more painkillers. Yes, but it had been weeks since the attack and he wasn't in any pain.

The feeling he had was more of ants climbing all over his skin. The feeling of bees buzzing around in his head. He could feel his skin almost vibrating and he hated it. Hated himself for allowing himself to become reliant on the tablets.

He'd do anything to have just one more. Just one more sweet pill, then he could sleep.

He was tired and his thoughts were becoming jumbled. He tried to lie down on the couch, hoping the change of scenery would help him fall asleep but it never came. He almost cried.

Everything at once came rushing at him like a freight train with no brakes.

His parents who never loved him, who he loved but would never see again.

His failures at University and his unhealthy obsession with chasing the impossible.

Seeing Ashley moving on with her life and becoming something with purpose, someone important.

Why hadn't the vampire just killed him?

He tossed and turned so much that he fell off the couch, landing awkwardly on his side and this time he felt actual pain.

He sat on the floor, on his dirty carpet, and rested his head in his hands. He felt tears prickling at his eyes and he did his utmost to fight them back.

What a sight he was, sitting on the ground; he had truly hit rock bottom, he thought.

Brushing away the liquid from his eyes, Chris picked himself up and searched the cupboards for any medication he could find. He'd take anything at this point. He opened a cupboard and found an old bottle of amber liquid.

It was better than nothing. Chris pulled the whiskey bottle down and poured himself a smallish glass. The liquid slid down his throat, burning him on the way down and he felt a small sense of relief. Finally, he was able to sit and be still. He didn't have the same urge to get up and go.

Was it the medication he was after? Or the alcohol?

He had been drinking a lot more on his nights searching for Mikael, he thought.

Probably a mixture of both.

He continued sipping the glass until he hit the bottom of it. Chris stared at himself for a second, before sighing, then he picked up the whiskey bottle and poured himself another.

Chapter Seventeen

Over the next couple of weeks his life spiralled out of control. He was off the medication, but instead of the painkillers, he had found a new hook. Every night he would use the excuse of searching for Mikael to allow himself to drink himself into a drunken stupor. He argued that it was the only way to sleep. Because when he tried to sleep without a drink of alcohol, his body went back to craving the medication that prevented so much pain.

He was painless – at least physically.

The night was the same as any other. He showered, had a bite to eat – toast and bran flakes – then headed out. After the taxi driver dropped him in town, he did his nightly walk around, looking in alleyways and down the generally avoided areas of Oakley. People generally stayed away from the southern part of the city because of the kidnappings that occurred the previous years. The people responsible were caught, eventually, but the taboo of going to that area at night was still there.

While he searched, his mind fell towards Ashley; she

was living the high life with her new agent and her new book deal. He also thought of Bryan, who every couple of days would text him looking for updates.

He started to worry the teacher was starting to lose patience with him. But Chris reminded himself he wasn't searching for Mikael to satisfy Bryan. Bryan told Chris what he wanted to hear: information that confirmed his belief he had spent time with the supernatural. Something that he wanted to experience more of.

With each passing night, his enthusiasm waned, and his frustration grew.

After searching for an hour, he headed back to the centre of town. Past the brightly lit Domino's and the barely lit Dentistry Office. Oakley Town Centre was nothing to brag about. Tourists visited the castle and the loch. Loch Rain was fifteen miles long and about half that wide – it was a hell of an attraction for people coming from England and abroad. People in Scotland were spoiled by the size of Loch Ness – most Scottish people weren't fussed about Loch Rain. Didn't help there is no monster.

Not for a rundown shopping centre where shops closed every week and for poorly run pubs and nightclubs.

He passed a couple, who were in the kind of love you saw in movies, holding hands and gazing lovingly at one another as they spoke. Chris noticed the guy pulled the brunette in closer when they passed. He passed the Domino's and took a brief glance at himself in the window – it wasn't a pretty sight.

Chris had put on a bit of weight, likely from the alcohol, and had let his beard grow out. The beard was at the awkward stage, the mid-length that no one wanted.

He walked through the town, taking the time to look down every street to see if he could catch a glimpse of

Mikael, and found himself realising how stupid the endeavour was.

Chris clocked The Wet Whistle.

He threw open the door and took a couple of steps inside. He had avoided the bar since the altercation with Greg, Tattoo Man and his fat friend, but at this point he didn't care. He wanted to get inside and get a drink.

Ignoring the looks from some of the couples having their dinner, the scruffy Chris walked towards the bar and took a seat on one of the barstools. He never saw himself as someone who would search for answers at the bottom of a bottle, but this is what he was now, wasn't it? *Pathetic*, he thought.

He got the attention of Colin by raising his hand.

'Jesus, mate, barely recognised you there. Long time,' Colin said, throwing the dirty tea towel over his right shoulder.

'Aye,' Chris said, stopping to stifle a cough. 'Wasn't too sure about showing up around in case those folk were here.'

'Sure. What can I get you? The usual?' Colin had already started to pour the cider out into a pint glass.

'Jack Daniels, please.'

'Oh, moving on to the strong stuff, are you? You want a mixer with it? Cola or something?'

'Just the JD, please. Thanks.'

Colin looked at Chris for a moment. 'Sure, mate. One second.' He poured the Jack Daniels into the glass and handed it to Chris who gave him a five-pound note in return.

Chris swirled the amber liquid around the glass, then suddenly threw the drink back in one gulp. He felt the alcohol run down his throat and into his stomach. It felt amazing, and he felt an immense pleasure and warmth. He leaned back in his chair and placed the glass on the table.

'You want another?' Colin asked, still holding the bottle in his hand.

'Yes,' Chris said. 'Double, please.'

'Are you alright, mate? You seem—'

'I'm fine,' Chris interjected, with a bit of sting behind the words. 'I just need a drink is all. It's been a rough time the past few weeks.'

Chris thought about the many sleepless nights. All the hours spent tossing and turning, wrapped in a hot duvet stinging his skin like a bunch of wasps. Failure to sleep was something he had a lot of experience of in the past while. His mind raced every night unless he had a glass or three of alcohol or had popped a hell of a lot of paracetamols.

'You want to come round the back and tell—'

'No. I don't really need to talk about anything. Would rather just have a drink. Do you mind?' Chris said, holding the glass out, waiting for Colin to pour it, getting more frustrated with each passing second.

Chris noticed a man at the end of the bar staring back at him. He was an older gentleman, around sixty, and he had his own glass of alcohol, looked like vodka. For a second he saw himself in that man, he saw his future.

He looked back at Colin and said, 'Please.'

Colin nodded then carefully poured the double Jack Daniels into Chris's glass. 'Let me know if you need anything else.'

Chris nodded, then took a sip of the double, savouring it this time and exhaling a sigh of relief.

He watched the people come and go for the next couple of hours. By shutting time he was absolutely plastered. So much so that he could barely see straight.

Chris was – besides two other lonely guys – the only person left still drinking, the rest were either wrapping or already on their way out the door. He hadn't run into Tattoo Man tonight which was a blessing, he had no idea how he'd cope with that again, not in the state he was in.

Being drunk numbed him to everything. All his feelings and emotions were either heightened or repressed. The tough ones – the ones that caused him pain and kept him up at night – were pushed to the back of his mind, whilst the other ones – the anger and frustration of life – came bubbling to the surface.

He had only left the bar stool a couple of times, each time needing to go to the toilet. And this was another of those times. He tried to stand, using the bar as a prop to keep himself upright. At any moment he could collapse on the floor, and what a laugh that would be. He was over any embarrassment now, mainly because the other people still there were either drunk or, at the very least, tipsy.

He felt his ankle roll and it reminded him of an accident he had on his way to school, where he had put his foot down at a wrong angle, and ended up falling to the side, losing balance but landing on his knee, right in the mud. The other kids had laughed at him then.

This time, he didn't fall over, instead he caught himself on the bar and this time he was one the laughing – laughing at himself for the state he was in. It was the first time in a very long time he was what you could call a legless type of drunk. But it felt damn good.

He made his way to the toilet and stumbled through the door. It was empty. He figured it'd be best to sit rather than stand, otherwise he might take a tumble and whack his head off a urinal. *What way to go that would be*, he thought. Found lying on a sticky toilet floor with blood gushing from his head. Cause of death: Death by urinal. Luckily, he survived the few steps to the toilet stall with no major incidents.

He did his business, making sure to wash his hands, because despite being drunk, he still cared about his hygiene. Even though you wouldn't have guessed it, looking at him.

Back at the bar, he sat on his stool and made eye contact with Colin. For much of the night, Chris had been served by another bartender. He knew Colin was avoiding him. Avoiding the mess on the other side of his bar. He hadn't done anything wrong – just had a few drinks. A boatload of drinks. And he hadn't made a fuss, never put a foot out of place. But he knew the look, the disappointed look.

It was the same look Ashley had given him when she found out he had failed the exam, or the time he had run out on her and her family.

Or the look his parents would give him when they returned to him after time away. The disappointed expression they had, realising they had a son they didn't want.

Bastards, Chris thought. *Screw the lot of them.*

'Colin,' he said, loud enough so Colin couldn't realistically say he couldn't hear him.

Colin walked over to him. 'Yes, mate?'

'One more drink, eh?'

'Last orders was a few minutes ago, bud.'

'Come on,' Chris said, smiling. 'One for the road. For your old buddy.'

'Sorry, but I can't serve you. I can get you water if—'

'Screw the water,' Chris said, standing up awkwardly. He stretched his arm and tried to reach one of the bottles behind the bar. Colin grabbed his arm and pushed it back.

'Stop it,' Colin said, trying to de-escalate a situation that could only get worse. 'This isn't you, man. Do you want me to get you a taxi?'

'No, I don't want a taxi,' Chris said, sitting back down in his chair. 'Just one more drink, please?'

His voice was softer this time, pleading almost.

Colin shook his head and leaned back against the back of the bar. Chris noticed the other patrons who were still there were finishing off their drinks, getting ready to leave.

'Two seconds,' Colin said and brought down a large pint glass and Chris smiled. He had got his way and he waited in anticipation of that final sweet drink before he headed home. Vampire hunting could wait. He wanted the drink, and he wanted to get home.

Colin disappeared out of sight with the glass then came back and Chris was supremely disappointed with what he saw in his hand.

Colin placed the tall glass of water, shimmering with ice cubes, condensation resulting in tears falling from the side of the tumbler. 'Drink this.'

Chris had already told him he didn't want water, and that was what angered him the most. He clenched his fist and smashed it against the glass, sending it to the end of the bar, water splashing everywhere and eventually the glass hit the hard floor and smashed, sending splinters sliding along the floor.

'Chris!'

The voice had come from the front door, and for a moment, Chris thought he had imagined it. *Not now*, he thought. He didn't want her to see him like this. He had just wanted a drink and to go to sleep.

He didn't want water. He didn't want judgement from Colin or any of the other people in the bar. And at that moment, he certainly did not want to see Ashley.

He turned slowly, and saw her standing in the doorway, staring at him in disappointment and his heart ached.

Chapter Eighteen

'Sit down. I'll get you a glass of water,' Ashley said, as she opened the front door and escorted Chris into the cold flat.

He felt like a kid being reprimanded by a strict teacher, like he had been caught doing something naughty.

Chris did as he was told though. He took a seat on the couch and glanced at the clock near the window, it had just gone two in the morning. His head had started to pound on the drive back. The journey was quick and silent. Ashley hadn't said much.

He tried to make small talk with her, but she never responded. He knew she was angry, but it was his right to get a bit drunk. She wasn't his mother, and he didn't answer to her.

She came back to the living room after filling a tall glass with cold water. She had poured a smaller one for herself. Chris watched her closely.

'Drink it,' she said. 'It'll help the hangover you'll get

tomorrow.'

Chris did as he was told, his head still swimming with the alcohol. He'd be lucky not to wake up with alcohol poisoning – let alone a hangover. 'Thanks,' he said meekly. 'How did you know where I was?'

'Colin messaged me to say you were there and weren't doing so hot.'

'You two best buddies now?' The words came out with a swig of vile hatred in them, and he immediately regretted it. 'Sorry, I didn't mean it like that.'

'We're not, but we are friends. He was looking out for you. That's what I was doing, and I thought you knew that.'

'What do you mean?'

'You don't get it,' she said, standing up and walking from the chair to the window. 'I'm not pissed off you went out and got drunk. We've all done that. But you did it because you're hurting, and I told you last time if you needed help – needed me – to tell me.'

She was right – in a way. She had said she was there for him, but he had tried to deal with everything himself. First the death of his parents. The failures at school and the belief he had failed at life. The assault. Medication. The alcohol.

It all came flooding at him like a dam had just collapsed. He thought about what he must look like. Unkempt, tired, like a drug addict who hasn't had their fix. He didn't consider himself an addict – not really.

'Maybe the dinner was a mistake,' she said, breaking him from his train of thought.

'It wasn't,' he interjected and felt a twinge in his temple. 'I had a good time, it's just – everything's been a lot these past few weeks.'

'I know,' she said, sitting back down, this time on the

couch next to him. 'I get it. You're going through a lot. Both physical and mental, but you have people around you to help. You have me.'

'Do I?'

'Eh?'

'I don't want to be a burden on anyone,' he said.

'Stop it,' she said. 'Don't turn this around. You're not a burden. I told you I'd be there for you to help you, especially after you came off the medication.' She paused. 'You are off them, right?'

He nodded.

'Is that why you were so drunk tonight? Replace one thing with another?'

He thought about it. She was right. He had simply stopped taking the painkillers and replaced them with alcohol. 'I suppose so.'

'You should have told me,' she said. 'Listen, you don't need the medication and you don't need the alcohol. Chris, we all enjoy a drink, but what I saw tonight was far too much.'

'I know.'

'If you continue on like that then I don't know what's going to happen. You say you struggle with living a boring life, but newsflash – we all live boring lives. This isn't a movie where excitement is around every corner. If you forget that, then you might realise where your priorities lie.'

'You're right,' he said, and he meant it.

For too long he had felt sorry for himself. About his parents not caring a jot about him. He had let his studies go chasing down a fairytale.

He felt his body craving another drop of the sauce. He thought about the amber liquid from the bar, and he felt his skin start to go red and hot.

Ashley looked at him, as if she knew what he was thinking. Then she said, 'You're thinking about drinking again?'

'I'm not addicted,' Chris said, a little too quickly.

'I know,' Ashley said, and smiled. 'But you will be if you're not careful. When you came off the meds how did you feel?'

He thought back to the day he had stopped and how awful it was to give them up. 'Terrible. I can't face that again.'

'What? Giving something up? Chris,' she said and grabbed his hand, 'listen, you were taking the pills because you were in pain, and you continued taking them because you were scared the pain would come back. But it's been a few weeks now, and you look fine. Well, you still look like you've been hit by a truck, but I can tell you're not in pain.'

No one said anything for a good minute.

'At least, not physically,' she said. 'Did you start drinking after you stopped the meds because—'

'Because,' he said and stopped. Chris looked at her, dead in the eyes and had to admit it to himself first before saying it. 'I started drinking because when I stopped the medication, I felt my brain craving it, and I felt the pain coming back.'

No one said anything again.

'I started drinking because it numbed everything.' Again, he paused. 'And, because it numbed all the pain I still felt about my parents dying and leaving me alone.'

She sighed. 'You're not alone,' she whispered.

'I started drinking because of that and I kept drinking because it was the only way to sleep, to live a life and – and because I was scared if I stopped then I'd start to feel, and it'd all come back.'

I reckon you took priority.'

The chat was back to their usual light-hearted ways, and Chris had felt a weight lift from his shoulders. He could tell she was no longer mad at him, but he would need to follow through on his promise.

He was confident he would, because he didn't need booze or painkillers to live a good life. He just needed a positive attitude and a friend like Ashley.

It'd still be good to find Mikael, to learn about his life and learn about that world, but, for right now, he was content with focusing on his studies and then maybe he would do what his parents did, and travel around the world. Hell, maybe Ashley would go with him? She could spend her days writing whilst he explored cities, and they could spend the evenings together.

'I'll message you tomorrow and we'll arrange something soon. Maybe another bungee jump,' she said and seemed excited for the hour it was. 'Or go-karting, I used to love that as a kid!'

'We'll get something sorted soon.'

'Oh, and get this place tidied up, eh?'

Chris agreed he would. He looked around and noticed how bad things had got. Maybe it reflected himself, he thought. Nothing was in its right place, and everything was either dirty or messy. He made a mental note to get up early – as early as he could after tonight – and get cleaned. The place would be gleaming by the next time Ashley saw it.

Suddenly, two loud bangs came from the door, stopping Ashley in her place as she was about to leave. 'Who could that be at this time?'

'No idea,' Chris said, and shook his head. He walked past Ashley, the drunkenness now almost completely gone, and carefully approached the door. The bangs were not your usual knocks – they were aggressive and dangerous. Was it the upstairs neighbours? If it was, then they'd get a piece of his mind about that damn patch on the ceiling.

Chris reached the door and popped his eye through the peephole. A coldness hit him in his stomach and his heart went into panic mode, quickly rising in beats per minute.

'Oh no,' Chris whispered, and had his eye almost pressed up against the hole.

'What is it?'

Chris turned. 'I think,' he whispered, 'it's those guys from the bar that night that attacked us.'

'You're joking,' she said and nearly laughed but Chris could tell she was spooked. 'Who is it really? It's not funny.'

Chris looked again through the blurry peephole. From what he could see, there were three men. He recognised one of them as Greg – Tattoo Man – because he saw the black star on his neck. The other two he wasn't sure about, but one of them seemed to be standing back, telling the others what to do.

He could hear them slightly.

'Greg, just kick the damn thing in!' the man at the back said, and Tattoo Man took a step back.

Greg suddenly rushed to the door, and kicked it with all his might, but the door only budged a little.

'Chris – we need to leave,' Ashley said. 'Is there another way out?'

'Just this door. Hell. How did they find me? Do you think they followed us?'

'I don't know. I'm calling the police.'

Chris watched her pull her phone out and then heard the man standing back tell Greg to get out of the way.

A few seconds later, Chris was blown backwards by the

force of the door coming off its hinges, narrowly avoiding smashing him in the face. Ashley screamed and Chris did all he could to make sure he didn't either.

Both were suddenly grabbed by Greg and the other two. One of them was the fat one from the bar. He had the same horrid stench. Chris tried to fight it but they were too strong. The two others had him under control and he tried to push them back, ramming them into the wall but all that did was annoy them, one of them wrenched his arm around his back and ran him face first into the opposite wall.

He felt a slight bit of blood trickle down his face, from the moment his forehead connected with the concrete wall. Chris could see Ashley fighting too, out of the corner of his eye. She could handle herself, he knew that, but the third man was far too big for her. He easily grabbed her by the arm and pushed her back onto the couch and held her down.

Chris had an uneasy thought that he pushed away, but it had given him the strength to get to his feet and take a couple of steps towards them.

But on the second step, he felt a hard clunk on the back of his head, and he saw the ground coming up towards him.

His eyes shut and everything from his hearing to his sight went dark.

Chapter Twenty

Blinded by the bright light, Chris struggled with his vision, adjusting to his new surroundings.

He was still attempting to cope with his sight after a minute. Finally, Chris could see, just barely.

He looked around the room. It was a box room. It wouldn't be a surprise if he was in a prison cell with the type of room it was. There was one door ahead of him. A heavy duty one, coloured blue with a slat in the middle of it, clearly this was a room used to keep someone in.

Chris tried to move but soon noticed he was stuck to the chair. His hands were tied with a thick rope, with the rope looping around the chair so he couldn't move. He tried to move the chair, but it seemed to be bolted to the floor.

He looked around and the memory of what happened came slowly back to him.

He recalled being steaming drunk in The Wet Whistle, then having a heart to heart with Ashley and – Ashley, where was she?

His heart rate had started to spike, and he felt his back beginning to sweat.

They had been taken from the flat. Roughly. He remembered seeing the hard wood coming towards his face and the last thing he could recall was smashing into the floor.

'What the hell?' Chris said to himself, looking around the room. He had no idea where he was, but he knew it wasn't good. He was also mightily concerned about Ashley. She would probably be in another room, but why? Why were they in this situation?

What was it the policeman said? To not mess with Tattoo Man – Greg – and the others. But he hadn't – he didn't go searching them out, he had left the fight how it ended and didn't bother about it, but, clearly, they still held a grudge.

Chris knew how dangerous these people could be, since he had been the victim of the beating and he knew what they had in mind for Ashley that night. The thought of Ashley alone in a room with one of these arseholes petrified him.

He tried to loosen the ropes around his wrist and chair but nothing was working. How did they do it in the movies? He couldn't exactly run and smash the chair on the floor since it was screwed into the concrete. He remembered a TV show he'd watched when he was younger called *Chuck* – where one of the characters was tied up and was told to break his thumb or dislocate it at least.

Did that work? Could he, do it? He pressed his right thumb into the palm of his other hand and all he could feel was pressure. *This was stupid,* he thought. He had no idea how to break his own thumb. There had to be another way.

He continued to try to loosen the ropes and he felt his body start to enter flight or fight and his heartrate quickened again, and his temperature skyrocketed. He was in trouble, and he needed help. Ashley needed help.

'Help!' he yelled, forgetting any sense of self-preservation. The rope loosening wasn't working, at least not quick enough for his body's reaction to calm, and yelling for help was the natural reaction. 'Help!' He tried again and heard some footsteps walking outside the door.

The slat on the door slid to the left and made a loud bang when it reached the end. He couldn't make out the face of the person peering back at him.

He waited, not saying anything. He'd no idea who it was, and he wasn't sure whether he was friend or foe. The logical thought was whoever it was wasn't there to get him out of here.

The slat closed and nothing happened for a minute. He heard muffled voices coming from outside and he struggled to make anything out.

Suddenly, the door was pulled open, and a man of sizeable bulk entered into the frame. It was if he took up the whole doorway. Bald, with a scraggly beard and dark eyes. The man wore a leather jacket and black jeans, but Chris could only focus on his eyes, which bore into him.

'My man tells me you're making quite the racket,' he said, stepping into the room and closing the door behind him, not before Chris caught a glimpse of a room opposite his with the same door.

The man took a few steps closer.

'What do you want?' Chris asked, failing at his first attempt before stuttering his way through it.

The man smiled and edged his way closer. 'Chris, is it?'

Chris looked him right in the eye. 'Aye, that's right.'

'Fantastic,' he said. 'Glad we got the right man. I'm

Steve, and you did something very stupid, son.'

'What's that?'

Steve smiled. Chris couldn't quite put an age to him, but he figured he was in his thirties or forties.

'Chris, you messed with my family. You broke my brother's nose, we can't just let that lie, can we?'

This is what the policeman had warned him about, but he hadn't bloody tried to seek them out. All he'd tried to do was forget about them. He didn't do anything wrong, only defended himself and that thought gave him the confidence to speak back, almost pleading his case.

'Look,' he said, pushing his chest out. 'Your brother – Greg – he started things with me. I didn't want any trouble, but he and his pals kept coming so I had to defend myself. Wouldn't you defend yourself?'

'Aye,' Steve said slowly. 'I would defend myself, but then again if I had broken your brother's nose wouldn't you want some kind of payback?'

Chris found himself wondering what it'd have been like to have a sibling and he had to admit he'd defend them if they had got into a scrap. Chris did not answer.

'I'll leave you now,' Steve said, turning his back on Chris and reaching the door to the outside.

'Where's Ashley?' Chris said desperately.

Steve turned, and Chris saw the slow grin appear on the bottom of his face. 'Don't you worry about that,' he said. 'Greg will be in soon to deal with you. We'll take care of Ashley for you.'

Chris felt utterly and truly helpless. He also felt like he was going to throw up at any moment. He no longer cared about the alcohol or the fact he had no medication. The pain was an afterthought – he only wanted to make sure Ashley was safe. Steve left him in the room with only his thoughts for company.

And his thoughts were not a pretty sight. He could only imagine what Greg had planned for him, or what they had planned for Ashley.

He knew he had to do something – anything at all to get out of the situation. He wriggled his arms back and forth, trying to see if he could get any of the rope to loosen. It seemed tight enough, but for a split second he thought he could feel movement in it.

Chris knew he wouldn't have long before Greg showed up, likely to do him even worse than before. Either he was going to be beaten within an inch of his life or killed. This thought, and the thought of Ashley alone with these people, spurred him on.

Finally, he felt the rope give way, loosen slightly, just enough for him to get his right hand out of the rope and use the free hand to get his left free. But, just as he did this, Chris heard footsteps outside.

It was Greg. He couldn't be sure but the sinking feeling in the pit of his stomach gave him a clue it was him.

He stayed seated on the chair, and as the door opened, Chris decided to keep his hands behind his back, hoping Greg wouldn't notice the ropes were no longer there – he held them loosely in his hands.

'Good to see you, old mate,' Greg said, standing in the door frame like his brother had. He wasn't as big as his brother, but he was just as intimidating. Chris stared him in the eye, frozen stiff with both fear and adrenaline.

'Wish I could say the same,' Chris said, not removing his gaze from Greg.

Greg slammed the door closed, causing a large echo in the room.

'Where am I?'

'Somewhere no one will find you. But then again, we made sure no one would be looking.'

'How long have you been watching me?' Chris wasn't sure if they had been watching, or if they spotted him earlier and took their chance.

'Long enough,' Greg said, then took a couple of steps closer. 'But we had to wait until we had both of you.'

'Where is she?'

'Safe,' Greg said with a sickening grin slowly appearing on his face.

'You better not have touched her,' Chris said through gritted teeth.

Greg's face switched from passive hatred to anger. 'Mate, you're not in any position to act the big man.' He pointed to his nose. 'You broke my nose. We couldn't let that stand.'

'What? So you kidnapped me and Ashley, who had nothing to do with that?'

'Exactly,' Greg said, moving forward so he was only a step away from Chris.

'What happens now? You kill me? You kill us?'

Greg got close in now, edging his face closer to Chris so they were eye level. Chris could smell the rancid smoke and alcohol on Greg's lips and he felt bile rise up from his stomach.

His window was coming.

'Not exactly,' Greg said, smiling. 'We'll kill you, and the hot thing you brought with you. Well, we'll keep her alive for—'

Chris immediately smashed the top of his forehead into the previously broken nose. Tattoo Man stumbled backwards, grabbing his nose and tripping over so he was flat on his back. He started to stand back up, muttering obscenities about how he was going to kill Chris, but he hadn't expected Chris to be untied, because when he sat up, he was met by a kick to the chest.

Chris saw red and booted Greg in the stomach a couple of times, before grabbing the man by the scruff of his neck and throwing him into the wall. Greg smashed back first, into the concrete, hitting the back of his head.

He slowly fell to the ground, his eyes closing and his mouth hanging there. Chris approached him gently, and then placed two fingers on the side of his neck, keeping the other hand clenched in preparation for a counterattack. But no counterattack came – he could feel a small pulse, so at least he hadn't killed him, only knocked him out, it seemed.

What was next? Part of him was screaming at him to get out of there and call the police, but he had no mobile on him, and he couldn't be sure where he was. For all he knew, he could be in the middle of nowhere, with no mobile reception.

He had to find Ashley. He wasn't about to leave her there with these people.

Approaching the prison-like door, he thought he heard Greg stirring but turned back and he was still sparked out. Chris grabbed the handle of the door and pushed it down, then slowly peeked out. The coast seemed to be clear. Outside was a narrow hallway, with a couple of doors on the other side of a similar nature.

Chris looked left to right. How long did he have? He hoped Greg would be knocked out long enough to give him time to find Ashley and get the hell out of there.

He decided to head down the corridor to the left where a T-Junction was about to meet him. Suddenly, he heard what sounded like a woman whimpering, but it didn't sound like Ashley, and he didn't think she was the whimpering type. It was coming from one of the other doors.

Chris reached out and grabbed the slat on the door. He

slowly pushed it to the side and his mouth dropped at what he saw.

Looking inside, he had to stop himself from being sick. In the room was around ten woman, all barely clothed and all looking either injured or sick. Most of them were asleep but some were awake and crying – all of them lying on the concrete floor. One of them saw him and immediately backed away from the door.

'Not tonight, please, not again!' the woman pleaded and the sound of her voice tore Chris apart.

He closed the slat and turned, resting his back against the door. He looked up at the ceiling and took a deep breath. These were dangerous people, so he had to tread carefully.

He could open the door and let them out. Or he could leave them there, find Ashley, escape and bring the police. Greg and the rest wouldn't know he'd have seen them, so they wouldn't know. But he couldn't face just leaving them there.

The choice was made for him though – because he tried the door, but it didn't budge. Locked.

He tried to tell the girls through the slat he wasn't a threat and wouldn't hurt them, but it only served to make them more terrified. The sound of his voice prompted some of them to shuffle further into the dark room like a group of scared mice scurrying from a predator.

It hurt him deeply to leave them, but he'd come back with help.

His priority was to find Ashley and then call the police.

Chris walked down the corridor to the T-Junction and looked left and right, it seemed clear. He had a decision to make, and he knew the wrong one could be terrible. If he went the wrong way, he could run into Steve, or the delay in circling back would give Greg enough time to recover.

The decision left him wishing he could have a drink. Opting for the left, he slinked down the corridor. There were no doors on this one and the end took a turn to the right. No sign of anyone still. That was good. He didn't have long, though.

He could hear himself breathing and he tried to still himself.

Chris turned right and this time there was another door on his left. This one was a black door rather than blue and there was no slat on it to peer through. No person guarding it. He grabbed the handle and pushed it down. It was stiff and he had to put effort in to move it.

The door screamed its protests as he used his shoulder to push it open. It was heavy. He clenched his teeth, pushing it further, wider until finally he could see into the room.

Ashley.

In front of him, sitting on the same kind of chair he had been – Ashley. She didn't look too bad, all things considered, her clothes were still intact and she didn't look roughed up. But her head was down, as if she was staring at the floor.

Chris edged his way towards her. 'Ash,' he whispered. 'It's me.'

She slowly raised her head, and he could see her eyes were red and one of them – the left one – was swollen. 'Hey,' was all she said.

'What happened to your eye?'

'Oh this,' she whispered, 'I may have kicked one of those bastards in the balls, so they did this.'

Chris smiled; he'd known she wouldn't go quietly.

'Come on, mate,' Chris said, reaching behind her and grabbing the ropes. 'We've got to go and get help.'

'Help?' she asked, as Chris undid the ropes.

'I think they're keeping people here. I don't know what for. Maybe trafficking or something like that. I saw a group of women locked in a room, and they all looked beaten and bruised and they were terrified of me.'

'From the way you look that's not surprising,' Ashley said, then her face turned grave. 'We need to get them out.'

'Let's worry about us right now. These people are dangerous and the sooner we get out the sooner we can get to a phone and the police. Then they can get the woman out.'

Ashley nodded as the ropes dropped to the ground.

'Can you walk?' Chris asked and received a nod in response. 'Come on then.'

'Are you sure we can just walk out? What if they have people around?'

Chris knew it wouldn't be a walk in the park to get out. 'We have to find a way out and quick. Greg won't be out for much longer.'

'Out? What? Did you knock him out?'

Despite himself, Chris smiled. 'Something like that,' he said. 'Let's go.' Chris reached the door; he pulled it open and looked both ways. No one was around, yet. 'The coast is clear,' he said.

Ashley followed him. He led her down the corridor, back the way he had come. He had no idea where they were, and the place seemed like a maze of corridors and doors. Judging by the layout and the height of the ceiling, Chris believed it to be a warehouse that had been customised.

For the first time, he had noticed the temperature. He felt the air get colder the further they went, and he figured it was a sign they were reaching the outside world. All they'd need to do is get out and grab a passerby and ask them to phone the police. It'd be that simple.

The only thing being, Chris turned a corner, and someone was at the other end, facing away. 'Crap,' Chris said, backing up into Ashley and pressing his back to the wall. 'Can't go that way.'

'Go back the way we came? Ashley asked, peeking round the corner.

'Wait,' Chris said and looked at the man and weighed up his options. He seemed no bigger than him, if anything he was a bit smaller. 'Do you think you could get him to chase you?'

'You're joking, right? And then what? You go all Liam Neeson on him?'

'No. I'd just try to take him by surprise when he turns the corner. Trust me.'

Ashley sighed. 'Fine,' she said.

Chris watched her edge out into the long corridor. It was like watching an actress at work. She keeled over, holding her stomach, gingerly walking down the corridor, making a bit of noise so the man heard her and turned round. Chris had a beady eye watching him and he could see a genuine handlebar moustache which deserved a beating even without the locked-up woman.

'Stop!' The man shouted and ran towards her.

Ashley turned and sprinted back towards Chris. The man seemed surprised, not expecting the woman to leg it that fast. That helped the situation because he certainly wasn't expecting what happened next.

Chris waited for the right moment – for Ashley to pass him, then he counted a couple of seconds. He heard the footsteps coming closer, louder with every step. Not long now. Any second now.

Bang.

Chris exploded from the wall, taking the man in his

stride, surprising him and pushing him backwards like an American Football tackle. The man stumbled, tripping over his feet and wincing at the impact of the blow.

His back hit the wall first, soon followed by the back of his head. He wasn't knocked out though – they weren't that lucky. He tried to stand back up, but Chris stuck out a knee, landing a blow to the chest then backing up and raising a hand, leathering him with a closed fist so this time he was knocked out.

'Damn,' Ashley said, a little out of breath.

Chris shook his hand back and forth. The bones were screaming in pain, unhappy at being used the way they had. 'I think I've broken my hand. That hurt like a bitch.'

The worst happened next – at the end of the corridor, Greg appeared, sporting a bloody hand, with Fat Man beside him. Both sneered at Chris and both jogged towards him.

He and Ashley turned, looking to escape in the other direction. They sprinted down the hallway but ran into a metaphorical dead end. Greg's brother, Steve, was in front of them. He was an intimidating man, which stopped both Chris and Ashley from moving.

Greg and the other man caught up, and now they were boxed in with no way out.

'We were going to make it quick,' Steve said. 'But this little stunt has cost you.'

Chapter Twenty-One

'Hold her there,' Steve said, pointing at the back of the wall. They were back in the original room where Chris had been locked up. 'If she makes a sound then make sure she regrets it, Jake.' The man who had been with Greg pulled Ashley by the hair to the back and pressed her up against the wall, holding his hand to her neck.

Chris tried to struggle but he couldn't move. He looked at Ashley, who had fear in her eyes but he also saw a hint of determination. She was scared, but she was angry too.

'Stop moving,' Greg said. He had his knee in the small of Chris's back and his hand on the back of his head, pushing it into the concrete floor. 'You broke my nose and you almost killed me by throwing me into that wall.'

'No more than you deserve, you bastard!' Chris said, his voice muffled by the pressure on his neck. Greg pushed harder, bringing a grunt of pain.

'Get him up,' Steve said. Greg picked Chris up, holding him by the neck with his arm around him. 'You've got some guts, mate. I respect that. I really do. But you messed with my family.'

Chris shook his head. 'Your brother started things with me. I was defending myself, <u>mate</u>.' The last word had been said with a vile hint of sarcasm.

'I don't care who bloody started it. I'm finishing it. We know you've seen what goes on here. What we do. I can't let you leave because you'll just go to the police and bring them here, won't you? Let me tell you, Chris, I won't enjoy what we're about to do.'

Suddenly, Chris pushed backwards, ramming Greg into the door, breaking his grip. Greg yelled at him, but Chris only had eyes for Steve. He reached him in two long strides and used his already sore right hand. He landed a hard punch, square in the jaw, which sent Steve stumbling backwards, only staying on his feet because he propped his hands on the wall.

Greg grabbed Chris again and contained him, despite Chris fighting back.

Steve looked down at the ground and then back at Chris. He smiled a little. He rubbed his lip with his thumb and showed Chris the blood on it. 'Big mistake,' he said. 'Jake, bring the girl here.'

Chris hadn't been thinking. He let his anger and feelings get the better of him. It had been a terrible night, filled with sadness and regret and addiction. He watched Fat Man grab Ashley by the hair again, but Ashley wheeled round and tried to kick him down below. Jake was wise to it and blocked her.

She wouldn't go down without a fight.

'You had the opportunity to take your death like a man,' Steve said. He took Ashley from Jake and told her to kneel in front of him. 'What happens next is on you.'

Steve reached behind himself, and seemed to be rummaging around with his belt. He pulled out a long, serrated knife which gleamed in the bright lights of the room.

'Wait,' Chris pleaded, hearing his voice break. 'Stop! You don't—' Greg smashed him in the back of the head with his elbow. Chris crumpled to his knees.

Ashley didn't look scared, nor did she have any tears in her eyes. Her face was a picture of determination. She wouldn't give them the satisfaction.

Steve tightened his grip around the knife handle, then used it to tear Ashley's shirt in two, pulling it off and throwing it to the ground, revealing her bare back and black bra. She instinctively covered her body.

'Remember, this is on you.' Steve backed up a step, then took his belt off.

Chris struggled again but Greg had a firm grip.

His belt was leather, and he held the end of it, before lashing it off Ashley's back, bringing a loud scream from her. Chris lost sight of everything but her. He wanted to get to her, to tell her everything would be fine and he'd get them out of there, but he couldn't move. He was frozen with shock.

Again, Steve smashed her in the back with the belt again, so hard that she fell forward, now on all fours and breathing heavily. Red marks had begun to appear where the belt had made contact. Chris could only imagine the pain – it put the whole idea about painkillers and alcohol into perspective for him. What he experienced during the bar fight had been nothing compared to this.

'Now,' Steve said, as he threw his belt to the side. He looked back at Jake. 'Hold her down.'

Fat Man did as he was told. He grabbed her by the hands and pulled her backwards so she was now lying on the cold hard concrete.

Steve walked to her legs and aggressively pulled her

jeans off.

Chris tried again to break free of Greg's grip, and almost made it, but now Jake had a handful of him. The two of them were enough to keep him down.

Steve looked at them. 'Make sure he watches all of this.' He made eye contact with Ashley. 'This won't hurt a bit. In fact, you might enjoy it.'

He was about to lower himself down onto her, but, as he did that, Ashley spat in his face, then slapped him across the cheek. From her position, it barely made an impact, but she wasn't about to go down without a fight. Steve wiped the spit from his cheek and rubbed his hand on his jeans. He shook his head. 'That was a mistake,' he said, and grabbed her by the legs, pulling her closer to him and grabbing her by the pants.

She squirmed and kicked out, using any part of her body to keep Steve from her. Chris tried again, yelling out for Steve to stop but he kept going.

Behind him, the door swung open and everyone bar him turned to the door.

'What the hell do you want?' Steve said angrily. He let go of Ashley and stood up. 'We're busy.'

'I know,' the man replied. Chris couldn't see him from how he was being held but he sounded like a small man. 'We have a major problem. There's someone here. I've found some of our guys—'

'Who?' Steve yelled.

'I don't—'

The grip on Chris was immediately loosened and he fell forward, but turned around just in time to see the man being yanked backwards, head first into the wall.

What happened next happened too fast for Chris to understand, but he saw the vampire: Mikael. Chris saw him enter the room, take Jake out by throwing him

161

forward, smashing his head against the floor, then deal with Greg swiftly, sinking his teeth into his neck and sending blood spurting.

Steve backed up to the wall. Chris did the same, but to the other one, and Ashley crawled over to him.

The three of them watched in awe at Mikael, who was feeding on Greg, sucking out all of the blood with his deep red eyes. Mikael stopped and threw Greg to the side. He was still alive. Barely.

'Stay away from me,' Steve said as he held out the knife he had.

'Mikael,' Chris said but the vampire didn't look at him. Ashley was cowering into Chris's body, petrified of what she'd seen.

The movement was quick and decisive – the vampire rushed forward, grabbing Steve by the neck, sinking his teeth into Steve's skin, sucking blood out, drinking most of it but spilling most of it down his chin and chest. Steve tried to fight back, digging the knife into Mikael's side but it hardly fazed the vampire.

Steve screamed out. Chris hoped Mikael would have enough self control to stop like he had done with Greg, but it didn't seem to be going that way. Chris left Ashley where she was and ran over to the vampire. He put a hand on his shoulder, but he was thrown backwards like a fly being swatted.

Finally, Mikael finished feeding on Steve, and Chris knew he was dead by how he fell to the ground. Steve's body was white. Mikael had drained Steve's body of every drop of blood.

Chris and Ashley stood by the door, watching the vampire who had his back to them. Mikael was breathing heavily, his shoulders moving up and down rapidly.

Mikael slowly turned to face them. His red eyes were

gone, but his white jumper was covered in crimson stains. Ashley screamed and told him to get away but Chris told her it was fine, she was safe. They were safe.

'Are you okay?' Mikael asked, his voice was raspy, like he had a cold.

'How did you find us?' Chris said.

'I followed you,' he said. 'It took a while because they had a vehicle and I had to go by scent.'

The three of them surveyed the scene. The place was a bloodbath.

Mikael looked at Steve, then his face turned downwards and he put his head in his hand. Chris was thinking he felt remorse, or guilt. 'He deserved to suffer for this,' Mikael said. He looked at Chris. 'We must go. Now.'

Chapter Twenty-Two

The building turned out to be an abandoned warehouse on the outskirts of Oakley, redesigned for the purpose that Steve and his people had wanted.

Chris and Ashley followed Mikael out of the building, past the knocked-out bodies and blood-smeared walls. Chris would do anything for a drink – a stiff one. Ashley stayed close to him, keeping one eye on the creature leading the way.

Mikael led them to a car. An old fashioned Renault Clio – yellow in colour, both inside and out. He climbed into the driver's seat and started the engine. It was an automatic – just a case of putting your foot down.

Mikael drove them back into the city. Ashley was quiet in the back and Chris stared at the road ahead. 'Thank you,' he said. 'For coming to get us. You didn't have to. Why did you?'

'I've been watching you for a while,' Mikael said, gripping the steering wheel tightly.

'Why were you following me?'

'I had to be sure you were not going to tell anyone.'

'I see,' Chris said, then turned back to Ashley. 'You alright?'

She smiled. Her lip was slightly swollen and she was hugging her stomach. 'Never better,' she said. 'I can't believe this. A vampire. How is that possible?'

'It's a long story,' Mikael said. 'One that you do not need to know or should care for. The important thing is we get out of here as I need to explain something in a safe place.'

His words sounded ominous, but it didn't stop Chris from seeing a phone box at the side of a desolate road. He asked Mikael to stop for a moment, and the vampire answered with a grunt then slowed the car down.

Chris grabbed the loose change in the glove compartment and opened the car door.

'Where are you going?' Ashley asked, glancing at Mikael.

Chris smiled and nodded. 'To make a call.'

He went into the phone booth, ignoring the smell of smoke, and dialled 999. While going through the details with the polite call handler, he noticed Ashley staring at the vampire and Mikael looking out into the road. She clearly was suspicious of him, and he understood why. Of course she would be, considering he had just killed someone and had dried blood all down him, looking like a toddler who had spilled their food.

He urgently relayed all the information they had about the place – he didn't have the exact location, but judging by the castle in the distance, he was able to tell them it was about five miles outside of Oakley and to the south. The call handler said they'd get patrols out there immediately. She asked for his name but he hung up.

He trusted they would do the job required – arrive, see

the mess and get the woman out of there. They'd get them to a safe place then immigration would handle them. He couldn't believe that kind of thing had been happening near his home city – Glasgow or Edinburgh he wouldn't be shocked if it happened but not here.

The Clio was warm compared to the outside. He rested on the chair, told Ashley he had called the police. She thanked him and also thanked Mikael for saving them. Mikael responded with a nod.

They drove in silence for around twenty minutes. Chris's flat was the destination, and on the drive there he found himself looking forward to having a drink. But he remembered the chat he'd had with Ashley.

'Just down this street,' Chris said, as Mikael approached the required junction. He easily turned the wheel, and Chris was amazed with how smooth he was at driving. *Must be those vampire reflexes*, Chris thought.

Despite the occasion, he felt an immense sense of pride and relief. Not for escaping Steve and Greg, but the vampire was real and he wasn't insane. It had been worth it. He'd need to phone Bryan and tell him.

Mikael twisted the key in the ignition, turning the car off, and stepped outside. Chris followed and watched Mikael open the door for Ashley. She flinched when he did it, but eventually came out of the car. Chris patted the small of her back reassuringly.

Chris led the way. The door was off its hinges – he'd forgotten about that. He'd have to tell the landlord. That'd be a pain. She wouldn't be happy. There would be a very real chance he'd get evicted.

Once inside, all three of them sat down on the couch and chair in the living room.

'I do not have much time,' Mikael said immediately. 'The sun will be rising shortly so I must make this quick. I am leaving.'

'You're leaving Oakley?' Chris asked.

'Yes. It is not safe here for me any longer. And it is not safe for you either.'

Ashley stood up, a little braver. 'What do you mean? You dealt with those people. Why isn't it safe?'

Mikael looked at Chris, he seemed to be weighing up the options of divulging whatever was in his mind. 'I have told you, Chris, already of Dragoslav and his coven.'

Chris nodded. Ashley listened, then said, 'Coven? Isn't that witch related?'

Mikael ignored the question. 'He and the rest of them will know where I am now. When a vampire kills a human, he knows where the kill happened. For that reason, I try not to kill.'

'How could he get here so soon?'

'Dragoslav is not just a vampire. Before he became a vampire, he was a witch.'

Mikael let that hang in the air for a moment. Chris and Ashley exchanged looks.

'He has the power of conveyance.'

'What does that mean?' Chris asked.

Mikael was about to answer, but Ashley beat him to the punch. 'It means he can move quickly from one place to the next. Teleportation.'

Chris looked at Mikael. 'You mean he can just pick and choose where he goes?'

'Almost,' Mikael said. 'He would have to have a reason, and my killing of that man will be reason enough. He has the ability to go deep. He can not only read the memories of your mind, but he can go further and tell you about your family's memories, your friends'.'

'How is that possible?'

Mikael shrugged. 'He is part witch. A lot of what

witches could do was unexplained. The power that he has is unmatched. When the witch who was safeguarding our tomb died – Dragoslav got his power back. Like I said, through dark magic he can see into your mind and through your soul, he can link in to any relative or friend you hold dear. Alive or dead and see their memories.'

'What does this mean for us?' Ashley asked. 'Why are we unsafe? If he's at the warehouse, he won't know where we are. He'll only know that you were once there, so as long as you move on, he won't be able to find you, or us.'

'Because,' Mikael began, pacing around the room. 'Vampires have the ability to track via scent. He will track my location and appear there, when he does he will smell where I have been, and he will smell you and he will be able to track you. Chris, the reason I did not kill you was because I didn't want Dragoslav to find me. I would rather die of starvation than be tormented to what Velkan and Nicholas would do.'

Chris felt hurt at the fact he'd not killed him because of that. He thought he had made a connection with the vampire.

'For that reason, I must go. The sun will be coming up soon, and I plan to get far away from here in the next hour. Once the sun is up, you both will be safe. You'll have until nightfall to get away from here and somewhere safe.'

'Can't we come with you?' Chris asked, glancing at Ashley.

'What about my mum and dad?' Ashley said to Chris. 'I can't just leave them.'

'It's too dangerous to come with me,' Mikael said immediately. 'I will forever be hunted by Dragoslav. You both will be better off forgetting about me and moving far from here and live your lives.'

'What about all the other people at the warehouse? He won't know which scent to follow,' Ashley said.

Mikael shook his head. 'Our scents will mix the further into the building he goes and he will eventually come for you. Dragoslav is smart. Powerful. He will stop at nothing to kill me and he won't hesitate to use you both against me, killing you if he needs to.'

'Can't you fight him?' Ashley asked.

'No. One of our coven – a poor woman – tried many, many centuries ago, but she was killed almost immediately by Dragoslav's former right hand – Vlad The Destroyer.'

'How would we kill a vampire?' Chris asked.

Mikael didn't answer immediately. He sighed. 'You kill a vampire with wood through the heart. But for Dragoslav, you would need to use a wooden stake, then take his head off. He is much more powerful than a regular vampire.'

The vampire walked to the door frame. Chris and Ashley followed him.

When Mikael got to the frame, he turned back. 'Good luck, I hope you both have long and wonderful lives.'

Chris nodded.

'Thank you for saving our lives,' Ashley said, smiling warmly.

The vampire lowered his head and smiled. He walked through the empty doorway, leaving Chris and Ashley in the hallway.

Ashley looked the door frame up and down, then turned to Chris. 'You'll need a new door.'

Chapter Twenty-Three

The two of them spent the remaining hour of darkness huddled in Chris's bedroom. Both sat on the bed. Chris held a sharp knife in his hand, ready for any attempt by the vampire witch hybrid to grab them. Silence was in the air, as neither of them spoke much. The odd bit of small talk was said, but both were tired and focused on staying awake. If they fell asleep they wouldn't know if anyone was about to attack.

The living room was a no-go zone. The door had been smashed off its hinges, lying in a battered heap in the hallway. For that reason, they had gathered refuge in the bedroom and barricaded the door with a heavy set of drawers. Chris looked at the barrier, and imagined, based on the strength Mikael had described, the chest of drawers wouldn't last very long.

He'd do anything for a drink. His mouth was dry and he could hear his blood flowing through his body. He was in his head. Far too much. He tried to focus on other things. It was a terrible sight that he had seen at the warehouse. All of those woman locked up and the look they had on their faces would haunt him for the rest of his life. No matter how short.

He was thankful Ashley hadn't seen what he did. She had enough to be concerned about. He noticed her feeling her back every so often. *She'd still be in a lot of pain*, he thought. Especially after being lashed in the back with a leather belt. Not to mention the emotional trauma from almost being raped.

Chris hated himself for failing to protect her. It was that thought that kept bringing him back to running through to the kitchen and grabbing a bottle of beer or a drink of whiskey.

The sun started to rise on the horizon. Chris watched it from the bedroom window. It came up slowly. He breathed a sigh of relief, then said, 'That's the sun up. We're safe now, Ash.'

Ashley stood up and watched the sun with him. 'What do we do now? We can't stay here and I don't want to head to my parents in case what Mikael had said was true about tracking by scent. Imagine he tracks us to my parents.'

Chris thought of George and Valerie and the shock they would have seeing a murderous vampire on their doorstep. 'Aye. We just need to get out of here. Doesn't matter where. As long as we get out of Oakley. How about we grab something to eat then have a shower each? We can then get on a train or drive your car to Glasgow or Edinburgh or even higher if you want to go further.'

'The further the better, I suppose.'

'Highlands, then?'

'Aye. We can drive. It'll be quicker than a train and more comfortable. This vampire can't follow us for that length of time or amount of miles.'

Chris nodded. He grunted as he pulled the chest of drawers away from the door. 'You can have a shower first, if you want? I'll go to the shop and grab us some bread and milk and we can have food. I'll have a shower after that and then we can get on the road.'

'This is crazy, Chris. I mean, vampires. How is that possible?' She didn't say anything for a moment, then looked at Chris. 'A few weeks ago you said you ran into a vampire. I thought it was a joke. Was that true?'

He nodded.

'Oh my God.' She sat down on the bed and rested her head in her hands. 'It's just so insane. And now look at us, running away from everything because of this.'

'We'll be able to come back. A few days or a week lying low and then we can come back. What will you tell your parents?'

'You mean instead of the fact we were kidnapped, almost killed, then we were saved by a centuries-old vampire?' She shook her head and smiled. 'What a night. I'll just tell them I have time off and we're going up north.'

'Fair enough. I'm sorry that you were involved in this. Thank you though.'

'For what?'

'I never really thanked you properly for helping me with the alcohol and painkillers.'

'Are you thirsty now?'

He smiled. 'Like you wouldn't believe.'

'Good. You'll drink the milk you'll get from the shop then.'

* * *

Chris left Ashley in the flat, safe in the knowledge that no vampire could reach them in daylight. Despite that, he couldn't help but look behind him every so often while walking to the local corner shop. He wasn't subtle about it either, every few steps he'd look around like a meerkat in the desert. People gave him strange looks, which only added to his anxiety.

Milk and bread were on the agenda and he found them easily. He grabbed the first ones he could find, a small bottle of full fat and a small loaf. At the counter, he paid in cash and asked for a bag. The cashier handed the bag to him and wished him a good day. *Chance would be a fine thing*, he thought.

On the walk back, he thought about the previous night and that thought almost made him turn back. He wanted to climb into the shop and beg the cashier to allow him to buy some alcohol at that hour. He knew the sale of alcohol was banned before ten AM, but he'd try. He was that desperate.

Instead of turning back, he pushed on. Cars and buses flew past him with people heading to work during the morning rush. People taking their kids to school and others taking their dogs for a walk. He saw no less than three people with dogs, letting them empty their bowels without picking up their mess. In other circumstances, he'd say something to them. He wished he could be like everyone else who passed him, without the worries and concerns he was landed with.

A crazy vampire was hunting him, he thought, and the absurdity of the idea almost made him laugh. He'd need to phone Bryan as soon as he got back to the flat.

Approaching the flat, he saw an older man hanging about outside the building. He ducked behind a low wall and peered through the green bushes shielding him from view. He had short grey hair and wore a black jumper. *Surely he wouldn't be a threat?* Chris thought, then remembered that vampires couldn't show themselves in sunlight.

173

For a moment, he wondered where Mikael had gone. Would he be hidden in some castle dungeon somewhere like all the old stories used to tell of?

Chris pressed his lips together, shook his head and stood up. He crossed the narrow street and walked towards his flat. The man spotted him from a distance, but didn't move. Chris approached with caution.

'Alright?' he asked, passing by the man.

'Do you live here?' The man looked Chris up and down.

'Yes. Why?'

'Oh, so you must be the downstairs neighbour.'

Chris's eyes tightened and he scrunched his brow. 'I live on that floor,' he said, pointing to the flat window, 'and who are you?'

'I live upstairs.'

Finally, he met the tenant from the upstairs flat. He wanted to shout at him for the damp patch, and he almost did, but then he figured he shouldn't bother. More important things to worry about.

'Why are you milling about out here?'

'My daughter's picking me up. I saw the door on the way down. Don't worry, I didn't look in. What happened?'

'Long story,' Chris said and left it at that.

'Hope you have a decent story for the landlord. She's a piece of work. Threatened to evict me twice over a late payment. Not my fault the pension comes in slowly.'

'Right. Aye. Well, I better get going. Good to meet you.'

'Andrew Walker Robinson.'

Chris had only known people who introduced themselves with their middle name to be either one of two things. A pretentious idiot or a bumbling moron. 'Chris

Winters.'

He left Andrew Walker Robinson outside and opened the door into the flat complex.

The door was still where he had left it. He was glad Andrew hadn't tried to take a look inside. *Imagine if Ashley had seen him*, he thought, *she'd have a fit.*

He had a think about what he'd tell the landlord. The upstairs tenant was right about her. She was certainly a piece of work. Besides paying for rent, Chris had no interaction with her. He'd have to think of a good reason, probably have to pay for the repairs out of his own pocket. That's if they survived the next couple of days.

He hated the fact they had to go on the run, to go into hiding. But he couldn't lie to himself – part of him liked the thrill of it and spending time in another city with a close friend wasn't too bad of a consequence.

Chris navigated his way over and through the debris sprawled across the hallway floor. Inside, Ashley was sitting on the couch, fully clothed but her hair still damp, and she was looking much better after a shower. He wondered how he must have looked to people in the streets.

'You alright?' Chris asked, as he put the bag on the counter top in the kitchen.

Ashley joined him and helped take out the milk and bread. 'My back's sore and I can't stop thinking about last night and what all this means. It's all just insane.'

'I know. How was your shower?'

'It was nice, but your shower doesn't have a lot of water pressure, does it?'

'Aye, you're not wrong. I'll go have one now. Feel free to make yourself some toast and tea. There should be some eggs in the fridge too, but might want to check they haven't gone off.'

Before he took his clothes off and headed into the shower, Chris took a seat on his bed and looked at the pillow. It sang to him, calling his name, instructing him to take a nap. Both of them were running on no sleep and a long drive to what could be classed as the Highlands was coming up.

Maybe Ashley would let him drive and they could take turns. *One drives while the other sleeps, that could work,* he thought.

Instead of closing his eyes, he grabbed his mobile from the bedside table. Almost out of battery but it had enough for a phone call. He dialled in Bryan's number and waited for the college teacher to answer.

At least thirty seconds passed before he was greeted with the shrill sound of a female voice telling him Bryan wasn't available and to leave a voicemail. The tone beeped.

'Bryan. It's Chris Winters. Call me back when you get this. Big news.' He hung up and placed his phone on charge. He left it there, hoping Bryan wouldn't call immediately, and took his clothes off in the bathroom. He caught a glimpse of himself in the mirror and noticed most, if not all, of the previous wounds had disappeared now. He realised then he wasn't in any pain anymore, but he still had the desire to crack open a beer to ease the stress of the previous night.

The shower was warm, but, like Ashley said, had very little pressure. He did his best to clean himself, washing away all the dirt and grime of the night before. He scrubbed his skin until it was raw, and felt the desire for a drink fall from him and wash down the drain. The cleaning lasted a few minutes, then he took a minute to stand in the middle of the shower, and let the water land on his neck and back.

He ducked his head down, stretching his neck muscles. Once he was finished, he dried himself with a damp towel and shoved on a simple white t-shirt and blue jeans. He roughly dried his hair, leaving it how it was, not bothering to style it.

The smell of eggs and toast came from the living room and it made his stomach growl. He'd thought he wouldn't have much of an appetite but the smell of the food told him otherwise.

His phone rang from its place on the bedside table and he almost fell over himself rushing towards it. Using his finger, he awkwardly answered the call. Bryan introduced himself and asked why he was calling – if he had found the vampire.

'He found me,' Chris answered. 'Told me some things. He said the leader of what he called his coven had the power to appear in different places almost instantly.'

'Like teleportation?'

'He called it conveyance. But yes, essentially that's what he meant.'

'Did he tell you anything else? Did you mention me at all? I'd love to have a sit down with him and get some quotes for my research.'

'I didn't get a chance. We're in danger, Bryan. Apparently the head of the coven, Dragoslav, has the power to see where all of his people are if they have made a kill. He's coming here and he'll follow the scene to me. I'm getting out of here so you might not hear from me for a while.'

'Hold on, did you say Dragoslav?'

'Aye. That's right. Why? Does that mean anything?'

'Dragoslav is a famous name in Romania. Dragoslav was the name of a famous witch family centuries ago. If you believe the stories, that is.'

'That makes sense. Mikael said Dragoslav was part witch and part vampire which is why he is able to have these connections with his people.'

'So it's true,' Bryan said, then coughed and sounded like he'd just sat down, 'what the stories say.'

'Must be,' Chris answered. 'I've got to get going, Bryan. I'm sorry I don't have more for you.'

'Don't be stupid. Chris, you've just confirmed decades of research and stories. Vampires, eh? It's amazing. Have you told anyone else?'

'No. Who'd believe me?'

'True. Thank you for calling, Chris. I hope you survive whatever is coming, and if you do, please call and let me know. I'd love to speak with you again, or this vampire, about Hoia Forest and how vampires were created.'

'There not any stories about it?'

'Tons, but none that have any concrete evidence. The only story that might make sense is the Dragoslav coven created vampires to protect them from humans. But the creation went wrong, and the vampires turned on them. I wonder if one of them turned this Drago.'

'Can't be. Mikael said Dragoslav was the first ever created vampire.'

'Maybe the spell that created a vampire needed something to latch onto and the Dragoslav coven sacrificed one of their own. Might explain why they were all but wiped out.'

Chris looked around the room and smiled. This was all interesting but terrifying at the same time.

'I'll let you go and continue to look into things. Keep in touch if you can.'

'Thanks, mate.'

'Bye.'

Chris was greeted with the shrill sound of the dial tone

and he placed his phone on the bed. If Dragoslav had been accidentally turned by his family, no wonder he had turned on them, created his own family and tried to move around Europe.

Eggs and toast filled his nostrils once again and it spurred him to leave the bedroom and sit next to Ashley on the couch. She had just finished her eggs and toast.

'Feel free to go for a sleep,' Chris said, in between shovelling food into his mouth.

Ashley nodded. 'I must look a state,' she said, laughing, 'so I think I'll take you up on that. Your bed okay?'

Chris nodded.

Chapter Twenty-Four

As Ashley snoozed in the other room, Chris spent his time fighting off tiredness and keeping his mind busy by tidying the flat. The place looked as though a bomb had gone off. From the previous days, there were plates and cutlery haphazardly lying all over the kitchen. The carpet in the living room needed a good clean. While cleaning, he did wonder what the point of it was, and wondered what Dragoslav was doing and where he would be. Surely if he was part witch, he'd be able to create a spell which allowed him to walk in daylight. Or perhaps the fact he was a vampire stopped him from doing major magic like that. Maybe conveyance was all he could manage.

With the flat looking sufficiently clean, he turned his attention to the hallway. As he stared at the carnage before him, at the door which had been smashed in the previous night, he felt his throat go dry and almost thought about opening up a beer or pouring himself a whiskey glass.

He started tidying up the wooden strips that had fallen off the door, but the thought of alcohol came flooding onto him when he bent down. He dropped the wood and rushed to the kitchen. He opened the kitchen cabinet and grabbed a glass, before aggressively twisting off the cap, and poured himself a large one.

The smell was intoxicating and made him forget all about the previous night. He could so easily put it all behind him, take the drink and drink more. Forget about it all. Head to the pub and wait for it all to blow over. Would he be welcome in The Wet Whistle anymore?

His body went cold. The glass got ever closer to his mouth, before he decided against it, showed some grit and determination, clenched his teeth and then emptied the glass down the sink. The bottle soon followed.

He walked backwards until his back was against the fridge. He stared at the sink, wide-eyed like a wild animal. Shaking his head, he rushed from the kitchen and sat in the living room.

Chris sat there for some time. Thinking about drinking it all away, but smiling at the fact he had managed to drop it all down the drain. He had no sense of time or how much of it has passed before Ashley had exited the bedroom.

She still had bags under her eyes and her skin was still white as a ghost but she seemed perky. At least, much more than she had been. 'You good?' she asked, taking a seat across from him.

Chris smiled. 'Aye. I'm good. How about you, did you sleep alright?'

'As good as I could,' she said and grabbed her phone from the coffee table. 'You need a new mattress because all I could feel was springs digging into my back. Not ideal when you have belt marks on your skin.'

Chris winced. The memory of the leather lashing against Ashley's naked skin echoed in his mind.

'When do you want to leave?' Ashley asked, dangling her keys in front of him. 'You can sleep in the car. I'd rather get up there as soon as we can so we're not rushing.'

'Can leave now if you like? Have you spoken to your parents?'

Ashley nodded. 'They bought it. Like I said last time, I told them we were having some bonding time up north. You know, I think they think we're a thing.'

'A thing?' Chris asked, raising his eyebrow and laughing. 'You wish.'

Ashley laughed too and for a minute they forgot about the perilous situation they were in.

'Let's get going,' Ashley said, standing up and throwing her hair back.

'Can I drive?' Chris asked, grabbing his jacket from the chair beside him and following her to the door. He didn't bother bringing any clothes – they had already decided to buy some clothes when they were up there and packing wasn't top of his priorities.

Ashley reached what was left of the door and turned, then said, 'No chance.'

She left him standing in the corridor. He looked back at his flat, wondering if he'd be there again. Before he left, he bent down and grabbed a decent-sized wooden piece of the door. It was sharp and pointed.

'This could do,' Chris said to the empty flat and closed the imaginary door on not only his home, but his empty, mundane and boring life.

Chapter Twenty-Five

It was a short drive out of Oakley and onto the motorway. Chris rested his head against the window as Ashley did the driving.

They drove in silence. The only sound in the car was the shrill sound of daytime radio. Chris listened periodically and from what he could deduce, someone had just won £500 in a call-in after answering a question successfully on a new musician's album.

Once they passed Perth, they were only around three hours from the Highlands.

'Do you want to search for a hotel?' Ashley asked, tightening her grip on the wheel, and swerving to the right into the fast lane to overtake an old dear in her Fiat.

'Sure,' Chris said, lifting his head from the window and opening his phone. 'Any preference? Luxury or are we talking B&B?'

Ashley shook her head and stretched her bottom lip out. 'Probably something that would be busy. The more people the less likely we're going to be attacked, right?'

It was a good plan, Chris thought. He scrolled through his phone and searched for hotels. A few turned up, but he figured going for a Premier Inn or a Travel Lodge would be the best option. They were always busy. Cheap and cheerful, but, more importantly, busy.

The Premier Inn was a bit more expensive, so he clicked on the Travel Lodge, and the cheapest came up in Elgin. The rates were decent – £50.00ish whereas Premier Inn was coming up at the higher rate of around £70.00.

'How about Travel Lodge?' Chris asked, reading the reviews which were fine for what the hotel was.

'No way,' Ashley said, shaking her head enthusiastically. 'I've stayed at a Travel Lodge before, and I had to go to a chiropractor for months after. The beds are awful. Like sleeping on Lego.'

'I know you're joking. Is it really that bad?'

Ashley grinned. 'Maybe I didn't go see about my back, but I should have. It was bloody awful. Anything else will do. How about Premier Inn? Every major city has one.'

'Would you class Elgin as a major city?'

Ashley looked at him. 'Wouldn't you?'

'Do you know what a city needs to be called a city?'

'Tell me.'

'Over 300,000 people, a cathedral and a castle,' Chris said, confident in what he was saying. He remembered a TV show he had watched as a kid that went into detail about what a city was and what a village or town was.

Ashley didn't look as confident. 'I don't think that's quite right. Anyway, Premier Inn?'

'It's a bit more expensive but I guess you pay for the quality, right?'

'Can't be worse than Travel Lodge.'

'I'll book it. They have a double room and a family room. A double is either a double bed or a twin and a family has an extra bed. Oh, the double apparently has air conditioning, but the family doesn't.'

'That's weird,' she said. She swerved back into the left-hand lane to allow a BMW driver to pass. 'Go for the double. Air con sounds like a dream.'

'I'll book it now.' Chris had done what he had to do, inserted his details, and clicked book. It took him to the payment page, and he put his bank card number in. The payment took a couple of seconds to through. 'I booked it for a few nights. Don't know how long we'll have to stay.'

'Hopefully not for very long.'

'My company that bad, aye?'

Ashley shook her head. 'You know I mean.'

Chris let Ashley drive in peace for a few minutes and felt his eyes start to close, watching the world pass by. 'Did you ever hear anything back from that agent you went to see?'

Ashley blinked twice then swallowed. 'It's only been a couple of weeks so hopefully I'll hear something soon. He seemed fairly happy with the book, but he was going to speak with his company to see if they want to represent me.'

'They will,' Chris said, smiling and nodding. 'I've seen your stuff. It's good.'

'What about you? Any writing on the horizon for you?'

Chris thought about the book he'd started. The book he had deleted. 'I did write something a few weeks back. About vampires, ironically. But I deleted it. Probably for the best, it'd never top what we're going through.'

'Guess that's true.'

Chris dozed off for what seemed like only a few minutes, but upon waking he found they were only an hour out from Elgin.

'Good sleep?' Ashley asked, still focusing on the road.

Chris rubbed his neck from the awkward sleeping angle. 'I've slept better.' He picked his phone up from the floor of the car and checked his notifications. He had a missed call from Bryan and, just as he was about to call him back, he had an email ping through from him.

Chris,
Hope you're doing good. Thanks for the chat this morning.

I tried to contact you, but I didn't get through. I've looked further into the information you told me about witches and vampires. I have a contact who lives in Romania who told me there are rumours of people going missing in Hoia Forest once again.

I called a Professor of the Occult in New York who I had dealings with a couple of years back. He wasn't best pleased to be woken up in the middle of the night. He's considered an expert in this sort of thing, and he told me the story of famous witch covens being wiped out in the early centuries.

Interestingly, I had a conversation with a local bookseller in London who sells some questionable books. He said he had a conversation with a man not too long ago about Hoia Forest. These vampires have clearly awoken recently, otherwise the whole world would have known about them by now. I wonder if this man has anything to do with this.

That's all I was able to find out. I'll keep digging. It's all very exciting.

Hope you're well and stay safe.
Bryan.

Chris relayed the message to Ashley.
'It's both amazing and terrifying at the same time,' she

said, tightening her eyes.

'How long are we from Elgin now?'

'Not long. About half an hour. How come?'

The clock had just gone past noon and his stomach rumbled. 'I'm starving. Guess that's what happens when you knock booze on the head. You want to grab food somewhere? We have around six hours before the sun starts to head down.'

'Sure. We can head to the hotel then grab a bite to eat. I'd like to buy some clothes too. I have nothing with me and I probably look a state. How are you coping with the no alcohol or painkillers?'

Chris tilted his head. 'Not bad. Don't get me wrong, I wish I was drinking a bottle now, but I'm not in any pain.'

'Just hungry then,' she said, as she pulled out into the middle lane and floored it past a slow car. 'That's good though.'

'How about your back?'

'Still sore. I guess it will be for a while. I've never been whipped before.'

Chris raised an eyebrow which Ashley glanced at.

'Enough,' she said. 'Why don't you just go back to sleep?'

'I think I might,' he said. He was absolutely shattered. Physically and mentally drained. Whilst Ashley had been able to sleep in the warmth and comfort of his bed, he was stuck with the bumpy Audi and the hard window as a pillow.

Chris rested his head and watched the green trees and the sky pass by. It was a chilly day but the Audi's heating had seen to that. He noticed clouds in the sky. Dark ones that looked ready to burst at any moment.

The Audi turned off the motorway and into Elgin. The Premier Inn was in sight and Ashley pulled into the busy car park. She found a parking space at the front. She shut the engine off and pulled the handbrake up.

'What time is it?' she said to herself, opening her phone. 'What time's check-in? I think we'll need to hold off on checking in. It's only just hit one and I'm sure check-in is at three.'

'Only one way to find out,' Chris said, throwing the door open and whipping his seat belt off.

'You could just search it online,' Ashley muttered.

Chris walked quickly across the large car park. A big truck was stationed outside the front door and some staff members were taking some duvets and pillows from the back of it. *Must be restock day,* he thought. The reception was a small square with a decent-sized desk at the back, with the door to the rest of the hotel next to it.

'Hello,' Chris said politely to the black-haired woman sitting behind the desk. She raised her head, glanced at the clock, then smiled.

'How can I help?' She glanced at Ashley who'd just joined Chris in the reception.

'We were wondering if our room was ready. For Chris Winters.'

'Check-in isn't normally until three, but I'll check to see if your room's been cleaned yet. Just a minute.' Gail – he knew from the name tag – stood and left the reception, disappearing into the hotel.

'She's a lot nicer than the last receptionist I spoke with,' Chris said, remembering his interaction with the woman he had spoken to when trying to phone Bryan. She was something else.

Ashley stayed quiet, scrolling through her phone. After a couple of minutes, Gail came back and sat back on the seat. She typed a few things into the computer then turned to them and smiled. 'Good news. Your room has just been finished. It's a policy to not let you in but judging by how tired you look, I bet you'd both love a place to sleep and refresh.'

'You're not half wrong,' Ashley said and smiled at the receptionist.

Gail rummaged around in a drawer behind her desk, then pulled out two purple cards with black stripes on the back. She placed them into a machine on the desk and typed a couple of things into the computer. A red light appeared on the card machine, then it disappeared, replaced with a green light.

She grabbed the two cards from the machine and slid them over the desk. 'Here you go. You're room 217 on the second floor,' she said, then pointed at the door to her left. 'Just head through that door then turn right, there'll be a lift or if you're feeling up to it you can take the stairs.'

'Brilliant,' Chris said, gently taking the cards from the desk. 'Cheers for your help, much appreciated.'

Chris walked towards the door and Ashley did the same, saying goodbye to Gail and smiling. The door made a loud beep as he opened it. 'Did you notice the restaurant next door?'

'Aye,' Ashley said. 'We should have some food there tonight before the sun goes down. It's weird having to arrange things around a murderous supernatural creature.'

Chris grinned. He found the lift at the end of the beige corridor and called it down. The lift shuddered to a halt and the doors opened. They stepped to the side to allow an old man to step out.

After they clicked the second-floor button, the lift came to life again, juddering once again. They arrived on the second floor and had to dodge multiple cleaners with their large cleaning stations. The decor was nothing to go bananas over, but it was homely. They reached room 217 and put one of the key cards into the slot on the door. A second later, they heard a beep then the locking mechanism turned.

When they entered and saw the bed, they both stopped and looked at each other.

'You did request a twin bed, didn't you?' Ashley asked, raising her eyebrow slightly.

'I did,' Chris said seriously. 'I can go down and ask for a switch. Two seconds.'

Chris started for the door, but Ashley sighed then said, 'It doesn't matter. I can't be bothered with changing and making a fuss. They've already been super nice to us, so we'll just have to put up with it.'

'Word of warning,' Chris said, returning to the room and feeling the soft, quilted bed covers, 'I like to sprawl out.'

Ashley shook her head, studying the air conditioning unit and working out how it worked. 'I bet you do.'

Chapter Twenty-Six

Before leaving to head into the town centre, both Ashley and Chris took turns sleeping on the double bed. Ashley had bunged the air conditioning on, the room turning crisp and cold – leading Chris to wonder if she had some kind of medical condition. With it being winter, and due to the fact the room was turning into an icebox, he opted to keep his jacket on. They had an hour of sleep each, just enough to get them through the rest of the day. While one slept, the other kept their eyes on the window and the door. They knew they weren't in danger since the sun was up, but they wanted to be sure. Despite the noise of the cleaners moving about outside the room, both had a good sleep and upon waking neither of them wanted to climb out of bed.

The room decor was nothing to get excited about. Besides the double bed, there was a small uncomfortable sofa where the non-sleeping person had kept watch. A small black television was mounted on the wall and below it was a long desk screwed into the concrete. The room had the normal provisions – tea bags, coffee sachets and a kettle for boiling water from the bathroom.

Chris had been in a Premier Inn before and was looking forward to using the shower – they always had good pressure, and it couldn't be anywhere near as bad as his shower at home.

While Ashley slept, Chris put together a simple text message to his landlord. He explained the door had been smashed in during a drunken escapade, which technically was correct. He said sorry and advised her he'd pay for the damage once he was back in Oakley. She wouldn't appreciate that, especially with the flat now being unsecured with no door. Chris didn't bother much about it – nothing in the flat was anything worth stealing except the University laptop but he doubted anyone would go looking, except maybe Andrew Walker Thompson. *What a name*, Chris thought.

Once both had a good hour of sleep, they left the hotel about four in the afternoon. They had around three to four hours left of sunlight depending on how the weather was feeling today. Outside, Ashley opened the Audi and ignored Chris asking if he could drive. She started the car and headed further into the centre of town.

'Where are we going first?' Chris asked.

'We need to get some clothes and some food for the room. Have you seen the prices of the vending machine and the mini bar?'

'Aye, quite expensive.' Chris thought about the cost of the clothes. He'd been eating into his savings for rent and would need to eat further into it to fix the door. He checked his bank balance on his phone, and it wasn't pretty. He'd need to stick to cheap clothes.

Ashley pulled into a multi-story car park and effortlessly parked between two big jeeps. She paid for parking – an extortionate £3.50 for two hours. 'I doubt we'll need the two hours but better to be safe than sorry. I'd rather not get a parking fine.'

They walked through the town centre, enjoying the nice breezy stroll. They felt safe amongst the people and walked close together. They passed many food stores and Chris felt his stomach rumble again, the smell of them all calling to him like a songbird. Ashley led them into one of the female clothing stores and he carried the basket like a good friend. He'd expected to spend hours shopping with her, but she was all about efficiency. She picked up a handful of t-shirts, a pair of jeans and a couple of pairs of leggings.

'How long do you think we'll be here for?' she asked him, as she calmly put a white vest into the basket.

'Just a few days. Enough for us to feel like we're safe to go back. I'm sure we can't be tracked for that long, or this far up north. Hell, maybe this guy might not search for us, and just go back to where he came from.'

'Hopefully.'

Ashley paid with her bank card, putting in the pin and smiled when the transaction went through. The polite cashier gave her the receipt and handed the bag over to her. *The people up here are a lot politer than the people down in Oakley*, he thought.

Chris led the way, this time to a male clothing shop. He searched the shop but was conscious of the price tag.

'How about these?' Ashley said, hanging back from Chris and showing him a multi-pack of black t-shirts.

'That could work,' he said and took the pack from her. He looked at the price and for what they were, they weren't cheap.

He pulled a pair of jeans off the rack and threw them in the basket and grabbed some boxers and socks too. With a complete outfit, he went to the cash desk and waited on the service. A man appeared from the back room. He was about Chris's age and had short blond hair. He barely looked at Chris, and just started scanning before bagging it up.

'£47.35,' the man said, without raising his eyes from the register. *Clearly the service up here isn't all good*, Chris thought.

Chris pulled his wallet out and put his card in. He could afford it. He'd have to be careful with money for the next while though. *Maybe I should get a part-time job*, he thought.

Once the goods were paid for, the cashier handed the bag over and shoved the receipt aggressively in the bag. Chris took the bag and left without saying thank you. Ashley followed him and they walked towards the car.

They had made good time. Forty-five minutes remained of the two hours Ashley had paid for. After navigating the maze of the car park, Ashley drove them around a mile out of the centre and stopped in at the nearest ASDA. The place wasn't too busy, most of the shoppers were school kids who'd just finished at the nearby High School.

As they walked round, gathering some essentials for the room – chocolate and sweets – he watched some of the kids. Smiling and happy, these kids didn't have a care in the world. Most of them were not from broken families and wouldn't have to worry about anything for a long time. He had always had something to worry about. Whether that be being left alone for long periods of time or paying for University or now trying to escape from a vampire who also doubled as a witch.

'I'll pay,' Ashley said, at the self-checkout area, as they scanned the items they had got. An elderly, sour-faced man in an ASDA uniform stood by the tills keeping a close eye on them.

Chris let her do what she wanted. He had no qualms with allowing a woman to pay for something if she had volunteered.

He carried the bag of food out of the shop and put the bag in the boot of the car. 'Time to eat?'

'Not yet,' Ashley said and checked her phone. 'We've still got a couple of hours, so we should head back to the hotel and change. You look awful.'

Chris looked at himself in the car window, then looked back at Ashley. 'You don't look so great either.'

'Best we go get changed then.'

Despite Chris changing this morning, he still looked dishevelled with the bags under his eyes becoming more pronounced as the day went on. Ashley hadn't had the luxury of changing, so was just wearing the same clothes from the night before, luckily with no blood stains. Chris wondered what Mikael would have done if he had been able to get clothes somewhere and change. For a moment, he blocked everything out and replayed the moment Mikael stuck his fangs into Steve and the image of the blood falling from him like a waterfall.

That could have been me, he thought. If Mikael had not stopped that night, then he'd be dead.

By the time he put that thought away, Ashley had already climbed into the driver's seat. Chris grabbed the door handle and sat down on the chair. Ashley twisted the key and drove from the car park.

It wasn't long before they had the hotel in their eyesight. 'What do you think of the hotel?' Chris asked.

'It's alright,' she said. 'Good for what it is. That air con is a dream though.'

'You think it'll be safe enough?'

She didn't answer for a minute and seemed to be thinking of what to say. 'I hope so. It's central so lots of people are around. And, like you said before, hopefully we've not been followed here. Surely Drago can't track us this far, especially with the fact he wouldn't have been able to make a move yet.'

Chris nodded. It was a good assumption. It had been a while since they found out he'd be after them, and because of daylight breaking they could go about in relative safety. Whether or not Dragoslav could track them all those miles was a question he couldn't answer, and he didn't want to consider the possibility that this powerful creature could do it.

Gail was no longer at reception, replaced by an older woman who barely acknowledged them when they appeared. Chris was tempted to mention the fact he had requested a twin bed. Instead, he followed Ashley through the main door and, because of the queue for the lift, they opted for the stairs.

'Nice and busy,' Chris said, too low for Ashley to hear.

Once they were back in room 217, they both quickly changed. Chris in the bathroom and Ashley near the bed. He looked longingly at the shower head – imagining what it'd be like to have a proper shower again. He'd have one after dinner he decided.

Both were changed into something a little more proper. 'Will that place next door do?' Ashley asked.

'I think it does the usual stuff we like: burgers, chips, wings, that sort of thing. Aye, aye – that'll be perfect. I need something salty and fatty I think.' He said it with one brain cell focusing on filling his desire for booze or painkillers with some nice bad food.

'I don't think we'll need to book,' Ashley said. She had tied her hair up in a ponytail and it was the first time Chris had seen her with one. It suited her. She turned the lights off in the room.

'How long do we have until sundown?' Chris asked, as they closed room 217.

'A couple hours.'

Water had broken from the clouds above like Chris had thought would happen. The rain wasn't heavy, but enough to get them wet if they didn't rush across the car park to the restaurant next door like they did.

It was called Meat and Grill and, surprisingly, it was as busy a restaurant as Chris had ever seen. The man at the front desk, dressed in nice white shirt and smart black trousers, told them it'd be a half hour wait.

'Feel free to take a seat at the bar, we'll give you a shout when your table is ready.'

'Perfect, thank you,' Ashley said, taking a small buzzer from the man which he explained would buzz when the table was ready.

Ashley led the way towards the bar and Chris noticed a few of the older men looking at her. She turned suddenly. 'I'm so sorry, I didn't even think.'

'About what?' Chris asked, looking a bit awkward at the rest of the restaurant.

She leaned forward a little, so close that their faces were almost touching. 'The bar! Drinking. I'm sorry, we can go somewhere else.'

Ashley pulled back and looked at the floor as she walked past Chris, but he told her to stop and then said, 'I can handle it. I'm not an alcoholic, Ash. Just because I had a bad few weeks doesn't mean I can't be around booze. Come on.' He took her by the hand and led her towards the bar. It wasn't the first time they had touched hands, but it was the first time they had ever held hands. Brief as it was.

They sat down on the bar stool and Ashley ordered a Coca-Cola and Chris ordered an Irn-Bru. He scanned the room. Every table was full of people. The ages ranged from teenager to elderly.

'You think I'll be allowed in The Wet Whistle again?'

Ashley smiled, stirring her black drink with a paper straw. 'It wasn't as bad as you remember. You were steaming. But you won't be the first, and certainly not the last, person to make a fool out of themselves in that pub.'

'Was Colin pissed off?'

Ashley laughed. 'Oh aye. He was fuming. But he'll get over it. When this all blows over, we can head there and you can say your sorries. I'm sure you're not barred.'

'Aye. Good.' Chris took a long gulp of his drink and sat back. There was no movement on the table front yet, but he caught the eye of the man who had served them at the front desk. The man looked at him and gave him his best customer service smile. Chris remembered putting on his customer service voice in the job he'd had last year.

Ashley was still stirring her drink and seemed to be in a world of her own with a glazed look on her face.

'Ash,' Chris said, breaking her from the trance she was in. 'You know – about last night, if you need to chat about it—'

'I don't,' she said almost immediately. 'I'd rather just forget it ever happened to be honest.'

He understood that. He didn't want to remember the night he had been attacked, and like her he wanted to forget about the previous night, especially the looks on the women's faces locked in that room. He hoped they would have found a safe place to get to. Hopefully they would be long gone – and the police too – by the time Dragoslav arrived.

'I get it,' he said. 'But if there ever comes a time where

you do, then you know where I'll be. You helped me get through some tough stuff, so I'll try to do the same for you.'

She smiled. 'Thanks. Hopefully after whatever happens next is done, we can both move on and get back to normality.'

He nodded. Would they ever get back to normality? It was one thing recovering after an attack, but forgetting all about the existence of vampires and knowing witches used to exist was another thing entirely. Did he want to go back to normality? Back to the grind of University and a dead-end job eventually?

The buzzer sounded off on the top of the bar just as Ashley finished her cola.

'That'll be us,' Chris said, drinking the last of his Irn-Bru. He looked around and saw the server giving them a wave by the side of a booth.

After they took their seats, the waiter asked if they wanted a drink, to which they requested two more of the same. The menu was small but looked rather good. He especially liked the look of the wings – fried and dripping in sauce apparently.

They were both starving and soon made up their minds. The waiter dutifully returned, laying the glasses on the table carefully. He took their order – five chicken wings which came with fries, and some veg, and for Ashley, the Triple Stack Burger.

Safe to say they were hungry.

No sooner had the waiter disappeared than Ashley's phone started vibrating on the table. Chris watched her stare at it like it was the first time she heard a phone ring. Her eyes were wide, and her mouth was slightly agape.

'You going to answer it?' Chris said, nudging the phone over to her with his fingers.

She looked at him, then back at the phone. She grabbed it and quickly answered, 'Hello.'

She listened carefully while Chris nursed his drink and tried to divert his attention. He never liked being watched or listened to by people when he was on a phone.

'Oh my God,' she said. 'Are you serious?'

Another silence. Chris was interested now. Could something bad have happened?

'That's amazing!'

Evidently not, Chris thought. He smiled because she was absolutely beaming with joy. It was the happiest he had ever seen her.

'No... yes... that's great. I'm just on a wee holiday right now but if you send the papers over email, I'll sign them and return them. We can chat when we're back.'

Chris studied her carefully but was interrupted when the food arrived. 'Any sauces or more drinks?' the waiter asked Chris, trying not to disturb Ashley.

'No. Thank you,' Chris said and gave him a nod of appreciation. He figured he'd better wait on Ashley finishing her call before diving into the food. It all looked and smelled delicious. It had been the first thing he'd eaten since this morning.

'Right. Thanks again,' Ashley said, taking the phone from her ear slightly. 'Bye.' She put the phone down, smiling, but stared at it for a good few seconds before looking at Chris with small droplets of water coming from her eyes.

'What is it?' he said.

'Remember the meeting I had with the agent?'

'Yeah.'

'Well,' she said and couldn't contain her huge smile. 'He said he's shopped it around and a publisher in London has made an offer for the rights!'

'That's amazing,' Chris said genuinely. It was his turn at failing to contain his happiness because he leaped up, almost knocking the table over and bashing into the bloke behind him. He hugged her, gently enough to not hurt her back, but enough so that she knew he was happy for her. 'We need to celebrate. You need to celebrate. You should get a drink.'

'Are you sure?'

'Of course,' he said. 'I'll stick with the orange stuff, but you get a wine or something. You deserve it after the past day and especially now you're going to be a famous writer.'

'Shut up,' she said, still smiling. 'This is so amazing.'

After that, Ashley called the waiter over and asked for a glass of wine to go with her meal. He asked Chris if he wanted anything, and it took all his strength to refuse.

Chapter Twenty-Seven

The meal went down a treat, but the saltiness of the food left them with a craving for something sweet. They ordered two desserts – chocolate brownie with ice cream and strawberry cheesecake. After scoffing the lot, Chris and Ashley called the waiter over, asked for the bill and Ashley paid by card – she insisted.

The waiter wished them a good night and Chris left some pocket change as a tip.

Outside, the night air had turned chilly, and the sky was darkening. It wouldn't be long before the sun would disappear. It was a short walk back to the hotel. They walked in silence, close beside each other and Chris could feel the warmth coming from her.

During the meal, the situation of the evening hit them.

They spoke about the fact that during the day they felt safe, but as night was approaching fear had begun to grow. *It's natural,* Chris thought.

As the sun went down, the risk went up.

To take their mind off it, during dinner they spoke

about the book deal and what it meant for her. Ashley said it wouldn't change much. She'd still get her degree. She never divulged how much she would be getting from the publisher, but from how she reacted, Chris imagined it'd be a sizeable chunk. *George and Valerie would be ecstatic he thought.* Their baby girl, brought up in a good home, made a success of herself.

Not like him. Brought up in a broken home with no prospects.

But he wasn't worried about the future right now. He was only concerned with surviving the night. If they survived, then it might be safe to return to Oakley. Although he thought they should stay a couple more nights, just to be safe. That, and the fact he was enjoying spending the time with her. And he believed she felt the same.

The hotel reception was warm. A far cry from the chilliness outside. Chris used some of his loose change to grab a can of Red Bull from the vending machine. A lot more expensive than buying it in a shop, but that would involve being out there in the dark and he had no intention of doing that. They'd both need a shot of stimulant to stay awake tonight.

After trudging up the stairs, they found their room and inserted the key card. Once inside, Ashley threw her bag to the side and turned on the air conditioning. Within a few minutes the room had started to cool.

'What do we do now?' Ashley said, sitting on the bed and taking her jacket off.

Chris idly walked by and peered outside. He couldn't see anything worrying. The sun was only slightly viewable. 'How about a movie? Take our minds off it.'

'Sure.'

The remote for the TV was on the bedside table and

Chris picked it up as he sat on the bed. He turned it on and started scrolling.

'*Twilight?*' he asked, glancing at Ashley from the corner of his eye, keeping the other on the screen.

She hit him playfully on the arm. 'That's so funny I forgot to laugh. Idiot.'

'Alright,' he said, shaking his head. He continued to scroll and, after many failed attempts, they settled on a movie called *Dumb and Dumber.* They paid £9.99 to the hotel, putting it on their room, and for that, they got the privilege of watching Jim Carrey and Jeff Daniels acting like idiots.

The film passed quickly, and it wasn't long before Chris broke into the bag of crisps and chocolate they'd bought at the supermarket. As they ate, they both couldn't help but glance every so often at the window and the door, expecting at any moment for someone, or something, to cave them in.

It was completely dark outside, and it made the room almost black, if not from the bright light from the TV. Chris was about to put on a lamp, but Ashley told him not to. She wanted to be extra careful.

Jim didn't get the girl in the end. The journey in the film was more important though, bringing together two friends. Chris enjoyed the film, and even though Ashley thought it was stupid in parts, he could tell she had enjoyed it too. After the film, the TV recommended the sequel, but Ashley quickly grabbed the remote and said, 'Don't even think about it.'

Not at those prices.

Chris stood up and stretched his legs, then walked over to the window and sat on the sofa's arm, peeking out behind the curtain. All he could see was the lights from the cars passing by in the night. 'What time is it?' he asked.

There was a short delay while Ashley checked her phone. 'Just gone eight PM.'

Chris nodded and tried to estimate how long it'd be until sunup. With it being March, he imagined the sun would start to come up earlier with winter ending, but he guessed it'd rise between six AM and seven AM. Maybe a bit later.

'I'm just going to have a quick shower,' Ashley said, grabbing some of the other clothes she bought from the shop. 'You be alright by yourself?'

Chris nodded. 'You should phone your parents when you're out and tell them the good news about your book.'

'Good idea. Be back in five.'

Chris listened to the water falling in the shower. The stream sounded heavy. He smiled at the thought of a proper shower.

He sat back, keeping an eye out of the window. *There's no way that Dragoslav could track us this far*, he thought.

Around ten minutes had gone by, and Ashley left the bathroom. Chris looked at her and his mouth fell open.

'Sorry,' she said, rushing past towards the bed in nothing but a white towel. 'Just forgot a change of pants.' She rustled in the clothes bag and grabbed what she needed then Chris averted his gaze as she stood up and looked at him. There was an awkward silence for a second, then she hustled back into the shower.

Chris replayed the moment he saw her in his head. The long, wet hair and the shimmering, soaked skin. He focused all his energy on what was going on outside, focusing on keeping watch, but he found himself thinking of her in that towel again.

After thirty seconds or so, his mind was clear, and he focused on the outside. He spotted a couple of people walking by the hotel on the road. They looked happy enough and didn't seem to be paying any attention to the hotel. He thought how crazy this was, to be hiding out in a Premier Inn, over a hundred miles from home and paranoid he'd be killed by a vampire and witch hybrid.

The door of the bathroom opened. Ashley – this time fully clothed – appeared and grabbed her phone by the bed. She smiled at him then grabbed the hair dryer near the bed and, without a word, started drying.

Over the noise, Chris said, 'Just going for a shower.'

Ashley nodded as Chris grabbed some clean clothes and one of the other towels from the cupboard that she hadn't used. This was one of the moments he was looking forward to most – turning on that sweet shower and feeling water hit him rather than just land on him. The water was scalding hot, just the way he liked it. The shower at his flat was always lukewarm, and the last time he'd had one that hot was when he lived at his dead parents' house: the house the bank had taken because they cashed out their life insurance policy to go gallivanting around Europe. *Did they ever go to Romania?* he thought.

He washed himself and let the water do most of the work. He scrubbed his hair and his nails then stood in the stream. The bathroom was clouded with condensation, and he felt as if he were in a sauna. It was glorious. Once satisfied, he twisted the shower knob and turned it off, stopping the flow of water. He clambered out of the bathtub. Once dry, he put on a white t-shirt, clean boxers, socks and soft black jogging bottoms.

He left the bathroom, making sure to close the door quickly to prevent the condensation setting the fire alarm off. *That would be the last thing they need,* he thought.

The alarm stayed quiet, and he walked towards the window, and took another look. Ashley had finished drying her hair. He left his own to dry naturally. She looked at him for a moment, then said, 'Do you feel safe?'

He thought about that for a second. He did feel safe, at least in the room he felt like he was hidden from the world, but he still knew that there was a danger out there. Something that was searching for them, so no, he didn't feel safe.

'Tough question,' he said. 'But aye, I feel safe here. Do you?'

Ashley looked down and rubbed her fingernails with her other hand. 'I'm not sure.'

'Think of it like this – we've travelled over a hundred miles, hidden inside a hotel, and passed umpteen different people today. No way he could track us this far without getting mixed up with other people. Besides, the hotel has security cameras. No one is getting in here without someone else knowing about it.'

He said the words but part of him felt they were hollow. He wished he'd asked Mikael how the tracking worked. How powerful it was. Was it powerful enough to track them this far? It probably would depend on how powerful the vampire was. Which, in this case, wasn't a good thought.

'Right. Aye,' she said, 'I guess you're right. I'm just over-thinking things. I reckon we should both take turns to keep watch though. Just in case.'

'Agreed,' he said, and smiled because he was glad she said it and not him. 'I'll take the first watch, let you get some sleep. Have you called your parents yet?'

She shook her head. 'I'll do it now,' she said, grabbing her phone from the bedside table. In the darkness of the room, her face looked ghostly white from the phone. She scrolled for a moment then raised the phone to her ear, smiling – ready to tell her parents the good news about her book deal. 'It's ringing.'

Chris gave her some privacy – as much as he could – by focusing on the outside again. Still nothing to report. It was calm in the streets of Elgin. He'd never been to the Highlands. Some people wouldn't even consider Elgin as the Scottish Highlands. They'd say you'd have to go as far as John O'Groats. Some would say even further to the little islands just off the coast.

'Not answering,' Ashley said with a panicked hint to her tone. 'I'll try again.'

Chris watched her face as she waited. But after a few more seconds, it changed into a beaming smile. 'Hey, Dad!' she said and gave Chris a thumbs up.

He zoned out from much of the conversation, but from what he did hear they were incredibly proud of her, and they had asked her how the trip was going. She told them how they had a great meal and the news about her book deal made it all even better. She told them about how Elgin was beautiful even though she had barely seen any of it. Chris thought about possibly touring the city as tourists in the morning. Some cities would have open top red buses that would take you to all the major attractions. *That would be good,* he thought. *If we survive the night.*

Ashley put the phone down and smiled. 'They're so proud,' she said and almost hugged herself.

Chris felt a strong sense of shame that he had been such a disappointment to his family. Or, had they been a disappointment to him?

'I reckon I'll try to get some sleep. Will you be fine by yourself?'

He knew what she meant. She meant would he control himself not to head downstairs and ask room service for a drink. 'I'll be fine,' he said. 'You get some sleep and I'll wake you in a couple of hours.'

'Feel free to put the TV on. I could sleep through a

thunderstorm.'

'I might do. Speak in a few hours.'

'Night,' she said, already tucking herself into the covers, facing the other way.

'Oh, by the way, can we turn the air conditioning off, it's freezing in this room.'

'Not a chance,' she yelled, and within seconds was asleep.

Chris smirked at the sound of her almost instant snoring. He turned to the window. It would be a long couple of hours, so he turned the TV on and kept the volume low. A rerun of *Two And A Half Men* was playing – the good episodes involving Charlie Sheen. He half watched it, half watched the road outside.

The number of cars had started to decrease, and a moon had risen high in the sky. He spotted a few more people – young ones – walking down the street and he made sure they didn't see him. A complaint about being creepy was the last thing he needed.

An hour passed, and in that hour, he thought of nothing but staying awake, watching the TV show and keeping an eye on the outside world. Ashley had tossed and turned a couple of times. At one point, she had twisted so violently Chris thought she had been possessed. After that, a bit of the duvet fell off, and he could see her shirt had ridden up a little, revealing some bruising and scarring on her lower back.

He walked across to her and put the blanket over her. Back on his perch, he settled into the cushions.

After another batch of time, he felt himself drifting. *Surely if they were to be attacked, it would have happened already*, he thought.

He didn't want to take any chances, so he reached into the mini-fridge and pulled out his second Red Bull of the night. This one was even more expensive than the one from the vending machine, and while he could have walked down to the machine, he didn't want to leave Ashley alone.

He downed the can, savouring the sickly-sweet taste and had to hold in a burp. He looked at his phone for a few minutes, reading the email from Bryan again. Despite the email, and despite what he knew, it all seemed too be too far-fetched to be real. But it was, and the danger was very real.

Thinking about the danger they were in, he remembered the wooden sheet he had taken from the door. He'd placed it in the boot of Ashley's car, and he'd taken it out earlier, hiding it behind his back from the receptionist. Ashley knew about it, but she hoped he'd never have to use it.

He took it out from underneath the bed and studied it in the moonlight. It was a decent shape. Long enough to hit deep and it had a sharp piece at the end which could do some damage. *Probably not enough to kill or damage a vampire, it had to be sharper,* he thought. With this in mind, he sat on the couch after grabbing a sharp knife from the countertop. He was surprised the hotel had left cutlery in the room, but it was a pleasant one.

He went to work for the next hour, using the edge of the knife and scraping away some of the wood at the end, shaping the stake as best he could into something that could be considered a weapon. After a painstaking hour, the wood resembled something like a stake you'd see in a vampire movie, sharp and powerful.

It was small enough where he could conceal it between his belt, but long enough and now sharp enough where it could go very deep, causing a lot of damage. Not enough to kill this creature, but enough for them to run if they had too.

He was no carpenter, but for a first attempt he was rather proud of himself. He didn't even notice the rising desire to break into a bottle of cider or beer. He could so easily run downstairs and head over to the local corner shop. They'd still be open and likely not have a rule about not selling after ten PM.

Instead, he kept the stake close, almost patting it as if you would a small cat. Outside, he heard noise and the hairs on his neck and arms stood on edge. He moved the curtains slowly to make sure he didn't attract attention and looked, gripping the stake tightly. He saw nothing and the rational part of his brain told him noises happen all the time. The other part – the idiotic part – told him to grab the stake and leg it out of the room and get in the Audi and drive.

With it now silent outside, he settled into the couch and waited. He didn't know how long he sat there until the shrill sound of Ashley's alarm jolted him from his half sleep.

Ashley groaned and turned, she reached out for the phone and switched it off. She sat up slowly, resting her back against the backboard of the bed. Her eyes were red and watery and she was struggling with the light from the TV. Seeing this, Chris turned it off, so they were in darkness, but they could still faintly see each other.

He slid the stake down the back of the couch. 'You can go back to sleep if you want,' Chris said.

She shook her head. 'It's my turn. Fair's fair. Come on.' Ashley stood up and pulled the back of her shirt down. 'Did you turn the AC off?'

'Guilty,' he said and smiled. 'Don't know how you can sit in that temperature. Far too cold for me.'

'I thought it was meant to be girls that felt the cold

more than guys.'

'Aye, well, not for me.'

She walked gingerly to the controls and switched it on, and Chris could hear the whirring of the machine doing its thing. He had turned it off earlier and hoped she wouldn't notice.

They switched positions, Chris taking her place in the bed and Ashley taking the couch. He snuggled into the covers and felt the warmth from her body. He could smell her on the pillows. Before trying to sleep, he checked the time and it had just turned two in the morning.

He tried to sleep, safe in the thought that if they were to be attacked, it'd have happened already.

He closed his eyes and tried to let sleep take him away. He thought of many things: Ashley's parents, the book deal, his parents, breaking open a cold bottle of booze. In the end though, he couldn't sleep. His mind raced and he was in no mood to lie there. He sat up, rubbing his eyes and throwing the duvet away from him.

'What are you doing?' Ashley said, standing up quickly. 'Something wrong?'

'No,' he said, standing up and stretching his back, 'I'll keep watch. You go back to sleep. I can't sleep anyway.'

'How come?'

'Just a lot going through my head. I struggle to sleep unless my mind is completely empty and—'

'You should easily be asleep most of the time then!'

He looked at her and shook his head but stifled a laugh.

'Bad joke,' she said. 'If you can't sleep then put the TV on and we can watch a movie.'

He shook his head and sat next to her on the couch. 'You go back to sleep, Ash. I'm too tired to watch a film and too awake to fall asleep. I'll keep watching though.

Anything happens and I'll wake you up.'

She studied him for a second. 'You sure?'

He nodded. 'Aye. Go,' he said, pointing to the bed. 'I'll wake you later.'

'Hold on,' she said and stood up. She reached under the bed and pulled out a laptop.

'Where did you get a laptop from?'

'It's mine,' she said. 'I took it out of the car earlier. You were there. Did you not notice?'

'Guess not,' he said, trying to remember if he had seen it. 'What are you doing?'

'Here,' she said, opening the laptop, turning it on and bringing it over to the couch. She typed in her password and opened a word document filled with around 90,000 worth of words. She handed the laptop over to him.

'Is this your book?'

'The manuscript,' she said, smiling. 'I want you to be my first proper reader. It's got to go through one more revision but it was good enough to get a book deal, so I hope you'll like it. It might make the next few hours pass quicker.'

'Or put me to sleep?'

Just like he had done, this time she looked at him, shaking her head and preventing a laugh from coming out.

'Bad joke,' he said. 'Thanks. Aye, this will help pass the time. I'll give my review in the morning.'

Ashley went back to bed, gave Chris a warm smile and turned over to go to sleep. He lay back on the couch with one eye on the window, although he couldn't see out of it. With his mind racing, he scrolled past the dedication page which stated: 'To Mum & Dad... for always supporting me.'

After the normal copyright, he reached the prologue and settled into a night of reading. It took him back to his childhood – staying up late with his head buried in the middle of a book. Likely a John Marsden book, or if his parents were feeling extra generous, a Stephen King or George R.R Martin novel.

The story was good. The writing was good. Chris was impressed. It was one of the better stories he had read in a while, and the neatness and easiness of the writing to read was a great element. She hadn't tried to fluff the piece up with flowery writing. She had an idea, and she did what she needed to do to convey the message.

It had been about a woman going about her normal life when an accident occurs, and she is paralysed from the waist down. The first few chapters were a depressing affair but soon after it became a lot more light-hearted. During the story, the woman found peace with her new affliction.

Thanks to the hours he had until sunup, he had read through the story in record time. It had only taken a couple of hours and a couple of breaks to keep an eye out the window for him to finish.

It had been freezing in the room, thanks to the AC, and once he was finished with the book, he turned off the laptop and placed it on the ground then wrapped himself up tightly in the blanket that had been on top of the duvet. He closed his eyes for a few minutes, confident that if they were to be attacked then it would have happened already.

He fell asleep and immediately went into a dream. Or a nightmare. He was walking through a forest with his wooden stake in hand. He could feel the wood on his skin, and it felt extremely real. The trees swayed in the wind and the forest animals scattered as he walked. His feet were bare, and he was shirtless, the only thing covering him was a pair of jeans. Despite the lack of clothes, he wasn't cold, in fact he was boiling.

The sky above was a strange mixture of green, red, and

yellow. The stars above were not stars, instead they were signs of the cross, only no matter the direction he looked, they were upside down. He continued to walk, feeling the mud and rocks on his feet. He came to a standstill; up ahead was a small derelict hut.

The hut couldn't have been more than ten feet wide and ten feet long. He approached it cautiously and almost jumped out of his skin when he heard a bird scream in the distance. The sound wasn't your normal bird sound, instead it cut through him like a knife, and he felt physical pain, wincing and grabbing his chest.

The cabin seemed to be calling him over. In his vision, it looked like the house was breathing, slowly getting smaller and bigger every second. Through the barred windows, he could see the faint glow of a light.

He reached the cabin. The front of it had a small lopsided porch with two steps. He put his foot on one and felt it almost give way. Once he was on the porch, Chris stretched his arm out and grabbed the knob. The knob was silver and cold to the touch, so much so that he had to withdraw his arm quickly.

Instead, he took a step back, then rushed forward and used his shoulder to barge the door in. The old door came clean off the hinges and fell with a thud to the ground.

Chris stood in the doorway, frozen still. He couldn't move. He tried and tried but his body was locked to the spot. He tried to take his eyes away, but he couldn't. It was as if his eyes were held open by someone.

He shook his head slightly, his eyes still locked. It was all he could do not to scream at the sight ahead of him.

His parents.

In the room ahead, the two people that he used to know were hanging from the ceiling. Below them were pools of dark, congealed blood.

Their faces were twisted in a sight you'd expect from a horror movie.

Chris heard footsteps behind him. It sounded like there were multiple sets, coming from several individuals. He tried to turn but he couldn't move. His heart was racing, and he could feel his lungs struggling to gather in air. His chest was expanding and expelling air, but it felt as though he wasn't getting enough oxygen.

After a moment, he felt his vision start to become blurry and the footsteps in the forest behind him quickened. He felt his legs go weak and he saw the floor start to come closer to him. His body fell through the air, like it had done when bungee jumping, only this time there was nothing to stop him from hitting the ground.

His vision went dark, like something had been put over his head.

He woke up violently, falling off the couch and landing on the floor – hard. His breathing was heavy and quick. He opened his eyes and they quickly adjusted. Ashley was still asleep.

He looked around the room for any threats. *Just a dream*, he thought, and realised that it was the first time he had dreamed of his parents.

Outside the window, the sun was starting to come up.

He sighed. They had both survived the night. They were in the clear and in a couple of days' time – they could go home and get back to normality.

Chapter Twenty-Eight

With the sun out, Chris could finally switch off and fall asleep. And, despite the nightmare, he fell back asleep almost instantly. The sleep was short lived, as Ashley woke up soon after the sun had broken the horizon.

She didn't aim to wake up Chris, but the movement of her standing up woke him. He bolted upright, reaching down behind the couch for the stake but he let it be after he realised it had been Ashley going to the bathroom. He listened to the water running and the sound of brushing of teeth then stood up and put on a new set of clothes.

He brushed his hair in the mirror and looked at the bags under his eyes. For a second, he thought he saw his parents hanging down from the wall in the mirror but once he blinked, they were gone. He sat down on the bed and rested his head.

Ashley stopped brushing and, after a flush of the toilet, appeared near the bed. 'Something wrong?'

She looked well rested. 'Besides the fact a murderous vampire is after us? Just a bad dream, is all.'

'Did you get much sleep?'

He shook his head. 'Not as much as I'd like, but I read your book.'

Her face lit up. Tiredness had been forgotten and she was totally awake now. 'What did you think? Be honest with me. Did you like it?'

He made a show of thinking about it for a few seconds, making her wait for what she knew was coming. 'I thought it was great. Genuinely. I read it in one sitting and you're going to make a ton of money when it is released. I wouldn't be surprised if your agent is shopping the movie rights around.'

She wrapped him in a hug which both surprised him and made him smile. He hugged her back, squeezing her tightly against her body and his mind went back to the moment she had left the shower with only a towel on. He quickly pushed that thought away.

'You have no idea how much that makes me happy,' she said, pulling away from him now. 'I don't know how it will sell but I'm proud of it.'

'That's all that matters, Ash.'

She nodded. 'Well,' she said, standing up, 'what do you want to do today? We survived a night so I figure we should make the most of the day while we have it, right?'

'Aye, we should go and explore the town. Got to be something worth seeing in Elgin. I'll have a quick shower. I know the hotel doesn't do dinners but I know they do have a breakfast bar so we could head down there after.'

'Do you want some time for more sleep? If you're running on only thirty minutes of sleep, then I don't want to be dragging you around. We could even take a drive out of Elgin and look at the scenery around it.'

He grabbed a towel from the front of the room. He didn't bother with clothes because he'd just put on the same ones on that he had changed into a few minutes ago. 'I'll be fine for sleep. Might have a nap a bit later in the afternoon. Besides, I'm a student, so I'm used to studying all nighters.'

'Studying? You – Chris Winters – studying?'

He looked at her then nodded, holding out his arms. 'Aye, fair enough. You know what I mean. If, while I have a shower, you want to search for some things for us to do today that'd be great. Won't be long.'

The shower was once again joyous. The warmth of the shower made him forget about the dream and the lack of sleep, and the stresses that he'd been feeling about the lack of alcohol or painkillers. The water pounded off him and he felt cleaner than he'd ever felt in his life. The bathroom was starting to steam up from the heat, so he turned the dial down to cold and felt the water change instantly.

His shower had two settings, cold or lukewarm, and when he did change it, the water didn't change nearly as quickly.

Once he was finished and sufficiently refreshed, he towel-dried himself then shoved on the clothes he had picked out. He patted his hair then brushed it and decided to let it air dry as normal. His stomach was rumbling now, and he was looking forward to a decent breakfast.

He met Ashley at the door to the bedroom. She opened it and led the way down the corridor. It was quite early, with only a handful of cleaners milling around, waiting for people to vacate their rooms. He thought they would be the only two down for breakfast, but once they reached the ground floor and made their way to the breakfast bar, he realised he was wrong.

The bar was packed with everybody from businessmen and women to families with small children. He even thought he saw a dog, but he couldn't be sure. Ashley told him to grab a table and she'd bring a plate of food over for him. He did as he was told, picking a clear table at the bottom of the bar near the window.

Even at this time, with the bar this full, it would have meant the hotel was nearly at capacity, meaning it would be even more difficult for them to be attacked at night, he thought. Not to mention the security cameras and reception staff working through the night.

Ashley arrived after a couple of minutes. 'Sorry,' she said, 'queue was murder. I got you a selection, I think I know you well enough to know what you'd like.'

She placed the oval plate on the table and Chris was in awe at what he was looking at. A huge selection of breakfast foods, both hot and cold. He counted four sausages, at least five strips of bacon with two fried eggs and a healthy portion of baked beans to go with it. There were also two slices of buttered toast and a pastry to go with it all.

After he was done drooling, he looked at Ashley and saw what she had. 'You're kidding, right?'

She looked at her bowl of cereal and laughed. 'I'm not hungry. Come on – you were up all night. You look awful and you need a good meal in you.'

'You sound like my mum.' The sentence was out before he realised what he was saying. Instantly, his face changed from happiness to sadness and regret. Ashley picked up on that and started eating, trying not to show she had noticed. The truth was she had never said anything like that, he thought. At least, not to him directly. 'Thank you,' he said finally. 'I don't know how I'll get through all this.'

'I may pinch a sausage or a slice of bacon eventually.'

He shook his head. 'The hell you will! You stick with your bird seed in milk, and I'll have my lovely fat-filled grease-laden breakfast.'

He cut into the first sausage and watched the amber liquid fill the plate, meshing with the bacon and beans. They ate in silence. Ashley watched out the window at the drivers passing by and Chris watched people. He focused on this one man, who was speaking frantically on an expensive mobile loud enough for Chris and the rest of the breakfast to hear him moaning about a big meeting that a client had cancelled on.

The families spent their time controlling their wild kids. Generally, the mother would look after the child while the dad stuffed their face with the same greasy food Chris had. A couple of hotel staff made their way through the tables periodically, taking plates and cutlery from the customers then disappearing for a few minutes.

It looked like a warm day for the time period. Chris had always preferred the colder temperatures of winter, but he did appreciate – like most people did – the odd hot day here or there.

'I've had a look at things we can do,' Ashley said, gulping down the last bit of her cereal. 'How familiar are you with the Loch Ness Monster?'

Chris remembered a story he had read when he was a child about a long serpent-like creature that prowled the lochs of Scotland, using underground water tunnels to swim between them. 'Not a lot,' he said. 'Why?'

'Do you remember a news report years ago, we must have been around eight or nine, where they showed footage of a dinosaur-like animal walking across a road near Loch Ness?'

'I can't say I do.'

'My dad used to tease me and tell me that if I didn't eat my vegetables or go to sleep then the dinosaur reptile thing would come and eat me.'

'Bird.'

'Eh?'

Chris swallowed down the last chunk of sausage meat then filled his fork with a good drop of beans. 'Dinosaurs are birds. They aren't reptiles.'

'Right,' she said, then took a sip of her water. 'Aye, anyway – Loch Ness is only a short drive from here. We could head there. We could get on one of those ships that go out on the water.'

'Sure,' he said.

'You don't sound too keen.'

The truth was he wasn't keen on going out on what was essentially a smaller version of the sea. 'Promise you won't tell anyone.'

She made a show of crossing her heart with her finger.

'I can't swim.'

'So? The boat isn't going to capsize. This isn't the Titanic we'd be going on!'

'Fine – we can go on the boat trip. But if it does fall apart and we hit the water, I'm the one getting on the life raft.'

'Deal. I also found a nice park we could go for a walk through.'

Chris finished off the last morsel of food and sat back as a pretty waitress took the plate from him and took Ashley's bowl. He enjoyed the idea of spending their day together and doing something they'd enjoy, but he couldn't shake the feeling they were being stupid when they had bigger things to worry about.

If they were going to die during the night, then they may as well spend their days doing something nice. He realised then that Ashley brought the best out in him. He hadn't once thought about alcohol or the painkillers during breakfast. Since he and Ashley started hanging out more, and since he told her about his parents and his lack of enjoyment of life, they had done a lot of fun things together. Bungee jumping, bar trips, shopping, going on long drives. Albeit, the long drive was a requirement rather than a choice, he thought.

Ashley went to the bar to get another glass of water and Chris asked her to get him an orange juice with no bits in. He hated having floaty bits of fruit in his drinks. She came back quickly since there was now no queue.

Chris checked his phone and he had realised they'd been there for over an hour. Most of the hotel would be up and going about their day, he thought. He spent the next few minutes sipping his orange juice while Ashley did the same in her water. They made idle chat about what the day would include, and they also spoke about when they could go home and how glad they were that they had survived the night. They reasoned if they survived one more night, then they could potentially go home the next day, as they both had work due in at the University soon.

Chris wondered what the lecturer would be doing. If only he knew that they had been involved in stopping a trafficking group and were now on the run from vampires. Would he question him then? Question what his family would think of him? He didn't care anymore what his mother or father would think. They didn't care about him, so why should he care about them?

The dream came back to him again. The image of them hanging from the ceiling with their faces twisted in shock horror.

His phone started buzzing, vibrating against the table, and bringing him out of his trance-like state. 'Bollocks,' he said, looking at the phone. He looked at Ashley and shook his head. 'It's the landlord.'

Ashley made a shocked face, then said, 'I think you

should answer it. I'll see you in the room.' She left him sitting at the table alone, staring at the phone and Mrs Kim's name.

He picked it up, took a deep breath and clicked to answer. 'Hello, Mrs Kim!' He heard it himself; his voice was far too cheery for that time in the morning.

'Where are you?' she said immediately. Mrs Kim wasn't one to mince words – Chris had known that from when they first met and agreed to the monthly payments. It had been the only time they had spoken face to face. He could tell from her tone she was not a happy bunny.

'I'm out of town at the minute,' he replied. 'Is this about the door?' Had she visited the flat? *Doubt it,* he thought. Perhaps the upstairs tenant had told her. Damn Andrew Walker Robinson.

'Yes, it's about the damn door,' she said, loud enough that Chris thought for a second she was in the same room. 'What the hell happened to it?'

'Well—'

'Save it. I don't want to know what happened. All I want to know is when it happened and why you haven't told me yet.'

'It happened a couple of nights ago. I've been out of Oakley for a bit—'

'Running because you don't want to pay for the damages. Listen here, Mr Winters, you aren't the first tenant to cause damage and do a runner. I will find you. And when I do you will be paying for this damage. When are you back?'

'I'm not sure. Couple of days.'

'Good,' she said, still shouting, and Chris was positive everyone in the breakfast bar could hear her. 'I'll be here when you come back. I will arrange for someone to replace the door and I fully expect when you are here to pay me back and then some.'

'While you do that, could you also fix the damp patch on the ceiling since you're in such a charitable mood for once?'

'Don't test me, Chris. The damp patch has nothing to do with me. I will fix the door and that's it. I'll give you an invoice when you're back and I'll be adding interest onto that.'

'Right, aye. Whatever you say.'

'I mean it, Mr Winters. I'm not in the mood to piss about and I can easily find another tenant. Let me know when you're back. Don't make me rely on the information from the other tenant, otherwise I will serve notice to evict.'

Chris was sure she wouldn't evict him, but she had reasonable cause with the damage done to her property.

'Are we clear?'

Chris looked around the room and decided he'd had enough. Not just of the landlord and her attitude, but of everything. 'Shove your flat,' he said with venom he didn't know he had. 'Shove it so far up your arse that you'll taste it. I don't want it. Are we clear?'

'Excuse me? You don't speak—'

'I'll speak to you however bloody well I like. The flat is disgusting and you as a landlord are just as bad. I'll be around to pick up my stuff from the flat and I'll pay whatever the door costs to replace, but it'll be the last penny you get from me.'

'I—'

Before Miss Kim could answer, Chris hung up the call and placed the phone face down on the table. He breathed heavily and noticed a young boy and his family watching him. He smiled at them and said, 'Landlord problems.'

He was sure he'd arrive back home to a pile of his stuff sitting outside the flat, likely with a brand-new door. But he didn't care. He stood up, waved goodbye to the wee boy staring at him and went to find Ashley in the room.

Chapter Twenty-Nine

Fuelled by the argument with his landlord, Chris stormed up the stairs to the room and slammed the door closed. Ashley jumped at the slam. Chris said he was sorry and explained what had happened. She laughed at the whole thing. After a few minutes, Chris had calmed down and saw the funny side of it.

He had nowhere to live now. *But at least I was able to tell that horrible woman where to go*, he thought.

Ashley put the rest of her make-up on and did her hair in a ponytail before putting on a black hat. The sun had broken the clouds now and it looked to be a scorcher of a day. She led Chris out of the room, past the cleaners who were now in full swing, and they traversed the stairs to the bottom floor. An older receptionist wished them a good morning and they left the Premier Inn, towards the car park and the Audi waiting on them.

'My turn to drive?' Chris asked, as they approached the white car. Despite being white, the car was immaculate. When he thought about getting a car a couple of years ago, before his parents died, he decided he'd get black rather than white, since white cars easily get dirty.

'Good joke,' she said, opening the vehicle with a click of her key fob.

Chris grabbed the door handle, yanked it wide and sat down. The car was like a small icebox. Ashley turned the engine on and blasted the heating in an attempt to clear the windshield of ice.

Ashley drove like she had been here before. Instead of using a Sat Nav, or her phone, she followed the signs. Soon, they were on the home stretch.

Chris could smell the water coming closer with every passing minute. Despite that, he felt his eyes start to tire. He felt like it was from the heat but also from the exhaustion he felt from the lack of quality sleep. He decided he'd have a nap on the drive back. It took them just over an hour to get there so a good nap of that length would set him right for the afternoon and another night of no sleep.

Turns out, Ashley had approached the loch from the wrong direction, and the tourist portion was on the other side, so they had to double back then take a turn they had missed. This added around ten minutes to the journey. Finally, they arrived, and thankfully the place wasn't too busy.

They parked in a quiet car park and locked the car. Not too far from the car park was an ice cream van, and, to perk himself up, Chris went over and paid for two ice cream cones for them. They ate them together near the car, the ice cream helping to cool them down.

He looked at Ashley and the amazing car they were leaning on, then at the scenery of the loch and the people around it. Ever since he'd met Mikael that night, his life had become a lot different. Good and bad things had happened to him. At that moment, he felt happy and content.

The journey across the loch on the boat took a fair bit of time. Ashley had purchased two tickets and they were welcomed on board by a friendly old Scottish man. They picked a seat at the top of the boat where most people had congregated. As they went over the water, the intercom speaker system told them stories of the loch and the fabled monster within it.

If vampires and witches were real, did that mean creatures like the Loch Ness Monster were real? Chris could only imagine what could be out there.

Despite the sun beating down on them, the coldness of the water seemed to be all around them, and the wind didn't help matters. Ashley and Chris huddled together on their bench, happy for each other's warmth. Most people sat in silence, appreciating the ambiance of the water and the sound of the captain talking to them through the history of the loch. A small batch of people – *tourists*, Chris thought – were being noisy though, taking pictures of each other. Chris couldn't understand their language, but it sounded Nordic.

The noise and disruption became so bad that it prompted another tourist – English speaking – to stand up and tell the group of four woman to be quiet while everyone listened to the captain. Chris wasn't sure if the group understood his words, but his demeanour made sure they knew to be silent.

The rest of the journey went off without incident and, nearing the end, Ashley had put her hand on his arm and rested her head on his shoulder. He paused for a second, then laid the side of his head on hers. Her hair smelled of strawberries and was soft against his skin.

They sat like that for a few minutes before the boat

pulled into dock at the station from where they had departed. The people on board left the boat in an orderly fashion – thanking the captain as they did so. Chris and Ashley nodded their thanks and stepped foot on solid land again.

'Lunch?' Chris asked, as they walked towards the car.

Once they were in the car, Ashley looked at him and said, 'How about we buy some stuff from the supermarket and have a picnic in that park I saw?'

'That'll be good. Aye, we can get something from ASDA or Tesco and head there. Any ideas for food?'

'Sandwiches. Crisps, maybe?'

'Ah, the healthy choice. Sure, let's go.'

Ashley put the car into drive and threaded the throttle down, easing her way out of the car park and onto the main road. The traffic was a little bit heavy, but Chris enjoyed the slowness of it. It gave him more time to rest his eyes. The lack of sleep had finally hit him, and it hit hard. He was asleep within a couple of minutes.

He woke up almost immediately – at least, that's what it felt like – by Ashley nudging him. 'We're here,' she said, turning off the engine. They were outside the same ASDA from the day before. 'I was thinking since we're going to that park, maybe we could go for a run? ASDA sell clothes so I reckon they'd have shorts.'

Chris hadn't been running for many years. He wasn't unfit by any means, but he was never the top performer at PE in High School. 'Eh, sure. Wouldn't you prefer pigging out on some chocolate?'

'Aye, I would. But I haven't been running in a few days now and I think you should come with me.

'Right, aye. Why not, what's the worst that will happen?'

They stepped out of the car and entered the

supermarket. Chris was thankful for the breeze coming from the shop's air conditioning, but it quickly dissipated the further they got into the shop. ASDA had a clothes section and in that he found a basic pair of blue shorts and some running socks. He'd have to make do with the trainers he had with him.

At the counter, they were served by an elderly lady with a beaming smile. She was very friendly and talked throughout serving them. She explained how she used to be in the army when she was younger but had settled down to have kids with her now-deceased husband. When Chris was paying – with what was left of his bank account – she said they were a beautiful couple.

Chris and Ashley looked at each other and smiled. 'We're not together,' Ashley said to the lady.

'Shame,' she said, passing over the receipt. 'Have a good day.'

They navigated their way out of the supermarket, through the car park and towards the car. Inside the car, Chris looked at Ashley and saw her the way the lady had. He had asked her out previously but that was when they had first met. They may not be together, but they had a connection like nobody else. He didn't need them to be together to be happy, just to be in her life was what he wanted.

'Are we going back to the hotel to change?'

Ashley shook her head. 'I'm wearing shorts and trainers already. You'll need to change.'

'Right here,' he said, looking around at the car park which was now teeming with life. 'I'm sure there's a school nearby, I'll get put on a register if we get caught.'

'Lucky for you the windows are tinted so no one can see in.'

'You can still see!'

She raised her eyebrow. 'You saw plenty of me the other night so get your kit off and get these shorts and socks on.'

Chris rolled his eyes. She was right, what he saw left little to the imagination. It was difficult to get into the right position to get his gear off and change, but after a few minutes of struggling, audibly grunting, he finally was ready. 'Right, we going for a run then?'

'Aye,' Ashley said, turning the engine on and pressing the throttle to pull them out of the parking space and towards the exit.

It wasn't long before they arrived at the park. They parked on a side street not far from the entrance. They left their mobiles hidden in the glove compartment and their purses and wallets underneath the car seats. The only thing Ashley had on her now was the car keys. 'You ready?' Ashley asked.

'For a heart attack?'

Ashley stepped out of the car and led him towards the entrance. 'How long you want to run for?'

Chris didn't know how fit he was. For all he knew, he could top out at one mile or ten. 'How long do you normally run?'

'About 10K.'

'10K! What is that – eight miles?'

'Roughly.'

'I guess we could try for that. Don't blame me if you have to carry me home on a stretcher though.'

The park was surprisingly quiet at lunch time. He'd expected to see groups of people hanging out in the sun, eating their picnics, and getting a tan or seeing dogs running and playing. Alongside one edge of the park was a stream of water about two car lengths wide. Soon after they entered the park, Ashley set off on a jog, catching Chris off guard. He had to push himself to catch up to her.

Her jogging wasn't what you'd expect a jog to be. He felt as though he was trying to keep up with a cross between Usain Bolt and Mo Farah. Ashley led the way through the park, past the people and their animals. She was breathing heavily but seemed to be enjoying herself as her ponytail swayed with each bounce. Chris felt as though his lungs were going to burst, and that was after only five minutes.

Ashley slowed her pace a little, allowing Chris to catch up. Running in the heat made for a lot of sweat. Primarily from him.

'Having fun?' Ashley asked, her voice shaking each time her foot hit the concrete.

Chris shook his head. He had no energy to speak. He was waiting for the runner's high he'd heard about. Maybe it would come in a few minutes, he thought, then he'd be able to sprint ahead and show Ashley up.

No runner's high came through, but he did manage to zone out and forget about the pain and tiredness for a minute. In that minute, his mind was clear, and it allowed him to think about the situation they were in. Hidden away in the Highlands of Scotland because they were on the run. The reminder made him think how stupid they had been. How stupid he had been searching out a vampire. How stupid he had been to develop a craving for painkillers and alcohol because of assault. In that moment, he hated himself for everything he had gone through and everything he had put Ashley through.

Because of him, she was locked away, hiding out, not able to celebrate her good news about the book. He made a mental note to buy her a celebratory gift.

Despite the feelings crossing his mind, part of him enjoyed the time spent up north. It was the excitement he had craved for so long, and almost made up for the couple of decades of boredom and neglect he felt at the hands of his parents. The same parents he'd seen the night before hanging from the ceiling. Was that how they died? Was the dream a sign of that? He knew Dragoslav was powerful, but could he implant dreams? Was he messing with them?

He remembered the look on Mikael's face when he explained how he would track them down and what he would do. From his expression, he gathered Dragoslav was not a man to wait around and if he was around, would have attacked already, likely in the hope they'd lead him to Mikael.

How had this happened? How were they roped into a feud between a vampire and his creator?

How many people had he turned? He seemed to remember Mikael speaking of a small group of vampires in Romania, the last of their kind. The ones who survived whatever war they fought centuries ago. He remembered him speaking about his partner who had been from Scotland – Rose.

Chris looked at Ashley and smiled. Despite it all, he was happy because he was spending time with her, and they both were enjoying each other's company. And that was despite his lungs being on fire and his heart beating out of his chest. She was his best friend – his only true friend. He'd protect her if it came to it, but the truth was it would likely be Ashley protecting him.

After reaching the halfway point of their original goal, Chris keeled over on the grass and lay down with his eyes pointed to the sun. He shielded them from the harmful rays and had to defend himself as a golden Labrador ran over to lick his face. The playful beast was called off by its owner, a young woman with long blond hair.

Ashley had noticed he was no longer behind her, and must have doubled back because he heard her voice from above, saying, 'Not got it in you to do the rest?'

'Listen,' Chris answered, sitting up and wiping the sweat from his brow. He covered his head as he looked at her. 'Mate, I tried. I can't keep up with you at that pace. I could barely keep up after a mile.'

'Aye, suppose so. Guess we can sit here then,' she said, sitting down next to him and staring out at the park with him.

They sat there for some time before Chris broke the silence. 'Sorry if I honk a bit. Who knew someone could sweat so much?'

'Just make sure we keep the windows down in the car on the way back.'

'I'll shower at the hotel, and we can go for a meal somewhere.'

'Oh. Another dinner – is this what dating Chris Winters would be like? Exercising, excursions and fancy meals every night.'

He raised a finger. 'If by exercising you mean a couple of ab crunches and if by fancy meals you mean burger and chips at the pub then of course!'

She rolled her eyes and stood up. 'You fit?'

He tried to get up but faked holding his chest then fell back to the lying position he had been in. 'I might not make it. Go on without me!'

She reached down, forcefully grabbing his arm and, with surprising strength, yanked him into a seated position before finally bringing him to his feet. 'Back to the car. Shower time for you. Remember, windows down.'

Chris stood to attention like a private addressing a drill sergeant and saluted. 'Aye aye, captain. Oh captain, my captain!'

By the time they reached the car, Chris had managed to catch his breath. Ashley barely looked as if she had broken a sweat and seemed to have a lung full of air. Once inside, he did as he was instructed and lowered the window – hoping the car air freshener would do its duty and mask the runner's scent coming from him.

If the vampire didn't have our scent before, he'd have it by now, he thought, but decided not to make the joke. It would be bad taste, he decided.

Ashley drove back to the hotel, it was now mid-afternoon and the sun was at its hottest. Chris necked a bottle of warm water from the back of the car and watched the people as they drove by. The women were clad in vests and shorts while the majority of the men walked around with their tops off. He never saw the appeal in that. Why walk around in public with your top off, especially if – like the majority of Scotland – you were pasty white with little muscle mass to show off.

The hotel receptionist – the same one as when they arrived – welcomed them with a smile. She had the fan blaring away, sending her hair flowing back like one of those *Baywatch* TV Shows.

The hotel had a decent air con, so once they reached their room and Ashley turned on the AC, the room became cool almost instantly. He had hated that AC the previous night but right now he could only wish that his future home had the same air conditioning.

Before heading for a shower, a thought crossed his mind that he had been avoiding all day. Where exactly would he live now? He had no home. He had no relatives in Scotland anymore. He had no ties whatsoever, if you discount Ashley, which he wouldn't do. But regardless of Ashley, the case was still the same – he was, as of this morning, technically homeless.

He'd need to get onto the council to see if they could arrange some accommodation. He didn't quite fancy the idea of kipping on Ashley's parents' couch, and he doubted Colin would be up for giving him a handout after their last interaction. He had some savings left, enough for a few nights at a hotel or more at a cheap B&B. He went to the shower with a sense of hope. He wanted to believe that everything would be alright.

Tonight, they would go to dinner, have a decent meal and fill their bellies, then go back to the room. He'd stay up again and watch out for any creatures lurking about in the night. He turned the shower on and welcomed the hot water just like he did this morning.

With only a couple of hours to go until the sun went down, he made sure he was quick in the shower this time. He made no attempt to enjoy the water, rather he did the usual and turned the shower off. He dried himself off and put on some clean clothes which didn't honk of sweat.

Ashley had a shower after him, and she didn't take long either. Once she was fully dressed, they left the hotel and got back into the car. Instead of going to the same restaurant they were at the previous evening, they opted for an Indian place a little further into the city centre. The car park was a decent size and it allowed them to get parked easily and, again, Chris's attempt at driving the car was rejected.

They got to a table easily, escorted to a booth by a young girl who looked as if she had barely broken sixteen. She gave them the menus and told them she'd be back in a couple of minutes with their drinks – two Irn-Brus.

True to her word, she came back with tall pint glasses of orange liquid filled with ice cubes. 'Are you ready to order?'

Chris looked at Ashley. 'You ready?'

Ashley nodded. 'I'll have the Chicken Korma please, with rice and a garlic naan.'

The waitress nodded and wrote the order down on her little notepad. She turned her attention to Chris.

'I'll go with the chicken tikka masala with chips and a garlic naan too, please. Can I also get a side of chicken pakora with that?'

'Sure,' the waitress said. 'It won't be too long, but we'll bring them out when they're ready. If you need anything else just give us a shout.'

'Thanks,' Ashley and Chris both said at the same time.

After the waitress was gone, Chris said, 'What do you think about going back tomorrow?'

'If it all goes fine tonight.'

'Aye,' he said, taking a sip of his drink. 'I'm sure it will. We were fine last night, and it doesn't seem like this guy is one to piss about.'

'That's fine then. We can head back tomorrow. You can get some sleep tonight, I'll stay up.'

'We can take it in turns.'

'You were up all night last night. I barely took a turn.'

'I couldn't sleep anyway,' Chris said. 'Besides, it gave me the chance to read your book.'

'I'm glad you liked it. It might be the only thing I'm able to write if we do end up dead.' She said it with a smile, but Chris could tell there was a hint of worry.

'We'd be dead already,' Chris said. 'Have you heard anything from the agent about the book today?'

Ashley shook her head. 'Won't hear anything for a couple of weeks probably. He explained these things can take time and not to worry if I didn't hear from them. Besides, I think we've got enough to worry about right now, don't you?'

'Aye,' Chris said. 'But remember, I think if this

vampire knew where we were, we would have been killed or used to find Mikael last night. Why would he wait?'

'Toying with us maybe?'

'If toying with us means letting us have a full night's sleep, then that's a strange way of doing it,' Chris said, and thought about the dream he'd had last night, about his parents' faces.

'What's wrong?' Ashley asked. 'Your face just turned white as a sheet.'

'Oh, it's nothing. Just remembered a bad dream that I had last night. Nothing to worry about – probably just because we've been thinking a lot about some really bad stuff.'

Ashley nodded, as if accepting his explanation, then pointed at the waitress, notifying Chris that she had their food and was bringing it to the table. She placed the plates down, expertly handling all five of them on a tray. The smell was delightful – it was that typical smell you'd get walking past an Indian restaurant, the smell of wonderful wood.

He grabbed a piece of chicken pakora, dipped it in their own homemade sauce and was about to stuff the whole in his mouth when his phone started to buzz in his pocket. He knew it was rude to answer your phone at a meal but when he checked who it was, he felt he needed to answer it. He apologised to Ashley then clicked answer. 'Bryan,' he said.

'Can you speak?' said Bryan Robson.

'Sure, I have a couple of minutes,' said Chris, stuffing a couple of chips in his gob.

'I did some more digging about that Dragoslav you mentioned. I found out some interesting things that I think you'd like to hear.'

'What's the source?'

'You might not know this, but there is a network of people around the world who study things like I do. I put the feelers out and one of them came back to me with more information about what happened to the Dragoslav clan.'

'How does it help us? We're on the run.'

'It doesn't. But better you have some more information about your enemy than none at all.'

'Go on then,' said Chris, as he watched Ashley take a spoonful of coconut-infused korma.

'It might not just be the one after you. There have been several rumours and sightings of different vampires in and around Romania over the course of the last few weeks. The deaths and attacks have been put down to animal attacks, but we know better.'

'Mikael did say they had a group of around six or so.'

'Have you heard from him since the last time you spoke?'

'Not a word.'

'Damn,' said Bryan then paused before speaking again. 'Anyway, Dragoslav was created by a witch's spell. He used the power of his coven to create creatures that would protect them from humans, but it backfired and he, himself, turned into that creature.

'You got this from your source?'

'A few people have confirmed this version of events. It's folklore in Romania but it seems to have some kind of backing to it. And it turns out, because of this, Dragoslav is the first vampire but, because he is a witch too, he has the power to turn humans into vampires. He was then shunned by his coven for being a monstrous creature, so he left and created his own family and looked to come back with many vampires to kill his old family. Piecing together stories from different countries, it sounds like he made his way through most of Europe before returning home.'

'Where he tried to kill his old family?'

'Correct,' said Bryan. 'But the coven saw him coming and got the help of covens from Denmark and Sweden to fend him off, killing the majority of Dragoslav's new family but putting him and just a few others to sleep, just in case they needed him.'

'Why go to that trouble?'

'Who knows – this is all a story, so we have no idea if it's true or not. If you do ever run into Dragoslav, be sure to ask him.'

'From how Mikael described him, I'd rather not.'

'I'm on the trail of someone that posted on a forum a year ago, asking for information on some kind of book. He mentioned breaking some kind of curse. I have no idea if it's legitimate it or not.'

'Will it help us?'

'Perhaps – apparently it is a witch's spell-book and the person on the forum said they procured it from some place in London. I'll keep you updated.'

'Thanks,' said Chris, and disconnected the call to allow them to get back to eating.

'What was that about?' said Ashley, swallowing a piece of her naan bread.

'Just information about what we're dealing with.'

'Anything that'd help us?'

He thought about that for a moment. 'Not really,' he said finally. 'Anyway, forget it. I'm starving.'

For the next hour, they stuffed their faces with Indian food and spoke about their day. Despite the painful muscles, Chris felt satisfied that he'd managed to keep up with Ashley for a good few miles before his body gave in. She had enjoyed the ferry ride over Loch Ness and admitted that she had enjoyed her time here so far but was looking forward to getting home the next day.

If they survived one more night, he reminded her. Once they had finished their meal, Chris called the waitress over and asked for the bill. He paid for the meal with the last of his savings – he'd need to find a part-time job at some point to gather up some more money. The waitress gave him his receipt and wished them a good night.

Chris held the door open for Ashley, letting her out of the restaurant first, and followed her towards the car. The restaurant was becoming busier and busier as dinner time was in full swing. They didn't have long before the sun would be down completely, so Ashley gunned it down the road and towards the hotel.

As they reached the roundabout before the hotel, Chris noticed two police cars outside and what appeared to be an unmarked car with the sirens showing on the dashboard. 'Wonder what's happening?' Chris said, peering out of his window.

'Hope no one's hurt,' Ashley said. 'Looks like a couple of police are at the front door. Should we wait to head in?'

Chris thought about it for a second and decided they needed to get to the room soon and the police weren't there for them so they would be fine. 'It'll be fine,' he said. 'Let's find a space and head up to the room. I'm shattered. A decent sleep before the sun goes down would be amazing.'

Ashley tightened her grip on the steering wheel and turned into the car park. Chris was sure one of the policemen watched them as they drove past the main entrance and reversed into a parking space at the end of the car park. Ashley had managed to get her Audi into a spot between a Land Rover and a BMW and Chris was impressed with how nimble the Audi had been, not to mention Ashley's impressive handling of the wheel.

Ashley turned the engine off and she stared at the main door. They were about thirty feet from the door. 'Something feels off,' she said.

'What do you mean?'

'I don't know. Police just throw me off, I suppose.'

Chris was reminded of the time the police had come to his door to tell him of his parents' death. Since he was technically an adult at the time, they didn't treat him with kid gloves and told him straight – his parents had been killed in an RTA. They explained that this meant a Road Traffic Accident where no one was at fault. The woman that had stopped by to let him know didn't stick around – she simply advised someone would be in touch. It took two days before anyone from the police force had given him a call and offered him a family liaison officer. Chris had refused.

The only other interaction he'd had with the police was the night he was attacked by Greg, the Tattoo Man. Aside from being in a hospital, the interaction was a positive one with the policemen seeming like top blokes. But Ashley was right, the way one of the policemen was looking at them seemed to suggest something was not right.

'If we drive away it'll look even more suspicious. We haven't done anything wrong. We're probably just being paranoid,' he said and gave Ashley's hand a reassuring tap. 'Let's go.' Chris stepped out first and closed the door. He waited for Ashley to join him before they approached the door.

'Evening,' Ashley said as they passed.

Neither of the policemen said a word, but one of them did nod a cursory greeting.

Inside, there was an older man who was suited and

booted. He turned when he heard the main doors slide open. The man was about six foot tall and had a handlebar moustache. He had bags under his eyes and his hair was receding massively. He looked back at the receptionist and said something that neither Ashley nor Chris heard.

The man turned to them as they were about to pass and stopped Chris by grabbing his arm. Chris was a little shocked by this and tried to take a step back, escaping the man's hold, but his grip only tightened.

'What are you doing?' Ashley said urgently.

The man leaned in close to Chris but spoke loud enough for Ashley to hear. 'Chris Winters, I presume. Listen, son, either come in quietly or I'll get those boys outside to wrestle you to the car. You're both under arrest.'

Chapter Thirty

They were placed in separate police cars and taken to a small police station in the centre of the town.

Chris was placed into the unmarked car and hadn't said a word to the driver and the other passengers. Ashley had whispered to him when they were taken away not to say anything and to ask for a solicitor, which he planned to do when he got to the station.

Over in the distance, the sun was starting to fade. At least stuck in a police station would be a relatively safe place to be. Before they were placed into the cars, both were read their rights.

Before Chris could protest, they were manhandled to the cars which was when Ashley gave him the advice to keep his mouth shut.

Chris speaking and getting himself into more bother wouldn't help the situation. He knew what the police were talking about. They were referring to the warehouse in Oakley. The driver, who had identified himself as Detective Chief Inspector Neish, was the arresting officer and his partner beside him, Detective Inspector Murdoch, was the one who practically threw him into the back seat.

The two men drove him downtown without a word between them. They arrived at the station. 'No funny business,' DI Murdoch said as he exited the car. He took a couple of steps from the car and waited for the other marked police car to join them. Once they arrived, the DI opened the door and grabbed Chris by the arm, tightening his grip and pulling him out of the car.

Ashley was getting treated much better. The uniformed policeman had opened the door and allowed her to step out herself. She was still handcuffed like Chris though.

'Right,' the DCI said to his colleagues. 'I want both of them put into holding cells before we get to questioning.'

'I want to call my solicitor,' Ashley said with more authority than Chris had given her credit for.

The DCI smiled. 'You'll get that. But for right now, you'll both go into a holding room until we're ready.' He turned to one of the other policemen, a young man with short black hair. 'Make sure they are put into separate cells.'

As they were being hauled away into the station, Chris overhead DI Murdoch say to his commanding officer, 'Bloody state of affairs this. All that blood, who'd have thought it would be these two.'

He didn't catch any more because he was forcefully pushed through the main two doors. Ahead of him was a makeshift reception. On his right was a square area of chairs and a table where leaflets made their home. On their left was another set of doors and a long corridor beyond it. He believed that was where they would be taken.

'We need two rooms,' the uniformed policeman who had Ashley said to the staff member on reception.

Chris didn't hear what was said but they were then moved beyond the doors, down the corridor and put into separate rooms. The room wasn't quite what he was expecting. From watching television, he thought the room would be a box room with a hard bench, but it had a comfortable sofa to sit on.

A few minutes passed before Murdoch opened the door to the room and stepped inside. 'Phone call,' he said.

'For me?' Chris said, standing up from the couch.

'I guess the girl is the brains then. No, not a phone call for you – you get a chance to call your solicitor before we take you in for questioning if you want one to be with you.'

'I don't have one,' Chris said.

'You can have one appointed for you but let us know now because I'll need to make a few calls to get one at this hour.' The sun was now completely down, and it had gone past seven at night. They wouldn't be questioning them now unless it was serious, he thought. They'd leave him to sit in the room for a night until the morning.

DI Murdoch was about to leave the room, but he stopped and stared at the floor, then looked up at Chris. 'I don't know how you can live with yourself after what you did.'

Chris wanted to defend himself, but he remembered Ashley's advice to not say a word without a solicitor. Chris simply looked away from the Detective and looked at the small window to his right – the moon had now risen, full and bright.

The Detective slammed the door closed and Chris sat back on the couch, resting his head on the back of it and imagining what Ashley would be thinking. They would question them separately, obviously, so they had to have matching stories but that'd be impossible. He thought about just telling the truth, but then he'd be put into a mental asylum.

From watching crime dramas, he knew the police could hold them for up to twenty-four hours before having to charge them. He knew due to the arrest they believed he, and maybe Ashley were murderers and traffickers. He reasoned the police force in Central Scotland must have found something at the scene, linking them to it and tracked them to the Highlands.

An hour passed without any update from the detectives, and it was an hour of worry and concern for Chris. *Ironic that we had been running from a vampire, to only then be tracked by the police*, he thought.

Suddenly, the door lock twisted, and the door was pulled open and DI Murdoch stood in the doorway with his arms closed and handcuffs dangling from one of them. 'Your appointed solicitor is here. Lot of good he'll do you. Do I need to use these?' He held up the cuffs with one hand.

Chris shook his head and stood up slowly. 'Do I speak with the solicitor one to one first?'

The Detective nodded. He stood in the doorway as Chris was forced to squeeze through the small gap. He walked to the right, down the narrow corridor. There were doors on either side and Murdoch told him to stop a couple down.

Through the door was the type of room he expected, without the one-way mirror. The room was small, box like, and painted grey with no windows. A small table was in the middle of the room with four chairs, two on either side, and an elderly man was sat on the far side. He was rummaging through a black briefcase, and barely looked up when Chris sat next to him.

'You'll have ten minutes to get your story straight, then we'll come in and we have some questions for you, Mr

Winters.' Murdoch closed the door and locked it from the outside.

Chris looked around the room awkwardly before setting eyes on his new solicitor. 'Don't we need to talk about this?'

The man turned to him and gave him a smile that Chris could tell was fake a mile off. 'The name's Edward Kerridge. I have the esteemed pleasure of dealing with this mess, so tell me straight. Did you kill those people?'

'I have no idea—'

He held up a hand then buried his head in it, sighing. 'Listen, son. From what they have told me, it's a cut and dry case, so there's no point trying to get out of this.'

'Isn't it your job to get me out of this situation?'

'Did you do it?' Edward asked, with no remorse.

Chris hesitated a little too long for the solicitor's liking.

'Listen, answer their questions honestly, and perhaps at best we can get some kind of settlement to reduce jail time, but from what I've heard you'll be lucky to get that. It's up to you how you want to approach this, you can either answer the questions they have, or you can say no comment.'

Chris nodded. The truth was too ridiculous to even be considered true, but he wasn't about to admit to the murders. He decided then he'd tell them everything about what went on with Steve and Greg and Ashley but take out the supernatural vampire element.

For the rest of the ten minutes, Kerridge barely looked at Chris and spent the time with his head on some papers which Chris managed a brief glance at and saw he was looking at another case for tomorrow. Clearly Chris was not a priority, and it didn't help that the call had come late at night.

DI Murdoch returned to the room with DCI Neish in

tow. The two men were about the same height, but Neish had an air of authority that Murdoch did not. Regardless, they both entered the room with their chests puffed up and took their seats across from Chris and Kerridge.

Nobody said anything for a good minute before Murdoch clicked a button on the tape recorder sitting on the table. 'Highlands and Islands Police Force Interview. Present – DI Murdoch and DCI Neish.' He paused, looked at Chris, then said, 'For the purposes of the recording, please identify yourself.'

Chris cleared his throat. 'Christopher Winters.'

'Accompanied by his appointed solicitor, Edward Kerridge of Lawson and Divine.'

DCI Neish cleared his throat and leaned forward on the table, tapping his pen on his little notebook. He looked Chris in the eye for a few seconds and it took all of Chris's strength not to look away. 'You have already been read your rights, Mr Winters. For the benefit of the recording, though: You do not have to say anything. It may harm your defence in court if you do not mention when questioned something you later rely on in court. Anything you do say can and may be used as evidence.' He took a breath to let it sink in. Chris had a feeling that Neish knew he wasn't a killer from the way he was looking at him, but it didn't stop Chris from looking guilty.

Neish continued: 'We need to remind you that you can refuse to answer our questions with either silence or no comment. Do you understand?'

'Yes,' Chris said and leaned forward. He felt warm underneath the collar but was conscious of not showing it.

Neish nodded at Murdoch who then said, 'I assume I can call you Chris. Do you know why you're here, Chris?'

Chris nodded.

'Please respond with either yes or no for the tape.'

'Yes.'

'Why?'

Chris paused. 'You said so when you read my rights. You said murder and trafficking.'

'So, it's true,' Neish said, less of a question more of a statement.

Chris looked at Kerridge for some support but realised he'd not be getting it from him. He'd rather be anywhere but there from the look of him.

'Let's circle back to that,' Neish said, before Chris could answer. 'When we did our usual search of you, the officer noted you had bruising on your side and back. He also noted that your friend, Ashley, had whip marks on her back. Can you explain why that is?'

Again, Chris stayed quiet then said, 'No comment.'

Murdoch glanced at Neish. 'Did it happen in the bedroom? Are you and Ashley in a relationship? Did you both get a little too rough in the sack one night?'

'How does this relate to the charges?' Chris said, extending his arms wide.

'If it wasn't bedroom related, then could it be related to the fact we found over eight dead bodies and evidence of trafficking at a warehouse in Oakley which had your fingerprints and DNA all over it?'

Chris could feel his face going red and he willed it to stop.

'Can I tell you what I think's happened?'

Chris stared back at Murdoch.

'I think that girl has no clue what you were into. I think something went wrong. I think you killed those people at your warehouse after something happened where the women that you trafficked got away.'

Chris shook his head. 'It's not true.'

Neish leaned forward this time. 'If that's not the truth,

then please tell us. You'll only be helping yourself by telling the truth, and if you care about that lass out there then that will help her too.'

'You won't believe it,' Chris said, an air of desperation in his tone.

Murdoch leaned back, evidently giving the floor to his higher up.

'Try me,' Neish said.

Chris spent the next five minutes telling them everything from the start, including the altercation with Greg at the bar, followed by the discussion with the police at Oakley then telling them of the kidnapping.

'How did you get out?' Neish said, again tapping his pen against his notepad. He hadn't written anything.

Chris had no response. Anything he said would be double checked with Ashley. He tried to think hard but nothing came to mind. He was half tempted to tell them they were saved by a vampire, but he knew how bonkers it'd sound.

'Well,' Murdoch said. 'If this is all true, then surely you can tell us how you got home? And if it was you that made the phone call, then why did you not give your name?'

Again, Chris couldn't answer.

Neish shook his head and finally wrote something down on his pad. 'Chris – we're going to take a quick break to verify some of the details you've told us here. We'll contact the Oakley police force to check this. If they tell us you're lying then it won't look good for you, son.'

Chris nodded. 'It's all true.'

Neish nodded at Murdoch who then said, 'For the tape, interview terminated at nine twenty-nine.'

Both detectives pushed their chairs out and stood up. They both looked down at Chris. He could tell he had almost convinced DCI Neish he was telling the truth, but

Murdoch was less than convinced judging by the snarl on his face. 'You have ten minutes with your solicitor,' DCI Neish said. 'We'll be back shortly.'

'You won't,' a low and raspy voice said from behind the detectives.

Both turned and were now face to face with a tall man who was not there before. He had long dark hair and his eyes were crimson. Chris knew straight away who it was, and his heart sank.

'Who the hell are you?' DI Murdoch said, reaching for his radio.

'How did you get in here?' DCI Neish said, taking a step forward and reaching out to the man.

Dragoslav glanced at Chris. 'I am here for this gentleman.' His voice had a foreign twinge, but his English was very good.

'He's under caution,' DCI Murdoch said, holding up the radio.

'I'll ask again,' DCI Neish said. 'How the bloody hell did you get in this room?' He reached out to Dragoslav and Chris was sure he saw a sly smile briefly appear on Dragoslav's face, as with no hesitation he reached out, grabbed the Detective's right arm, and snapped it behind his back, almost taking the arm out of the socket.

DI Murdoch saw what had just happened and his mouth widened. From where Chris stood, it looked like the Detective Inspector was frozen to the spot. Kerridge on his right had backed away to the back of the room. Murdoch rushed forward to protect his superior, but Drago spun the DCI around, so he was facing Murdoch, then ripped his head off. Blood spurted around the room and the lifeless body hit the floor with a thud. Dragoslav threw the head to the side and moved so quickly that Chris couldn't see him.

The next thing he knew was DI Murdoch was on the ground with his throat ripped out and Kerridge was lying in the foetal position on the floor, hugging his briefcase to his body and begging God for help.

Dragoslav stood above him. His black suit was now a shade of dark red and he confidently nudged Kerridge with his foot. He leaned down next to Kerridge who refused to lift his head and look at the vampire. 'Edward Kerridge,' he whispered, his eyes closed, and Chris knew he was using his witch powers to learn about the solicitor. 'God won't help you here.'

Dragoslav snapped the solicitor's neck quicker than Chris Winters could see it happen. Dragoslav stood to attention, staring at him. Chris could feel the vampire working through his mind, learning his thoughts and his feelings, perhaps learning of his relatives' thoughts and feelings.

He rummaged around Chris's mind for a good minute while Chris looked at the chaos around him. There would be no point in running. He could only hope that he'd take him and leave Ashley alone.

Finally, Drago's face lit up, and he grinned. 'We have lots to discuss, Christopher.'

Chapter Thirty-One

He felt as though his body had been on a roller coaster. His muscles and bones ached. He opened his eyes and stared up at a dark sky with a full moon staring back at him. His back was wet, and he realised he was lying on green grass. He slowly sat and looked around him.

Ahead of him was a large church with gorgeous multi-coloured windows running down beside the main doorway. Behind him, he saw long rows and columns of gravestones. He was in a cemetery.

He remembered what had happened only a few minutes ago. Drago had touched his arm and his vision had gone immediately. His body twisted and turned and suddenly he was in a cemetery. But not just any cemetery, it was the one where his parents had been buried side by side.

Chris wasn't sure where the grave was in relation to where he was, but he knew he had to get out of there. He looked for Drago but couldn't see any sign of the vampire witch. Chris took a deep breath and pushed himself off the wet grass and walked through the graveyard.

He heard a sudden scream in the distance. It was female and it sounded petrified. It wasn't your average scream; this came right from the depths of whoever it was screaming's stomach. Chris ran towards the scream, rushing past multiple gravestones, stepping over the ground where dead people were laid to rest.

He reached a clearing in the middle of the cemetery. It was a small, circular patch of grass. At the centre lay Ashley.

'Ash,' Chris said, reaching her and wrapping his arms around her. 'Ash, we need to go. Come on.'

Chris tried to pick her up, but her body was limp. She was alive, but it was as if she was frozen.

'Ashley, listen to me,' Chris said, lifting her face up so she was looking at him. 'We need to go.'

'He found us.'

'I know,' Chris said. 'Let's go.'

Ashley nodded as Chris stood and helped her to her feet.

They both turned to find the exit of the cemetery. Chris wasn't sure what direction the exit was, so he decided to keep going the way he had come. Away from the church.

'How did he find us?' Ashley said, slowly jogging beside him.

'I'm not sure. That's not important right now,' he said, starting to breath heavily. 'We just need to get out of here and far away.'

If only I had the stake on me, he thought. He'd left it at the hotel, which no doubt would have been ransacked by the police. At least if he had it with him then he could do some damage to the vampire to give them time.

'Do you see him anywhere?' Ashley said, looking side to side.

'No,' Chris said, and was thankful he wasn't there, at least for now.

'I think he's toying with us,' Ashley said.

Chris couldn't argue with that. Drago had the chance to kill him and likely had the chance to kill Ashley but he had moved them here using his witch power. Chris had no idea what the vampire intended but he knew it wouldn't be good.

'Wait,' Chris said, coming to a standstill. Ashley stopped a couple of paces in front of him.

'What is it?' she said. 'We need to go.' She was bouncing on both balls of her feet, looking around at her surroundings.

'It's my parents,' he said, looking at the two gravestones to the right of them. He turned to face them. His parents, Harry Winters and Amanda Winters, lay before him, under the cold ground. It was the first time he'd been there since the funeral a couple of years ago.

'Chris,' Ashley said softly. 'Come on. Now's not the time.'

'It's the perfect time,' Drago said. He appeared behind them, and the twosome almost jumped out of their shoes. The blood had disappeared from his suit, but he still had some in his long dark hair.

Dragoslav walked by them and raised a dark eyebrow when Chris stood in front of Ashley. He almost smiled. Drago reached the two gravestones and put one hand on each.

'What are you doing?' Chris said, stepping forward, but Ashley held onto his arm and held him back.

'Silence,' Dragoslav said, and suddenly Chris's vocal cords were snapped shut. He couldn't say a single word. He couldn't even make a sound.

Chris watched him for the next two minutes. He

watched as he closed his eyes and muttered some kind of incantation. After another couple of minutes, the vampire smiled. 'Interesting,' he said, and then looked at Chris. 'If only you knew.'

Was he reading their dead minds? Was he looking into their past? Chris tried to question him, but his voice was meek and barely audible.

Drago waved a white palm in the air and Chris felt his throat open again, able to make sounds now. He was about to speak, but suddenly it was Ashley that had stepped forward. The clouds in the sky broke open at that point, raindrops falling on all three of them.

'How did you find us?' she said, only a couple of steps from him.

Drago smiled. 'You truly believed you would be able to run from me. I imagine Mikael has informed you of my power. You should not have been so naïve as to expect you could get away.'

'Mikael has got away.' Ashley said, her jaw tight and her teeth clenched.

'Has he now?' Drago said, brushing his hair back and again running his cold hand over the top of the gravestones. 'He will appear soon,' he said, and looked at Chris, 'I'm sure of it.'

'You didn't answer my question,' Ashley said and Dragoslav's gaze snapped back to her.

'You were right about one thing,' he said, taking a step towards Ashley, but to her credit she remained where she stood. 'Travelling this far north was a very good idea. Despite my power, scent can only travel so far and because you had travelled miles – I simply couldn't find you.'

Chris felt as though they were being toyed with because Dragoslav was smiling as he spoke with no hint of annoyance, like he was setting them up for something.

Ashley watched him as he started walking back and forth in front of her. 'Answer my damn question! I don't care about what you thought of our idea to run. I just want to know how the hell you found us?'

Chris had a sinking feeling in his chest which his heart almost dropped into. He knew how Drago found them and he knew what was coming.

'Ashley, is it?' Dragoslav said. 'My my, you are a pretty one.' He almost reached out to touch Ashley's face, but she stepped back, slapping his hand away like swatting a fly.

Here it comes, Chris thought.

'Your parents spoke very highly of you.'

There it was. Chris knew it was coming but it seemed Ashley hadn't, because her mouth fell open and her brow furrowed. She shook her head. 'I don't believe you. You didn't!'

'Didn't I?' Drago said, feigning shock and awe. 'Tell me, Ashley. Are your parents called George and Valerie?'

'You know that already because you can see into my mind, you bastard! You're going to need to do better than that.'

Dragoslav paced again with his right hand resting on his chin. 'You're right. I can see into your mind. I can see into your friend's mind.' He nodded to Chris. 'If I wanted to, I could touch any grave here and know how these people died. I can see that Mr Winters here is starting to harbour some feelings for you which I can see you are starting to reciprocate. Shame you both won't be alive to act on them.'

He continued pacing, glancing at both Ashley and Chris periodically. The rain had started to get heavier but neither of the three bothered about it. Ashley and Chris were transfixed by the vampire witch and, despite the fact he could now speak, he simply couldn't, because, the truth was, he was petrified and it was all he could do not to show it.

'Listen to me when I tell you this,' Drago began. 'Your parents, George and Valerie, told me where you were. They told me you had travelled to the North of Scotland. It has changed since last I was here but once I was in the city, I could track you for miles. Although, as we both know, I knew where you were just from looking at them.'

'My parents wouldn't do that! You're lying. You're messing with my head,' Ashley said, putting her hands to the side of her head and closing her eyes.

'Here,' Drago said and closed his eyes. He muttered some kind of phrase and then Chris felt the world go black.

Chapter Thirty-Two

Chris was inside the house that belonged to George and Valerie. The house that not too long ago he had visited for dinner and some good company. The laughter and happiness that he had known from the house before had disappeared.

The house looked as though it had had all the colour stripped from the walls and furniture. He looked around and his vision felt hazy, like it could only focus on things directly in front of him. He tried to step forward but found his feet were bolted in place.

He looked to his right and saw Ashley standing there too. She was looking back at him and tried to speak but Chris heard no sound. She looked at him with sadness in her eyes and Chris felt the sadness coming through loud and clear.

Drago could read their minds and had revealed what Chris had been thinking for a couple of days now, that he had started to have proper feelings for Ashley. And, the surprise was, she had started to feel them too.

He understood Drago knew where they were the second he spoke with George and Valerie, meaning this was all for show, a way to intimate and cause grief.

He wanted to reach out to Ashley, and to tell her that everything would be alright but he knew that would be a lie.

Suddenly, three figures appeared in front of them. Dragoslav had his back to them and even he was colourless. Beyond him were George and Valerie. The head of the house, George was gritting his teeth and trying to pull his way out of the chair he was tied to. Valerie, on the other hand, was more subdued, looking down at her feet and not making eye contact with the vampire.

What Chris saw next was something he wouldn't wish on his worst enemy. He'd even take a beating from Steve and Greg before witnessing what he saw again. He effectively sat through what was a long torture session.

Dragoslav used a multitude of tools including a hammer, a pair of pliers and a needle.

Chris tried to tell Ashley to look away, but his voice wasn't heard. She watched the whole thing, trying to push her way forward out of the force blocking her.

George had to watch as Valerie was tortured and Dragoslav inflicted a lot of pain on her by hitting her arm with the hammer and then using the needle to stick underneath her nail bed. Chris could feel the pain and he winced with every howl that came from her.

George had to relent. Any good man would have. He told Drago to stop and he'd tell them where Ashley was. Valerie told him not to, proud until the end, but he wanted to save his wife.

Drago thanked him for his understanding, but then picked up the pair of pliers. 'Weak. A friend of mine called Vlad taught me how to use torture to my advantage

– he taught me this.' He then used the pliers to rip out two of George's front teeth. George screamed out in pain, a sound that Chris didn't know a human being could make.

Again, he looked at Ashley who had finished shouting and screaming. She was now resigned to watching what was going on.

Eventually, the torment stopped as Drago turned to face the two of them. Chris couldn't tell what was real and what was a vision anymore. Dragoslav looked directly at them though and smiled. He closed his eyes and said something in Romanian, then the world went black for a few seconds.

Chris opened his eyes, and they were back in the graveyard. Ashley was on her knees on the cold grass, her knees now covered in wet mud. Chris ran over to her and knelt beside her.

Drago walked over slowly, and Chris felt ready to attack him, but he had no weapon, and he knew if he did they would be killed. He couldn't see a way out, but he knew he had to buy them time.

Drago lowered his body, so he was in front of them. Ashley kept her head down, but Chris met his gaze. Dragoslav smiled. 'I told you: I do not lie.' He nodded behind Chris and Ashley.

Ashley didn't turn but Chris did, and he saw what at first looked like his parents hanging from one of the large trees in the cemetery. It looked amazingly like the dream he'd had.

He blinked twice and knew it wasn't his parents. They were already dead. It was George and Valerie – their throats cut open and dangling from two ropes in a tree. Their bloated bodies swayed in the wind and blood was dripping onto the ground.

Chris kept Ashley's head down and hugged her tightly.

He looked at Dragoslav and said, 'You made me dream of that, didn't you?'

Dragoslav nodded. 'If you had paid more attention, you'd have seen it was Ashley's parents and not your own.'

Chapter Thirty-Three

Ashley had cried for a good few minutes before the tears were all used up and she had gone silent.

Chris knelt beside her. He had his arms wrapped around her and she leaned on his chest. His shirt was wet from her crying and his jeans were wet from the grass.

Finally, Dragoslav said: 'Come with me' to Chris.

Chris looked up at the vampire and shook his head. 'I'm not going anywhere with you.'

'You don't have a choice.' Dragoslav reached his hand out to Chris.

Chris felt as though he had a rope around him, and his body moved without his legs doing anything.

His body was walking as if he was taking a morning stroll, but he wasn't the one moving his muscles. 'What about Ashley?' Chris said as he was forced to walk.

Dragoslav laughed. 'She won't be going anywhere.'

It was then Chris realised he couldn't see further than the cemetery. 'Where are we?'

'Your parents' cemetery, of course. However, I've

cloaked it so nobody can enter or exit without my saying so. Your friend won't be going anywhere, and after what she's just seen I doubt she'll be fit to move.'

'Why did you do that? What is so important about tracking us down and finding Mikael?'

Dragoslav stopped in place which made Chris do the same. 'Mikael was part of my family. As you experienced, family can be difficult, and Mikael left our coven without my permission. Because of that, I must track him down and kill him, otherwise others may feel they can leave too.'

Chris shook his head. 'It's their own choice.'

'They are my family,' Drago said. 'It is not up to them. All of them want to stay by my side, all but one. Tell me, Christopher – why are you involved in this? Why was Mikael with you?'

Chris thought back to the night he had run into the vampire. 'He tried to kill me.'

'Hunger must have got the better of him. Shame. He really thought he could avoid killing to survive as a vampire.'

They started walking again. 'He stopped himself. He said he didn't want to kill humans anymore. He said he was in Scotland because his previous partner—'

'Rose,' Dragoslav said, and smiled. 'Mikael was madly in love with her and at his request I turned her into a vampire, but she never took to the life. Mikael thinks she died in the war between the vampires and the witches but—'

'But you killed her.'

Dragoslav nodded. 'You're a smart man, Christopher. Due to her opinions on humans, she threatened to reveal us to the world, which is something we couldn't have.'

'I don't understand. If you are so powerful, then why are you worried about humans finding out you exist?'

Dragoslav looked at the dark sky, his pasty white face illuminated by the full moon. 'There are only six of us. There are over one million humans on earth. The odds are not in our favour, no matter how strong we are.'

Chris realised then he was walking and talking with the man that killed Valerie and George and he felt bile rise from his stomach. 'What is it you want with us?'

Dragoslav stopped underneath a large green tree, but thankfully there were no bodies hanging from this one. 'I have been tracking Mikael for the past three months. I have left my coven in the Hoia Forest to search for him. I need to get back to them and to do that I need to find Mikael and kill him.'

Dragoslav stopped speaking for a minute and shook his head. 'I do not want to kill him, but I must. And you, Christopher, are going to do two things.'

'What?'

Dragoslav grinned, two of his fangs showing. 'You are the reason Mikael will come here, so you being here has done something already.'

Chris folded his arms across his chest. 'And the second?' Chris knew he was in mortal danger being around this vampire, but he was still pissed off about what he had done to Valerie and George, not to mention the way he caressed his parents' gravestones.

'You are going to tell him to stop running and tell him he must submit himself to me and I will then execute him.'

Chris shook his head. 'Why would I do that?'

'Because,' Drago said, turning to face him, his pupils dilated, and the whites of his eyes turned red. 'If you don't comply, you won't find out what really happened to your parents.'

Chris stared at him for a good thirty seconds.

'And I will kill your friend, Ashley. I will leave you

alive, just so you can be alone again. Wondering about your parents and knowing you were the reason Ashley died.'

Chris could feel a chill in the air and the coldness spread down his back. 'Aye, but what makes you think Mikael would do that? We've only spoken twice.'

'You saved his life. He saved yours. Let's call it a bond you two now have. I'm positive he wouldn't let two of his favourite humans die now.'

'I can't do it,' Chris said, looking down at his feet. 'Let Ashley live and kill me instead. I don't care about how my parents died; I know how they died. A car crash. Simple. End of.'

Drago started walking once again and Chris felt his body move with him. 'That's not how they died. Your parents were very interesting people, Christopher. Travelling the globe, uncovering huge discoveries but ultimately leaving their baby boy to rot. You blame them for so many things. I can give you the true reason why they were gone so much.'

'I don't care!' Chris said, and tried to walk away but he was kept in place by whatever spell Dragoslav had conjured up.

'You will,' he said, his voice low and calm. 'Besides, if you don't do what I ask, then Ashley will die. And judging from what I gathered, that is the last thing you would want. Is that correct?'

Chris avoided Dragoslav's eyes, looking at a gravestone in the far distance.

'Well,' Dragoslav said, stepping close enough to Chris that he could smell his blood-stained breath. 'Do we have an agreement?'

'Yes,' Chris said, finally. He had no idea if he could go through with it or not, but the idea of Ashley dying wasn't one he wanted to have happen. It was because of Mikael they were in this mess, wasn't it? Why should he protect him over Ashley? *Because he saved your life.*

'I'll tell him,' Chris said and Dragoslav nodded and grinned, looking like the cat that got the cream.

Chapter Thirty-Four

The concept of time was completely lost on Chris and Ashley. They had no idea how long they had been with Dragoslav in the cemetery or how long it had been since they were in the police station. Chris wondered what would be happening there. Would they be getting the blame for the two dead detectives? *More than likely,* he thought.

The rain had continued for the last ten minutes as he sat beside Ashley on the cold grass. Underneath the moonlight, the grass had a white sheen to it which helped illuminate the area they were in. Ashley hadn't said a word since he had been brought back. She was still in a daze and emotional from seeing her parents like that. They were still there, hanging in the wind, but Ashley had stopped looking at them.

'How long is this going to take?' Chris said, a hint of annoyance in his voice. He was looking ahead at the back of Dragoslav who was standing with his eyes closed, his head bowed.

He did not answer. Instead, he continued to speak under his breath, so faint that Chris and Ashley could barely hear it. *If only he had the stake, Chris thought.* He could quickly rush across the grass and shove the wood into the bastards back and through his heart, then everything would be alright.

But who was he kidding – taking on the most powerful creature in existence. It was stupid, really.

Drago opened his eyes and turned to face both of them. He slapped his hands together and smiled. Chris couldn't take his eyes off the two large fangs showing from the top of his mouth – they were caked in blood and what looked like bits of meat, likely from the two detectives, he thought. Despite the fact they were questioning him, he held no contempt for them and wished they were still alive. They did not need to die, nor did the solicitor, Edward Kerridge.

He thought about Bryan Robson – he'd love to be here to speak to Dragoslav and ask him all manner of questions.

'The deed has been done,' Drago said. 'The die has been cast. Mikael – if he cares about either of you – will be here soon. Then you will do as we discussed.' He glared at Chris and turned back to face the other way – safe in the knowledge that neither Chris nor Ashley could do anything to hurt him.

'What's he on about?' Ashley whispered, nearly causing Chris to jump.

It was the first time he had heard her speak in a while and it caused his heart to race. 'Never mind,' he said. 'I can get us out of this, I promise.'

Ashley surveyed him with justified scepticism.

Chris returned the look with a reassuring smile then looked back at Dragoslav. 'One thing I've been wondering,' he said, and watched as Drago turned round. 'Where are the rest of your family? Why did they not come with you?'

'I must do this alone,' Dragoslav said.

'Yet, you have us here,' Ashley whispered.

'Christopher is here as a required pawn in this game,' he said, glancing at Chris. 'You, Ashley, are here because you were in the wrong place at the wrong time.'

'So let her go,' Chris said, an air of desperation in his voice. He knew the answer would be a no from the terms of the agreement, but he had to try.

Dragoslav simply shook his head and faced the opposite direction. He ran his hands through his hair and pushed it behind his shoulders. He wasn't what Chris had expected as the ever-powerful vampire witch. He expected someone bulkier and someone a bit darker. While Dragoslav was tall, he was rather skinny. Chris expected him to be dressed in centuries-old fabrics, but he was rather dapper in the navy suit.

'How long will it take him to get here?' Chris said.

Dragoslav didn't answer for a minute, then said, 'He's already here.'

Chapter Thirty-Five

From out of the mist appeared Mikael, standing proudly a few feet from them.

Mikael stepped forward but did not look at either Chris or Ashley. His eyes were locked to Dragoslav. His face was stern and his eyes pinched.

'You came,' Drago said, his grin wide. 'You put too much value on human life.'

Mikael shook his head. He took one step forward. 'I came because of what you told me in that message. You were going to kill two more innocent people if I didn't come here. Say what it is you want to say, Drago, and be done with it. Let the two of them go and then we can all go our separate ways.'

'Why?' Dragoslav said, waving his hand in the air, as if blowing off what Mikael had said. 'Who said anything about going our separate ways? You made a mockery out of our family. That cannot be forgiven, and it certainly cannot be forgotten.'

The two creatures watched each other for a minute.

Chris and Ashley watched with bated breath at what was going on. It seemed as if they were having a conversation between them – every little twitch of their body giving something away.

'Besides, I believe it is your friend here that has something to say,' Drago said, and grabbed Chris by the arm and urgently pulled him to his feet. 'Go on, Christopher.' He pushed him in the back towards Mikael. 'Tell him what we discussed.' The look on Dragoslav's face was one of absolute glee.

Chris took a deep breath, then let it out with a large sigh. He walked forward to Mikael, so he was standing in front of the vampire. Being this close to him reminded Chris of the night he had almost been vampire meat.

'What is it?' Mikael said, watching Chris carefully, but keeping one eye on Dragoslav behind them in the distance. Ashley knelt beside him.

'I'm sorry,' Chris said, gritted his teeth and wiped his nose. 'You need to stop running.'

Mikael glanced at Dragoslav then looked at Chris thoughtfully. 'What did he tell you?'

'If you do not do this one thing – then he will not tell me the true fate of my family, and he'll also kill Ashley.'

A loud yelp came from Ashley behind them, then she said to Dragoslav: 'You bastard.'

She got a backhanded slap from Dragoslav for that, and Chris winced at the sound. Mikael took a step forward, as if to protect Ashley, but Chris put his hand on his chest, pushing him back – he was cold to the touch. They were very close now, only a few inches separating them.

'Fine, I'll do it,' Mikael said. 'I owe you both and it's my fault you're here. I'll be glad when it's over.'

'Splendid!' Drago said behind them and took a step back behind Ashley and yanked her off to the side.

While that was happening, Mikael leaned close to Chris, reached behind him, and handed Chris the wooden stake he had carved in the hotel room – the same one he'd taken from the broken door.

The two men – one a vampire – met each other's gaze and Chris felt as if they knew what the other was thinking. Chris nodded at Mikael who nodded back. *Who knew Greg and Steve might come in handy?* Chris thought.

'Come on now,' Drago said, waiting for Mikael in the centre of the cemetery, surrounded by the dead. 'I haven't got all night. The sun will be up soon, and I would like to get back to my family.'

Mikael grunted and thrust past Chris, whacking him in the shoulder with his arm – Chris knew he was playing the part, but it still hurt like a bitch. Mikael walked towards Dragoslav, and it wasn't long before he was standing in front of him.

'Do your worst,' he said. 'If anything, once I'm dead, I'll no longer need to worry about being on the same earth as a monster like you.'

'You mean the monster that gave you immortality?' Dragoslav said, grinning.

'No.' Mikael stepped forward so that he was eye to eye with the coven leader. As he did that, Chris crept his way behind Dragoslav, joining Ashley, the stake firmly tucked between his back and the waistband of his jeans. 'The monster that took me from my real family as a young man and brought me into a life that I did not want.'

Dragoslav shook his head rapidly. 'Ungrateful,' he said. 'Kneel before me and say your last words.'

'I've said all that I need too,' Mikael said, kneeling on the cold ground and looking up at the man who would kill him.

Drago nodded. He grabbed Mikael by the neck and

was about to rip his head off, but then Chris rushed forward, taking three long strides, and sliced through Dragoslav's back with the wooden stake, carved from his own front door.

Dragoslav screamed in pain and staggered forward into Mikael, pushingd the vampire away. Mikael fell a few feet from him. Dragoslav was still strong, Chris realised, and soon he worked out he hadn't quite hit the heart, it was too far to the right.

Even with the stake bedded through him, Dragoslav swivelled and grabbed Chris by the chest and neck. He opened his mouth, bared his fangs and his eyes turned crimson – he was a split second from digging his teeth into Chris when Mikael jumped on him from behind.

The vampire wrestled him from Chris and threw him off his feet and into a tree nearby. Dragoslav quickly got up, ripping the wooden stake out of his body, and screaming in agony. He threw it to the side. 'I don't need weapons or tricks to kill you, Mikael. And once I'm finished with you, I will kill your friends.'

Chapter Thirty-Six

The noise of the two supernatural creatures going toe to toe would be something that Chris would never forget.

As he and Ashley ran through the cemetery, through the mist that had descended upon the grave site, all he could hear was the screams and yells of Mikael and Drago fighting to the death.

Mikael had told them to run and that's what they were doing, but Chris had no idea where to go. They couldn't escape the cemetery – it was cordoned off by whatever spell Drago had inflicted on it. Could they wait until morning? For the sun to rise? He thought about it, but he knew that wouldn't work because Drago would kill Mikael and come after him for betraying him.

'What do we do?' Ashley said, stopping and holding her breath. Chris had a brief thought about gloating that his lungs had held out longer but decided against it. 'We can't get out of here and do you hear what is going on back there?'

'I hear it.' Chris looked around – everything looked the

same, like they were running in circles. All the gravestones had meshed into one and he didn't recognise any of them anymore. He saw in the distance the tree where Ashley's parents were hanging. 'We need to think of something, because sooner or later Dragoslav is going to kill him and then he's going to kill us.'

Ashley looked around frantically and spotted the tree in the distance. 'There,' she said, and set off running.

'What are you doing?' Chris said. She was running to the tree where her parents were hanging. 'That's where—'

'I know!' Ashley said, her tone showing she wasn't in the mood to argue. 'I have an idea.'

They reached the tree just as they heard what sounded like a cat's screech not far from them. They were at the bottom of the tree and on the other side were her dead parents. And somewhere in this graveyard were Chris's dead parents – who didn't die in a car crash.

'Give me a boost,' Ashley said, resting her hands on the tree trunk.

'Eh aye, sure.' Chris held his hands out and Ashley put her wet foot onto them. Chris gripped her shoe but felt it slide from his hand when she tried to jump up. She almost fell flat on her back, but Chris caught her. 'One more time.'

Ashley put her foot in his hand and grabbed onto the tree trunk. 'Push as I jump.' She bent down slightly, then rose, pushing her body off the ground with her foot and Chris raised his hands at the same time, sending her higher into the air.

She reached out with her hands and grabbed onto a thick branch. She used all her strength, gritting her teeth and grunting to climb up and swing her leg over. She was able to stand on the branch now. She shimmied her way to the far end of it and held onto the branch above for support.

'What's the plan?' Chris shouted from down below. The drop wasn't far – but it was still around seven feet, so it'd be a painful landing. He hoped she wouldn't turn round because her parents were almost right behind her.

'I'm going to jump and kick the end of this branch down. It should be sharp enough for us to use on him.'

'You mean we're going back?'

Ashley nodded. 'Yes – Mikael came to save us and we can't let him die and sit here waiting for that bastard to kill us.'

Chris agreed with that and let her know with a smile and thumbs up. He watched as she moved up and down, swaying the branch below her. She then jumped up, using the branch above to pull herself higher with her hands, and she landed on the end of the bottom branch with her feet. The impact snapped the branch from the tree, and it fell to the ground below. Ashley tumbled with it and Chris saw her ankle twist in a way he knew it shouldn't.

To her credit, she didn't whine or complain – she used the tree to help herself back to her feet as Chris checked on the branch. It was a decent size, about the same length as his arm, and the part where it had broken off had a nice arrow shape to it – enough to pierce someone's body, he hoped.

This time he wouldn't miss.

Chapter Thirty-Seven

The scene in front of them was one of those moments you hate looking at but can't look away from. Like witnessing a car crash in real time.

Chris and Ashley huddled behind a large gravestone. The ground below was soft and marshy from all the rain. Their clothes were now almost see-through from the wetness. They watched the two go at it for a few minutes – they couldn't make their move just yet.

They knew they had to wait for the best time to do it. Move too early and Dragoslav would know something was going on. Move too late and the chances were Mikael would be dead and they would be next.

'We need to do it now,' Ashley whispered.

Chris watched Drago push Mikael off him and threw him against a nearby gravestone. The stone shattered into pieces and the vampire lay on the ground for a second longer than Chris would have liked.

'Make the distraction and I'll do it,' Chris whispered.

Ashley nodded and sneaked away from him. They

were only a few feet from Drago as he put his knee under Mikael's chest. Mikael tried to push the knee off, but Dragoslav was too strong.

'I told you I didn't need witchcraft to kill you,' Dragoslav said. Chris was just close enough to hear it.

Mikael grunted and tried to speak but couldn't get the words out. Drago's knee was preventing any sound from appearing. Finally, Dragoslav lifted a little, allowing him to speak and he said, 'Kill me. Do it. I'll be glad to get away from you and see Rose again.'

Dragoslav grinned. *Don't do it,* Chris thought. *Don't tell him.*

'Let me tell you something about Rose.' Dragoslav grinned and leaned closer to Mikael. 'I – Killed – Rose.'

Chris wished they had attacked sooner, because the look on Mikael's face was twisted with sadness and horror. The blood on his face dripped down the side of his cheeks. He roared like a lion then opened his mouth and looked like he used all his strength to reach his head up and bit into Dragoslav's neck.

Dragoslav stumbled back with his hand to his neck, but he was smiling.

'HEY!' Ashley was behind him, with her hands cupped to her mouth, getting his attention. Dragoslav turned and grinned.

Drago advanced on Ashley. Chris made his move. He crossed the muddy grass in a few long strides with the heavy branch in his grip. He reared his arms back and dived towards Dragoslav, with the branch pointed to his black, dead, heart.

Drago must have known. He swivelled on the spot with lightning-quick reflexes and grabbed Chris by the throat, knocking the branch from his grasp. 'Wrong move,' Drago said, and lunged forward, looking for the killing blow, and

Chris saw the fangs appear and his eyes turn red.

Drago stopped and blood spurted from his chest.

Chris dropped to the ground and landed hard. He wiped the mud from his face and looked up. Dragoslav was stumbling forward with the wooden stake Chris had carved at the hotel in his back, right where his heart would be.

Ashley was behind him, her hands covered in blood, she looked both terrified and glad at the same time.

Mikael was up quickly; he jumped on Dragoslav and took him to the ground. Mikael grabbed him by the neck and looked to twist – to rip – the head from the body.

'Wait,' Drago said, his voice raspy and desperate. He was surrounded by the three of them, but his eyes were fixed on Chris. 'Spare me and I will tell you of your parents' true death.'

He choked out every word, and Chris could see the arrogance and confidence had left him, now he was pleading, on his knees and about to die. Did he want to know how his parents died? What would be the point?

As if Drago could tell what he was thinking, he said, 'Trust me, you will want to know. And you, Mikael,' he said, looking up at him, 'you will want to know too because it threatens every vampire.'

'I do not care about the vampires,' Mikael simply said, ready to twist and rip Dragoslav's head off.

Drago looked at Chris again. 'Please – you'll want to know. Spare me and I'll tell you.'

Chris looked at both Mikael and Ashley and both shook their heads.

'Fine,' Chris finally said, his desire to know the real reason they died was too strong.

Drago smiled and the weight seemed to lift from his shoulders. 'Your parents were not killed by a car crash.

Your uncle knew this. Witches and vampires aren't the only supernatural creatures.' He glanced at Mikael who was listening intently now, blood still dripping from his mouth. 'Your parents were killed by a Lycan.'

Chris stared.

He glanced at Mikael who looked just as shocked as he did.

'Now – let me go and I will forget about Mikael. I'll forget about you and Ashley.'

Chris looked at Ashley for a long time. He thought about his parents lying dead in their grave and Ashley's parents hanging from the tree.

'I wish to get back to my family,' Dragoslav said.

The final words from Drago decided Chris's next actions. He looked at Mikael and nodded. Chris then said, 'Don't we all.'

Deep down, he knew he missed his family, and he knew Ashley would never be the same and he knew Mikael had Dragoslav to blame for the death of the love of Rose. Dragoslav did not deserve to live any longer.

He made a deal – but deals can be broken.

Chris and Mikael met eyes once more, as if Mikael was checking Chris was sure. 'Do it,' Chris said.

Mikael tightened his grip on the neck and ripped it from his body, but not before Dragoslav had screamed one more time.

Blood spurted from the lifeless body and Dragoslav landed on the soft ground, sending mud flying in all directions.

The head rolled on the ground away from them and the soulless eyes stared back at him. Chris let out a large breath and he could finally let his body calm down – he almost lost feeling in his legs, and he sat down on the ground to prevent him falling flat on his face.

Ashley came over to him and sat next to him. The two of them sat in the rain, both parentless and both unsure of what would happen next.

Mikael stood before them, but then sat down as well. He wiped the blood from his face and his hands. He looked at the two of them and smiled slightly. 'Thank you, both.'

Chris and Ashley nodded. 'Thank you,' Chris said.

He knew Mikael would be feeling the sting of finding out the love of his life was killed by the person he considered family for so long.

Ashley rested her head on his shoulder.

The haze around the cemetery started to fade away until they could see the outside of the area and Chris was confident, they could leave now. The sun would be up soon, so they'd need to move quickly for Mikael to live.

'What happens now?' Ashley asked.

Chris didn't know what the answer was – technically they were on the run, and he wasn't sure how the detectives' deaths would be explained.

Chris shook his head, glanced at the severed skull of Dragoslav and then looked at the full moon above.

His world was a lot bigger than he'd ever expected – and he knew this was only the beginning.

Chapter Thirty-Eight

TWO WEEKS LATER

Jenny's Grill was a quiet American-style dinner just off the M74 motorway near the services. It had been there for quite some time and opened when the call for Americanised food and drink had become popular in the United Kingdom. Cheap and cheerful, it served as a hub for heavy goods drivers and for families on their way up and down the country. Beside it were the usual buildings you'd expect from a services – a Burger King, a cheap hotel and, of course, a petrol station.

Outside, it looked inviting. The building was a rectangular shape, smaller in height than the rest. Inside, the tables were lined up in a row against the windows at the front of the building, adjacent to a long bar and behind that was the kitchen. It was your typical American diner.

Chris had driven down from Oakley for about twenty miles before turning off and parking outside. He turned off the engine to his rental car – a Nissan Juke – and took a seat inside, ignoring the stares from the lorry drivers. He felt like an invader on their patch, but he tried not to show it.

He sat down and waited. A waitress came over, her hair tied up in buns and her make a up a little too out there, with a pot of coffee and tried to pour him a drink. He held up his hand. 'Just water, thanks.'

'Suit yourself,' the waitress said. 'Can I get you anything to eat? Piece of cake?'

'No,' Chris said, he wanted to sit in silence and wait for her to arrive. 'Thank you, though,' he added, not looking to be rude.

The waitress came over with the glass of water – tap, no doubt – and was soon back at the bar. He had to admit, the smell from the kitchen was making him hungry but he didn't want to eat because his stomach felt like it was doing jumping jacks. He stared at the rental. He'd managed to afford it because after learning of his parents' death – and finally having the guts to look into things – he learned of a savings account they had where they had a decent stash, nothing life changing but enough to help him pay for the damage to the door of the flat and rent the car.

He sipped his lukewarm water and watched the waitress carry out two platefuls of burgers and chips to the table a few booths down. He almost called the waitress over, but the sight of the white Audi pulling into the services stopped him.

He thought this would be a good place to meet and chat, since it was on the same road they'd be going, albeit in different directions. They were on differing paths now, both physically and emotionally.

She stepped out of the car, slamming the door shut and clocking him from where she stood. She gave a wry smile and walked into the diner.

'Hey,' Chris said, standing up and giving her a large hug, and he noticed the stares she had got from the men in the diner. She was wearing a small tank top and jean shorts – it was a scorching hot day.

'Hey, yourself,' Ashley said, letting go of the hug and sitting down across from him. The waitress toddled over and smiled at her and stood waiting with her notepad. 'Just coffee, please.'

The waitress turned to Chris and grinned, as if she took it personally that he'd rejected her offer of caffeine. She was quick with bringing the pot over and poured the black liquid into a basic white mug. Ashley broke up a small milk pod and dropped it in, followed by two teaspoons of sugar.

It took a couple of minutes for them to start talking as the friends they were. It was to be expected after what they had been through. After all, neither had seen the other for a couple of weeks since what had happened.

'How's the book deal coming?' Chris asked. 'That's why you were down in Manchester, right?' He had known this already, but he figured it was a way to make conversation.

She nodded, sipping her coffee. 'It's good. We're pushing for a Christmas time release and, even better news, it's been optioned to be turned into a television show. That's why we were in Manchester – meeting at ITV.'

'Sounds great,' Chris said, and he couldn't help but feel a bit envious. 'How are you getting on with—'

'The fact that my parents are dead?' she said, staring at the milky coffee.

Chris nodded, and let the silence hang in the air before him. He never truly knew what it was to grieve. At the time of his own parents' death, he felt they didn't care about him, but that had been wrong. He wished he had mourned them at the time.

'It's really hard,' she said. 'Every morning I wake up and I think about them. Every night I think about them. Sometimes I even dream about them. But you know what the worst thing is?'

'When you dream about them, you only see their bodies in that cemetery.'

Ashley nodded and sniffed. 'I hate the fact they never got a proper burial with all their friends and family.'

'We did what we could. You know it'd be too difficult to explain to everyone.'

'Everyone thinks my parents upped and left, Chris.'

'I know,' Chris said. He paused. 'Aye, it sucks. They'd be proud of you, you know.'

Ashley nodded and smiled. She glanced out of the window and landed on the Nissan. 'Is that yours? How'd you afford that?'

Chris shook the keys. 'Rental. Not quite as fancy as your Audi, but it gets the job done, I suppose. Turns out my parents had a bit of money saved after all, so I used some of it to rent that bad boy and pay off Mrs Kim for the door.'

Ashley eyes widened. 'How did that go? Can't imagine it was a fun conversation.'

'Lots of shouting,' Chris said, laughing. 'But she got her money and I'm rid of her now. Remember that damp patch? It had grown so wide that a bit of the ceiling had fallen. She tried to blame me; can you believe that?'

The waitress was back and had poured her another cup of coffee. 'Any food for you two?' Both shook their heads and she went back to serving the other tables.

'You know,' Ashley began, stirring the coffee with the spoon, 'I can't quite believe we got away from all of that. Even the police, nothing seemed to come of that.'

'We stuck to our story and refused to comment on

anything, so they dropped it.' It was true – after the night in the cemetery they had gone back to the police station and sat through no end of questions. They both agreed not to say a word and it seemed to work. The police had no evidence to charge them with the crimes they had been accused of.

'Did Mikael have anything to do with it?' Ashley asked.

Chris knew that he did. He knew the vampire had gone into both the Highlands and the Central Police Forces' records and removed all traces of them, including documents and any CCTV tapes. For all the police knew, they had lost all the documentation which meant they had lost all leads. 'I think he might have,' Chris said.

'Have you seen or heard from him?'

'Not since that night,' Chris said. 'He took it hard about Rose.'

'I can imagine. I wouldn't want to be near a betrayed vampire,' she seemed to stare at Chris for a minute, and he knew she was thinking about that night. 'It's just all so crazy. Turns out it's a bigger world than any of us thought.'

Chris nodded and let his brain think about all he'd learned in the past few weeks. He had made new friends and made enemies – escaped from the police and helped kill a powerful vampire. The world certainly was an interesting place, and he no longer believed his life was the boring thing he thought it to be.

'What are your plans in England?' Ashley said, finishing off the second cup of coffee. Her hands were rattling slightly with the cup. The caffeine seemed to be doing its job.

'Drago said my parents were killed by Lycans and my uncle knew about it. I need to find out what happened and what my uncle has to do with it.'

Ashley looked around, then spoke in a hushed tone.

'Isn't a Lycan a Werewolf?'

'Aye, that's right,' Chris said, it was a suggestion he'd have laughed at not too long ago. 'Bryan is going to help me. He was quite excited about the prospect.'

'It'll be dangerous, no doubt.'

Chris almost laughed. 'No more than the previous couple of weeks.'

His hand lay on the table in front of them, and Ashley reached hers out and put it on top of his. She idly rubbed his skin with her thumb. Chris stared at it like he had been transfixed. 'I wish things would be different,' she said, looking into his eyes. 'I get why you need to do it though.'

'Aye, I know the feeling,' he said, and smiled. He wished he could stay in Scotland with her, but he knew he needed to find out more about his parents and his uncle. 'We're going in different directions, I suppose. No point in me holding you back.' He thought about her book deal and the new TV series and knew he couldn't force her to travel and search for a Lycan.

'You'll stay safe though, right? And keep in touch – I'd hate to find out you've been killed by Bryan after annoying him too much.'

'As if,' he said, stroking her hand with his thumb this time. 'We'll hopefully see each other sooner than later.'

Acknowledgements

With most books, it takes more than one person to write it. Therefore, I need to thank a handful of people for making this book possible.

The first being my partner, Nicola, who is the reason this book was written and the reason why it was published, being my first beta reader and suggesting improvements.

I need to say a huge thank you to my publisher and everyone involved in the process to help get this book prepared – particularly the books cover artist and editor who improved the book tenfold and ultimately the reason why it's in your hands.

And lastly, a big thank you to you, the reader, for purchasing this story, and supporting my dream of being an author. If you enjoyed this story, please consider leaving a review on Amazon, Goodreads, and any other social platforms you are a member of.

About The Author

Calum France is a Scottish writer born in the beautiful city of Stirling. His passion for writing began at a young age and has only grown stronger with time. He holds a BA in English Literature and will pursue a master's degree in creative writing.

When not immersed in writing, Calum enjoys playing squash and exploring the pages of a good book. He is also the proud owner of a beloved Dalmatian.

Calum's love for writing stems from his desire to create stories that capture the imagination and offer unique perspectives.

Instagram: @calumfranceauthor
Website: www.calumfrance.com

www.blossomspringpublishing.com

Printed in Great Britain
by Amazon

25166524R00169